Clare Victor Dwiggins

MADAME BOVARY

A TALE OF PROVINCIAL LIFE

BY
GUSTAVE FLAUBERT

WITH A
CRITICAL INTRODUCTION
BY
FERDINAND BRUNETIÈRE

Of the French Academy

AND A
BIOGRAPHICAL PREFACE
BY
ROBERT ARNOT, M. A.

———

VOLUME I.

———

SIMON P. MAGEE,
PUBLISHER,
CHICAGO, ILL.

CONTENTS

PART I.

PART II.

CONTENTS

ILLUSTRATIONS

CRITICAL INTRODUCTION

Domi mansit, lanam fecit: "He remained at home and wrote," is the first thing that should be said of Gustave Flaubert. This trait, which he shares with many of the writers of his generation,—Renan, Taine, Leconte de Lisle and Dumas *fils*,—distinguishes them and distinguishes him from those of the preceding generation, who voluntarily sought inspiration in disorder and agitation,—Balzac and George Sand, for instance (to speak only of romance writers), and the elder Dumas or Eugene Suë. Flaubert, indeed, had no "outward life;" he lived only for his art.

A second trait of his character, and of his genius as a writer, is that of seeing in his art only the art itself—and art alone, without the mingling of any vision of fortune or success. A competency,—which he had inherited from the great surgeon, his father, —and moderate tastes, infinitely more *bourgeois* than his literature,—permitted him to shun the great stumbling-block of the professional man of letters, which, in our day, and doubtless in the United States as well as in France, is the temptation to coin money with the pen. Never was writer more disinterested than Flaubert; and the story is that *Madame Bovary* brought him 300 francs — in debts.

A third trait, which helps not only to characterise but to individualise him, is his subordination not only of his own existence, but of life in general, to his conception of art. It is not enough to say that he lived for his art: he saw nothing in the world or in life but material for that art, — *Hostis quid aliud quam perpetua materia gloriæ?* — and if it be true that others have died of their ambition, it could literally be said of Flaubert that he was killed by his art.

It is this point that I should like to bring out in this Introduction, — where we need not speak of his Norman origin, or (as his friend Ducamp has written in his *Literary Souvenirs* with a disagreeable persistence, and so uselessly!) of his nervousness and epilepsy; of his loves or his friendships, but solely of his work. We know, in fact, to-day, that if all such details are made clear in the biography of a great writer, in no way do they explain his work. The author of *Gil Blas,* Alain René Lesage, was a Breton, like the author of *Atala;* the Corneille brothers had almost nothing in common. Of all our great writers, the one nearest, perhaps, to Jean-Jacques Rousseau, who died a victim to delirium from persecution, was Madame Sand, who had, without doubt, the sanest and best balanced temperament.

Other writers have sought, — for instance, our great classical authors, Pascal, Bossuet and perhaps Corneille, — to influence the thought of their time; some, like Molière, La Fontaine, and La Bruyère, to correct customs. Others still, — such as our romantic writers, Hugo or De Musset, — desired only to express their personal conception of the world and of life. And then Balzac, whose object,—almost scientific,—was to make a "natural history," a study and description, of the social species, as an animal or vegetable species is described in zoölogy or botany. Gustave Flaubert attempted only to work out his art, for and through the love of art. Very early in life, as we clearly see from his correspondence, his consideration for art was not even that of a social but of a *sacred* function, in which the artist was the priest. We hear sometimes, in metaphor and not without irony, of the "priesthood" of the artist and the "worship" of art. These expressions must be taken literally in Flaubert's case. He was cloistered in his art as a monk in his convent or by his discipline; and he truly lived only in meditation upon that art, as a Mystic in contemplation of the perfections of his God. Nothing outside of art truly interested him, neither science, nor things political or religious, nor men, nor women, nor anything in the world; and if, sometimes, it was his duty to occupy himself with them, it was never in a degree greater than could benefit his art. "The accidents of the world"—this is his own expression—appeared to him only as things permitted *for the sake of description,* so much so that his own existence, even, seemed to him to have no other excuse.

It is that which explains the mixture of "romanticism," "naturalism," and I will add, of "classicism"—which has been pointed out more than once in Flaubert's work. *Madame Bovary* is the masterpiece of naturalistic romance and has not been surpassed by the studies of Zola or the stories of De Maupassant. On the other hand, there is nothing in Hugo, even, more romantic than *The Temptation of*

Saint Antony. But it is necessary to look for many things in romanticism; and the romanticism of Hugo, which was one of the delights of Flaubert, did not resemble that of De Musset, (Lord de Musset, as Flaubert called him) which he strongly disliked. What he loved in romanticism was the "colour," and nothing but the colour. He loved the romanticism of the Orientals, of Hugo and Chateaubriand, that plastic romanticism, whose object is to substitute in literature "sensations of art" for the "expression of ideas," or even of sentiments. It is precisely here that naturalism and romanticism — or at least French naturalism, which is very different from that of the Russians or the English — join hands. In the one case, as in the other, the attempt is made to "represent"— as he himself puts it; and when one represents nothing except the vulgar, the common, the mediocre, the everyday, commonplace, or grotesque, he is a "naturalist," like the author of *Madame Bovary;* but one is a "romanticist" when, like the author of *Salammbô,* he makes this world vanish, and recreates a strange land filled with Byzantine or Carthaginian civilization, with its barbaric luxury, its splendour of corruption, immoderate appetites, and monstrous deities.

We have done wrong in considering Flaubert a naturalist impeded by his romanticism, or a romanticist impenitent, irritated with himself because of his tendency to naturalism. He was both naturalist and romanticist. And in both he was an artist, so much of an artist (I say this without fear of contradiction) that he saw nothing in his art but "representation," the telling of the truth in all its depth and fidelity. *Les Fileuses* and *La Reddition de Bréda* are always by Velasquez; but the genius of the painter has nothing in common with the subject he has chosen or the circumstances that inspired him.

From this source proceeds that insensibility in Flaubert with which he has so often been reproached, not without reason, and which divides his naturalism from that of the author of *Adam Bede* or that of the author of *Anna Karenina* by an abyss. Honest, as a man, a good citizen, a good son, a good brother, a good friend, Flaubert was indifferent, as an artist, to all that did not belong to his art. "I believe that it is necessary to love nothing," he has written somewhere, and even underscored it — that is to say, it is necessary to hover impartially above all objective points. And, in fact, as nothing passed before his eyes that he considered did not lie within the possibility of representation, he made it a law unto himself to look nothing in the face except from this point of view.

In this regard one may compare his attitude in the presence of his model to that of his contemporaries, Renan, for example, or Taine, in the presence of the object of their studies. With them also critical impartiality resembles not only indifference but insensibility. Not only have they refused to confound their emotions with their judgments, but their judgments have no value in their eyes except as they separate them from their emotions, — as they emancipate themselves from them or even place themselves in opposition to them. In like manner did Flaubert. The first condition of an exact representation of things is to dominate them; and in order to dominate them, is it not necessary to begin by detaching yourself from them? We see dimly through tears, and we are too much absorbed in that which gives us pleasure to be good judges of it. "An ideal society would be one where each individual performed his duty according to his ability. Now, then, I do my duty as best I can; I am forsaken. . . . No one pities my misfortunes; those of others occupy their attention! I give to humanity what it gives to me —*indifference!*" Is not the link between Flaubert's "indifference" and his conception of art evident here?

But Flaubert said besides: "Living does not concern me! It is only necessary to shun suffering." Should we not change the name of this to "egotism" or "insensibility?" We might, indeed, did we not know that this egotism germinated in Flaubert as a means of discipline. The object of this discipline was to concentrate, for the profit of his art, those qualities or forces which the ordinary man dissipates in the pursuit of useless pleasures, or squanders in intensity of life.

We may take account at the same time of the nature of his pessimism. For there are many ways of being a pessimist, and Flaubert's was not at all like that of Schopenhauer or Leopardi. His pessimism, real and sincere, proceeded neither from personally grievous experiences in life, as did that of the recluse of Recanati, nor from a philosophic or logical view of the conditions of existence in which humanity is placed, like the pessimism of the Frankfort philosopher. Flaubert was rather a victim of what Théophile Gautier, in his well-known *Emaux et Camées,* calls by the singularly happy name of "the Luminous Spleen of the Orient." To tell the truth, what Flaubert could not pardon in humanity was that

it did not make enough of art, and so his pessimism
was a consequence of his æstheticism. "As lovers of
the beautiful," he tells us, "we are all outlaws!
Humanity hates us; we do not serve it; we hate it
because it wounds us! Let us love, then, in art, as
the Mystics love their God; and let all pale before
this love."

These lines are dated 1853, before he had published anything. Therefore, Flaubert did not express
himself thus because he was not successful. His
self-love was not in question! No one had yet criti-
cised or discussed him. But he felt that his ideal of
art, an art which he could not renounce, was opposed to the ideal methods, if they are ideal, held by
his contemporaries; and the vision of the combats
that he must face at once exalted and exasperated
him. His pessimism was of the élite, or rather the
minority of one who feels himself, or at least be-
lieves himself to be, superior, and who, knowing
well that he will always be in the minority, fears,
and rightly too, that he will not be recognised. It is
a form of pessimism less rare in our day than one
would think, and Taine, among others, said practically the same thing when he averred that "one
writes only for one or two hundred people in Europe, or in the world." It may be that this is too
individual a case! A more liberal estimate would be
that we write for all those who can comprehend us;
that style has for its first object the increase of such
a number; and, after that, if there still be those who
cannot comprehend us, no reason for despair exists
on our part or on theirs.

Let us follow, now, the consequences of this
principle in Flaubert's work, and see successively all

that his work means, and the dogma of art which
proceeds from it.

At first you are tempted to believe that Flaubert's
work is diverse, though inconsiderable in volume;
and, primarily do not see clearly the threads which
unite the *Education Sentimentale* with the *Tentation
de Saint Antoine* or *Salammbô* with *Madame Bovary*.

On the one side Christian Egypt, and on the other
the France of 1848, Madame Arnoux, Rosanette, and
Frederick Moreau, the Orleanist carnival, and the
"underwood" of Fontainebleau.   Here, Carthage,
Hamilcar, Hannibal, Narr' Havas, the Numidian hero,
and Spendius, the Greek slave, the lions in bondage,
the pomegranate trees which they sprinkled with
silphium, the whole a strange and barbaric world;
then Charles Bovary, the chemist Homais, his son
Napoleon and his daughter Athalie, provincial life in
the time of the Second Empire; *bourgeois* adultery,
diligences and notaries' clerks.   Then again Herodias,
Salome, Saint Jean-Baptiste, or Saint Julien l'Hospitalier, the middle ages and antiquity,— all, at first sight,
seem far removed, one from the other.   At first one
must admire, in such a contrast of subjects and
colors, the extraordinary skill, let us say the *virtuo-
sité*, of the artist.   But, if we look more closely, we
shall not be slow to perceive that no work is more
homogeneous than that of Flaubert, and that, in
truth, the *Education Sentimentale* differs from *Salammbô* only as a Kermesse of Rubens, for example,
or a Bacchante of Poussin differs from the apotheoses
or the Church pictures of the painters themselves.
The making is the same, and you immediately recognise the hand.   The difference is in the choice of
subjects, which is of no importance, since Flaubert is

only attempting to "represent" something, and in the choice of material, when he is "representing," he is no longer free. That is the reason why, if one seek for lessons in "naturalism" in *Salammbô*, he will find them, and will also find all the "romanticism" he seeks in the *Education Sentimentale* and in *Madame Bovary*.

From the other lessons that flow from this work, I find some in rhetoric, in art, in invention, in composition, and two or three of great import, eloquent in their bearing upon the history of contemporary French literature.

A master does not mingle or engage his personality in his subject; but, as a God creates from the height of his serenity, without passion, if without love, so the poet or the artist expands the thing he touches, and, on each occasion, brings to bear upon it all the faculties that are his by toil but not innate. Nothing is demanded of the workers, and they make no confessions or confidences. Literature and art are not, nor should be, the expression of men's emotions, and still less the history of their lives. That is the reason why, while from reading *René*, for example, or *Fraziella, Delphine, Corinne, Adolphe, Indiana, Volupté*, or some of the romances of Balzac — *La Muse du Departement*, or *Un Grand Homme de Province à Paris*, — you could induct Balzac's entire psychology, or Sainte-Beuve's, or Madame Sand's, Benjamin Constant's, Madame de Staël's or Chateaubriand's, you would find in *Madame Bovary* or *Salammbô* nothing of Flaubert, except his temperament, his taste, and his ideals as an artist. Let us suppose another Flaubert, who did not live at Rouen, whose life is not that related in his correspondence, who was not the friend of Maxime Ducamp or of Louise Colet, and the *Education Sentimentale* or the *Tentation de Saint Antoine* would not be in the least different from what they are now, nor should we see one line of change to be made. This is a triumph in objective art. "I do not wish to consider art as an overflow of passion," he wrote once, a little brutally. "I love my little niece as if she were my daughter, and I am sufficiently active in her behalf to prove that these are not empty phrases. But may I be flayed alive rather than exploit that kind of thing in style!" It has been but a short hundred years since, as he expressed it, romanticism "exploited its emotions in style," and made art from the heart.

"Ah! strike upon the heart, 'tis there that genius lies!" But, for a whole generation, *Madame Bovary, Salammbô* and *Education Sentimentale* have been teaching the contrary. "The author in his work should be like God in the universe, everywhere present but nowhere visible. Art being second nature, the creator of this nature should act through analogous procedure. He must be felt in each atom, under every aspect, concealed but infinite; the effect upon the spectator should be a kind of amazement." Furthermore, he remarks that this principle was the core of Greek art. I know not, or at least I do not recall, whether he had observed (as he should, since Anglo-Saxons have been quick to notice it) that this "principle" underlies the art of Shakespeare.

To realize this principle in work you must proceed scientifically, and, in this connection, we may notice that Flaubert's idea is that of Leconte de Lisle in the preface to his *Poèmes Antiques,* and of Taine in his lectures upon *L'Idéal dans l'art.*

Romanticism had confounded the picturesque with the anecdotal; character with accident; colour with oddity. *Han d'Islande, Nôtre-Dame de Paris* and some romances of Balzac, the first and poorest, not signed with his name, may serve as an example. The classic writers on their side, had not always distinguished very profoundly the difference between the general and the universal, the principal and the accessory, the permanent and the superficial. We see this in the French comedies of the eighteenth century, even in some of Molière's — in his *L'Avare* and his *Le Misanthrope*, for example. Flaubert believed that a means of terminating this conflict is to be found in method; and that is the reason why, if we confine ourselves wholly to the consideration of the medium in his works, we shall find the *Tentation de Saint Antoine* entirely romantic; while, as a retaliation, nothing is more classic than *Madame Bovary.*

The reason for this is, that in his subject, whatever it was, Carthaginian or low Norman, refined or *bourgeois,* modern or antique, he saw only the subject itself, with the eyes and after the manner of a naturalist, who is concerned only in knowing thoroughly the plant or the animal under observation. There is no sentiment in botany or in chemistry, and in them the desideratum is truth. Singleness of aim is the primary virtue in a *savant.* Things are what they are, and we demand of him that he show them to us as they are. We accuse him of lying if he disguises, weakens, alters or embellishes them.

Likewise the artist! His function is ever to "represent:" and in order to accomplish this, he should, like the savant, mirror only the facts. After this, what do the names "romanticism" or "classicism" signify? Their sole use is to indicate the side taken; they are, so to speak, an acknowledgment that the writer is adorning the occurrence he is about to represent. He may make it more universal or more characteristic than nature! But, inversely, if all art is concentrated upon the representation, what matters the subject? Is one animal or plant more interesting than another to the naturalist? Does a name matter? All demand the same attention. Art can make exception in its subjects no more than science.

If we ask in what consists the difference between science and art, on this basis, Flaubert, with Leconte de Lisle and with Taine, will tell us that it is in the beauty which communicates prestige to the work, or in the power of form.

"What I have just written might be taken for something of Paul de Kock's, had I not given it a profoundly literary form," wrote Flaubert, while he was at work on *Madame Bovary;* "but how, out of trivial dialogue, produce style? Yet it is absolutely necessary! It must be done!" He went further still, and persuaded himself that style had a value in itself, intrinsic and absolute, aside from the subject. In fact, if the subject had no importance of its own, and if there were no personal motives for choosing one subject rather than another, what reason would there be for writing *Madame Bovary* or *Salammbô?* One alone: and that to "make something out of nothing," to produce a work of art from things of no import. For though everyone has some ideas, and everyone has had experience in some kind of life, it is given to few to be able to express their experience or their ideas in terms of beauty. This, precisely, is the goal of art.

Form, then, is the great preoccupation of the artist, since, if he is an artist, it is through form, and
in the perfection or originality of that form, that his
triumph comes. Nothing stands out from the general
mediocrity except by means of form; nothing becomes
concrete, assuming immortality, save through form.
Form in art is queen and sovereign. Even truth
makes itself felt only through the attractiveness of
form. And further, we cannot part one from the
other; they are not opposed to each other; they are
at one; and art in every phase consists only in this
union. It is the end of art to give the superior life
of form to that which has it not; and finally, this
superior life of form, this magic wand of style, rhyth-
mic as verse and terse as science, by firmly establishing the thing it touches, withdraws it from that law
of change, constant in its inconstancy, which is the
miserable condition of existence.

> All passes; art in its strength
> Alone remains to all eternity;
> The bust
> Survives the city.

This it is that makes up the charm, the social
dignity, and the lasting grandeur of art.

This is not the place to discuss the "æsthetic"
quality, and I shall content myself with indicating
briefly some of the objections it has called forth.

Has form indeed all the importance in literature
that Flaubert claimed for it? And what importance
has it in sculpture, for example, or in painting? Let us
grant its necessity. Colour and line, which are, so to
speak, the primal elements in the alphabet of painting and of sculpture, have not in themselves deter-

mined and precise significance. Yellow and red, green and blue are only general and confused sensations. But words express particular sentiments and well-defined ideas, and have a value that does not depend upon the form or the quality of the words. You cannot, then, in using them, distinguish between significance and form, or combine them independently of the idea they are intended to convey, as is possible with colours and with lines, solely for the beauty that results from combination. If literary art is a "representation," it is also something more; and the lapse in Flaubert, as in all those who have followed him in the letter, lies in having missed this distinction. You cannot write merely to represent; you write also to express ideas, to determine or to modify convictions; you write that you may act, or impel others to act: these are effects beyond the power of painting or of sculpture. A statue or a picture never brought about a revolution; a book, a pamphlet, nay, a few fiery words, have overturned a dynasty.

It is no longer true, as a whole generation of writers has believed, that art and science may be one and the same thing; or that the first, as Taine has said, may be an "anticipation of the second." We could not in the presence of our fellow-creatures and their suffering affect the indifference of a naturalist before the plant or the animal he is studying. Whatever the nature of "human phenomena" may be, we in our quality as man can only look at them with human eyes, and could temptation make us change our point of view, it would properly be called inhuman.

One might add that, if it is not certain that nature was made for man, and if, for that reason, science is wholly independent of conscience, as we take it, it is otherwise with art. We know that man was not made for art, but that art was made for man. We forget each time we speak of "art for art's sake" that there is need precisely to define the meaning of the expression and to recall that but for truth art could not have for its object the perfecting of political institutions, the uplifting of the masses, the correction of customs, the teachings of religion, and that although this may lead finally to the realization of beauty, it nevertheless remains the duty of man, and consequently, is human in its origin, human in its development, and human in its aim.

Upon all these points, it is only necessary to think sensibly, as also upon the question — which we have not touched upon,— of knowing under what conditions, in what sense, and in what degree the person of the artist can or should remain foreign to his work.

But a peculiarity of Flaubert's,— and one more personal, which even most of the naturalists have not shared with him, neither the Dutch in their paintings, nor the English in the history of romance (the author of *Tom Jones* or of *Clarissa Harlowe*), nor the Russians, Tolstoï or Dostoiefski,— is to despise the rôle of irony in art. "My personages are profoundly repugnant to me," he wrote, *à propos* of *Madame Bovary*. But they were not always repugnant to him, at least not all of them, and, in verification of this, we find that he has not for Spendius, Matho, Hamilcar, and Hanno, the boundless scorn that he affects for Homais or for Bournisien, for Bouvard or for Pecuchet.

We recognise here the particular and special form of Flaubert's pessimism. That there could be people in the world, among his contemporaries, who were not wholly absorbed and preoccupied with art, surpassed his comprehension, and when this indifference did not arouse an indignation which exasperated him even to blows, it drew from him a scornful laughter that one might call Homeric or Rabelaisian, since it incited more to anger than to gaiety. And this is the reason why *Madame Bovary*, *Education Sentimentale*, *Un Cœur Simple*, and *Bouvard et Pecuchet* would be more truly named were they called satires and not representations.

The exaggeration of the principle here recoils upon itself. That disinterestedness, that impartiality, that serenity which permitted him to "hover impartially above all objects" deserted him. A satirist, or to be more exact, a caricaturist, awoke within the naturalist. He raged at his own characters. He railed at them and mocked them. The interest of the representation had undergone a change. He was no longer in the attitude of mere fidelity to facts, but in a state of scorn and violent derision. Homais and Bournisien are no longer studies in themselves, but a burden to Flaubert. His *Education Sentimentale*, in spite of him, became, to use his own expression, an overflow of rancour. In *Bouvard et Pecuchet* he gave way to his hatred of humanity; here, as a favour, and under the mask of irony, he brings himself into his work, and, like a simple Madame Sand, or a vulgar De Musset, we perceive Flaubert himself, bull-necked and ruddy, with the moustaches of a Gallic chief, agonizing at each turn in the romance.

It is not necessary to exaggerate Flaubert's influence. In his time there were ten other writers, none of whom equalled him,—Parnassians in poetry,

positivists in criticism, realists in romance or in
dramatic writing,— who laboured at the same work.
His æstheticism is not his alone, yet *Madame Bovary*
and *Salammbô* shot like unexpected meteors out of a
grey sky, the dull, low sky of the Second Empire.
In 1860 the sky was not so grey or so low; and the
Poèmes Antiques of Leconte de Lisle, the *Études
d'histoire religieuse* of Renan, and the *Essais de Cri-
tique* of Taine, are possibly not unworthy to be
placed in parallel or comparison with the first writings of Flaubert.   An exquisite judge of things of the
mind, J. J. Weiss, very clearly saw at that time what
there was in common in all these works, in the
glory of which he was not deceived when he added
the *Fleurs du Mai* by Charles Baudelaire, and the
first comedies of Alexandre Dumas *fils*.   But the
truth is, not one of these works was marked with
signs of masterly maturity in like degree with *Madame Bovary*.

It is, then, natural that, from day to day, Flaubert
should become a guide, and here, if we consider the
nature of the lessons he gives, we cannot deny their
towering excellence.

If there was need to agitate against romanticism,
Madame Bovary performed the duty; and if in this
agitation there was need to save what was worth
salvation, *Salammbô* saved it.   If it was fitting to recall to poets and to writers of romance, to Madame
Sand herself and Victor Hugo, that art was not invented as a public carrier for their confidences, it is
still Flaubert who does it.   He taught the school of
hasty writers that talent, or even genius, is in need
of discipline,— the discipline of a long and painful
prenticehood in the making and unmaking of their

work. He has widened, and especially has he hollowed and deepened, the notion that romanticism was born of nature, and, in doing this, has brought art back to the fountain-head of inspiration. His rhetoric and æstheticism brought him face to face with Nature, enabled him to see her, a gift as rare as it is great, and to "represent" her—the proof of the preceding. It is the artist that judges the model. Poets and romance-writers, like painters, we value only in as much as they represent life—by and for the fidelity, the originality, the novelty, the depth, the distinction, the perfection with which they represent it. It is the rule of rules, the principle of principles! And if Flaubert had no other merit than to have seen this better than any other writer of his age, it would be enough to assure for him a place, and a very exalted place, in the Panthéon of French Literature.

F. Brunetière

BIOGRAPHICAL PREFACE

GUSTAVE FLAUBERT was born at Rouen, December 12, 1821. His father was a physician, who later became chief surgeon in the Hôtel Dieu of that city, and his mother, Anne-Justine-Caroline Fleuriot, was of Norman extraction.

Fourth of a family of six children, as a child Flaubert exhibited marked fondness for stories, and, with his favourite sister, Caroline, would invent them for pastime. As a youth, he was exceedingly handsome, tall, broad-shouldered and athletic, of independent turn of mind, fond of study, and caring little for the luxuries of life. He attended the college of Rouen, but showed no marked characteristic save a pronounced taste for history. After graduating, he went to Paris to read law, at the École de Droit. At this time disease, the nature of which he always endeavored to conceal from the world, attacked him and compelled a return to Rouen. The complaint, as revealed after his death by Maxime Ducamp, was epilepsy, and the constant fear of suffering an attack in public led Flaubert to live the life of a recluse.

The death of his father occurring at this critical period, Flaubert abandoned the study of law, which he had begun only in obedience to the formally expressed wish of his family. Having a comfortable income, he turned his thoughts to literature, and from that time all other work was distasteful. He read and wrote incessantly, although at this period he never completed anything. Among his papers were found several fragments written between his eighteenth and twentieth years. Some bear the stamp of his individuality, if not in the substance, which is romantic,—at least in the form, which is peculiarly lucid and concise, —for instance, the slight, romantic, autobiographic sketch entitled *Novembre*.

Flaubert wrote neither for money nor for fame. To him, art was religion, and to it he sacrificed his life. Perfection of style was his goal; and unremitting devotion to his ideal slew him. That he was never satisfied with what he wrote, his letters show; and all who knew him marvelled at his laborious and pathetic application to his work. He settled first in Croisset, near Rouen, with his family, but shortly afterwards went to Brittany with Maxime Ducamp. On his return he planned *La Tentation de Saint Antoine*, which grew out of a fragmentary sketch entitled *Smarh* (a mediæval Mystery, the manuscript tells us), written in early youth. *La Tentation* proved a source of labor, for he never ceased revising it until it appeared in book form in 1874. In 1847, he wrote a modern play, entitled *Le Candidat*, produced in 1874 at the Vaudeville. It was not his first dramatic effort, as he had already written a sort of lyric fairy-play, *Le Château des Cœurs*, which was published in his *Œuvres Posthumes*.

In 1849 Flaubert visited Greece, Egypt, and Syria, again accompanied by his friend Maxime Ducamp.

After his return he planned a book of impressions similar to *Par les Champs et par les Grèves,* which was the result of the trip to Brittany; but the beginning only was achieved. Still he gathered many data for his future great novel, *Salammbô.* The year 1851 found him back in Croisset, working at *La Tentation de Saint Antoine,* which he dropped suddenly, when half finished, for an entirely different subject — *Madame Bovary,* a novel of provincial life, published first in 1857 in the *Revue de Paris.* For this Flaubert was prosecuted, on the charge of offending against public morals, but was acquitted after the remarkable defense offered by Maître Senard.

Flaubert's fame dates from *Madame Bovary,* which was much discussed by press and public. Many, including his friend, Maxime Ducamp, condemned it, but Sainte-Beuve gave it his decisive and courageous approval. It was generally considered, however, as the starting point of a new phase in letters, frankly realistic, and intent on understanding and expressing everything. Such success might have influenced Flaubert's artistic inclinations but did not, for while *Madame Bovary* was appearing in the *Revue de Paris,* the *Artiste* was publishing fragments of *La Tentation de Saint Antoine.*

In 1858 Flaubert went to Tunis, visited the site of ancient Carthage, and four years afterwards wrote *Salammbô,* a marvellous reconstitution, more than half intuitive, of a civilisation practically unrecorded in history. This extraordinary book did not call forth the enthusiasm that greeted *Madame Bovary.* Flaubert, in whom correctness of detail was a passion, was condemned, even by Sainte-Beuve, for choosing from all history a civilisation of which so little is known. The author replied, and a lengthy controversy ensued, but it was not a subject that could be settled definitely in one way or another.

In *L'Education Sentimentale, roman d'un jeune homme,* published in 1869, Flaubert returns momentarily to the style which brought him such rapid and deserved celebrity. In 1877 appeared *Trois Contes,* three short stories written in the impersonal style of *Salammbô,* contrasting strangely with *La Legende de Saint Julien l'Hospitalier* and *Herodias,* wherein Flaubert shows himself supreme in the art of word-painting.

Death came to him on May 8, 1880, as he was writing the last chapters of a new work, *Bouvard et Pecuchet,* which was published in part after he died and later appeared in book form (1881).

At the age of twenty-five, Flaubert met the only woman who in any way entered his sentimental life. She was an author, the wife of Lucien Colet, and the "Madame X" of the Correspondence. Their friendship lasted eight years and ended unpleasantly, Flaubert being too absorbed by his worship for art to let passion sway him.

He remained unmarried because his love for his mother and family made calls upon him that he would not neglect. He was indifferent to women, treated them with paternal indulgence, and often avowed that "woman is the undoing of the just." Yet a warm friendship existed between him and George Sand, and many of his letters are addressed to her, touching upon various questions in art, literature, and politics.

The misanthropy which haunted Flaubert, of which so much has been said, was not innate, but was acquired through the constant contemplation of human

folly. It was natural for him to be cheerful and kind-
hearted, and of his generosity and disinterestedness
not enough can be said. At the close of his life fi-
nancial difficulties assailed him, for he had given a
great part of his fortune to the support of a niece,
restricting his own expenses and living as modestly
as possible. In 1879, M. Jules Ferry, then Minister of Public Instruction, offered him a place in the Bibliothèque
Mazarine, but the appointment was not confirmed.

Flaubert's method of production was slow and
laborious. Sometimes weeks were required to write
a few pages, for he accumulated masses of notes and,
it must be said, so much erudition as at times to im-
pede action. He thought no toil too great, did it but
aid him in his pursuit of literary perfection, and when
the work that called for such expenditure of strength
and thought was finished, he looked for no reward
save that of a satisfied soul. Alien to business wis-
dom, he believed that to set a price upon his work
disparaged it.

In Flaubert, a Romanticist and a Naturalist at first
were blended. But the latter tendency was fostered
and acknowledged, while the former was repressed.
He was an ardent advocate of the impersonal in art,
declaring that an author should not in a page, a line,
or a word, express the smallest part of an opinion.
To him a writer was a mirror, but a mirror that reflected life while adding that divine effulgence which
is Art. Of him a French Romanticist still living
says:

"Imagination was espoused by Unremitting-Toil-in-Faith and bore
Flaubert. France fed the child, but Art stepped in and gave him to
the Nations as a Beacon for the worshippers of Truth-in-Letters-and-
in-Life."

The city of Rouen reared a monument to Flaubert's memory, but on the spot where he breathed his last are reared the chimneys and the buildings of a factory, a tribute — possibly unconscious — to reality in life.

Before writing *Madame Bovary* Flaubert had tested himself, and an idea of the scope and variety of his ideas may be gained from the following list of inedited and unfinished fragments:

HISTORICAL

The Death of the Duc de Guise, 1835.
Norman Chronicle of the Tenth Century, 1836.
Two Hands on a Crown, or, During the Fifteenth Century, 1836.
Essay on the Struggle between Priesthood and Empire, 1838.
Rome and the Cæsars, 1839.

TRAVELS

Various notes on Travels to the Pyrenean Mountains, Corsica, Spain and the Orient, from 1840 to 1850.

TALES AND NOVELS

The Plague in Florence, 1836.
Rage and Impotence, 1836.
The Society Woman, fantastic verses, 1836.
Bibliomania, 1836.
An Exquisite Perfume, or, The Buffoons, 1836.
Dreams of the Infernal Regions, 1837.
Passion and Chastity, 1837.
The Funeral of Dr. Mathurin, or, During the XVth Century, 1839.
Frenzy and Death, 1843.
Sentimental Education (not the novel published under same title). 1843.

PLAYS

Louis XI, Drama, 1838.
Discovery of Vaccination, a parody of tragic style; one act only was written.

CRITICISMS

On Romantic Literature in France.

MISCELLANY

Quidquid volueris? A psychological study, 1837.
Agony (Sceptical Thoughts), 1838.
Art and Commerce, 1839.
Several nameless sketches.

Unfortunately, nearly all the works of Flaubert's youth were mere sketches, laid aside by him. Their publication would have added nothing to his fame. Still, the loss of some would have been deplorable, to wit, such gems as *Novembre*, *The Dance of Death*, *Rabelais*, and the travels, *Over Strand and Field*. These sketches will be found in this edition.

Robert Arnot

MADAME BOVARY

PART I.

I.

THE NEW BOY.

WE WERE in class when the head-master came in, followed by a "new fellow," not wearing the school uniform, and a school servant carrying a large desk. Those who had been asleep woke up, and every one rose as if just surprised at his work.

The head-master made a sign to us to sit down. Then, turning to the class-master, he said to him in a low voice:

"Monsieur Roger, here is a pupil whom I recommend to your care; he'll be in the second. If his work and conduct are satisfactory, he will go into one of the upper classes, as becomes his age."

The "new fellow," standing in the corner behind the door so that he could hardly be seen, was a country lad of about fifteen, and taller than any of us. His hair was cut square on his forehead like a village chorister's; he looked reliable, but very ill at ease. Although he was not broad-shouldered, his short school jacket of green cloth with black buttons must

have been tight about the armholes, and showed at
the opening of the cuffs red wrists accustomed to being bare. His legs, in blue stockings, looked out
from beneath yellow trousers, drawn tight by braces.
He wore stout, ill-cleaned, hob-nailed boots.

We began repeating the lesson. He listened with
all his ears, as attentive as if at a sermon, not daring
even to cross his legs or lean on his elbow; and
when at two o'clock the bell rang, the master was
obliged to tell him to fall into line with the rest of us.

When we came back to work, we were in the
habit of throwing our caps on the floor so as to
have our hands more free; we used from the door to
toss them under the form, so that they hit against
the wall and made a lot of dust: it was "the thing."

But, whether he had not noticed the trick, or did
not dare to attempt it, the "new fellow" was still
holding his cap on his knees even after prayers were
over. It was one of those head-gears of composite
order, in which we can find traces of the bearskin,
shako, billycock hat, sealskin cap, and cotton nightcap; one of those poor things, in fine, whose dumb
ugliness has depths of expression, like an imbecile's
face. Oval, stiffened with whalebone, it began with
three round knobs; then came in succession lozenges
of velvet and rabbit-skin separated by a red band;
after that a sort of bag that ended in a cardboard poly-
gon covered with complicated braiding, from which
hung, at the end of a long, thin cord, small twisted
gold threads in the manner of a tassel. The cap was
new; its peak shone.

"Rise," said the master.

He stood up; his cap fell. The whole class began to laugh. He stooped to pick it up. A neigh-

bor knocked it down again with his elbow; he picked
it up once more.

"Get rid of your helmet," said the master, who
was a bit of a wag.

There was a burst of laughter from the boys,
which so thoroughly put the poor lad out of countenance that he did not know whether to keep his cap
in his hand, leave it on the floor, or put it on his
head. He sat down again and placed it on his knee.

"Rise," repeated the master, "and tell me your
name."

The new boy articulated in a stammering voice an
unintelligible name.

"Again!"

The same sputtering of syllables was heard,
drowned by the tittering of the class.

"Louder!" cried the master; "louder!"

The "new fellow" then took a supreme resolution,
opened an inordinately large mouth, and shouted at
the top of his voice as if calling some one the word,
"Charbovari."

A hubbub broke out, rose in *crescendo* with bursts
of shrill voices (they yelled, barked, stamped, repeated
"Charbovari! Charbovari!"), then died away into
single notes, growing quieter only with great difficulty, and now and again suddenly recommencing
along the line of a form whence rose here and there,
like a damp cracker going off, a stifled laugh.

However, amid a rain of impositions, order was
gradually re-established in the class; and the master
having succeeded in catching the name of "Charles
Bovary," having had it dictated to him, spelt out,
and re-read, at once ordered the poor devil to go
and sit down on the punishment form at the foot of

the master's desk. He got up, but before going hesitated.

"What are you looking for?" asked the master.

"My c-a-p," timidly said the "new fellow," casting troubled looks round him.

"Five hundred verses for all the class!" shouted in a furious voice, stopped, like the *Quos ego*, a fresh outburst. "Silence!" continued the master indignantly, wiping his brow with his handkerchief, which he had just taken from his cap. "As to you, 'new boy,' you will conjugate '*ridiculus sum*' twenty times." Then, in a gentler tone, "Come, you'll find your cap again; it hasn't been stolen."

Quiet was restored. Heads bent over desks, and the "new fellow" remained for two hours in an exemplary attitude, although from time to time some paper pellet flipped from the tip of a pen came bang in his face. But he wiped his face with one hand and continued motionless, his eyes lowered.

In the evening, at preparation, he pulled out his pens from his desk, arranged his small belongings, and carefully ruled his paper. We saw him working conscientiously, looking out every word in the dictionary, and taking the greatest pains. Thanks, no doubt, to the willingness he showed, he had not to go down to the class below. But though he knew his rules passably, he had little finish in composition. It was the curé of his village who had taught him his first Latin; his parents, from motives of economy, having sent him to school as late as possible.

His father, Monsieur Charles Denis Bartolomé Bovary, retired assistant-surgeon-major, compromised about 1812 in certain conscription scandals, and forced at that time to leave the service, had then taken advantage of his fine figure to get hold of a dowry of sixty thousand francs that offered in the person of a hosier's daughter who had fallen in love with his good looks. A fine man, a great talker, making his spurs ring as he walked, wearing whiskers that ran into his moustache, his fingers always garnished with rings, and dressed in loud colors, he had the dash of a military man with the easy air of a commercial traveller. Once married, he lived for three or four years on his wife's fortune, dining well, rising late, smoking long porcelain pipes, not coming in at night till after the theater, and haunting cafés. The father-in-law died, leaving little; he was indignant at this, "went in for the business," lost some money in it, then retired to the country, where he thought he would make money. But, as he knew no more about farming than calico, as he rode his horses instead of sending them to plough, drank his cider in bottle instead of selling it in cask, ate the finest poultry in his farm-yard, and greased his hunting-boots with the fat of his pigs, he was not long in finding out that he would do better to give up all speculation.

For two hundred francs a year he managed to live on the border of the provinces of Caux and Picardy, in a kind of place half farm, half private house; and here, soured, eaten up with regrets, cursing his luck, jealous of every one, he shut himself up at the age of forty-five, sick of men, he said, and determined to live in peace.

His wife had adored him once on a time; she had bored him with a thousand servilities that had only estranged him the more. Lively once, expansive and affectionate, in growing older she had become (after the fashion of wine that, exposed to air, turns to vinegar) ill-tempered, grumbling, irritable. She had suffered so much without complaint at first, when she had seen him going after all the village drabs, and when a score of bad houses sent him back to her at night, weary, stinking drunk. Then her pride revolted. After that she was silent, burying her anger in a dumb stoicism that she maintained till her death. She was constantly going about looking after business matters. She called on the lawyers, the president, remembered when bills fell due, got them renewed, and at home, ironed, sewed, washed, looked after the workmen, paid the accounts, while he, troubling himself about nothing, eternally besotted in sleepy sulkiness, whence he only roused himself to say disagreeable things to her, sat smoking by the fire and spitting into the cinders.

When she had a child, it had to be sent out to nurse. When he came home, the lad was spoiled as if he were a prince. His mother stuffed him with jam; his father let him run about barefoot, and, playing the philosopher, even said he might as well go about quite naked like the young of animals. As opposed to the maternal ideas, he had a certain virile idea of childhood on which he sought to mould his son, wishing him to be brought up hardily, like a Spartan, to give him a strong constitution. He sent him to bed without any fire, taught him to drink off large draughts of rum, and to jeer at religious processions. But, peaceable by nature, the lad answered only poorly to his notions. His mother always kept him near her; she cut out cardboard for him, told him tales, entertained him with endless monologues full of melancholy gaiety and charming nonsense. In her life's isolation she centered on the child's head all her shattered, broken little vanities. She dreamed of high station; she already saw him, tall, handsome, clever, settled as an engineer or in the law. She taught him to read, and even on an old piano she had taught him two or three little songs. But to all this Monsieur Bovary, caring little for letters, said: "It is not worth while. Shall we ever have the means to send him to a public school, to buy him a practice, or to start him in business? Besides, with cheek a man always gets on in the world." Madame Bovary bit her lips, and the child knocked about the village.

He went after the laborers, drove away with clods of earth the ravens that were flying about. He ate blackberries along the hedges, minded the geese with a long switch, went haymaking during harvest, ran about in the woods, played hop-scotch under the church porch on rainy days, and at great fêtes begged the beadle to let him toll the bells, that he might hang all his weight on the long rope and feel himself borne upward by it in its swing. Meanwhile he grew like an oak; he was strong of hand, fresh of color.

When he was twelve years old his mother had her own way; he began his lessons. The curé took him in hand; but the lessons were so short and irregular that they could not be of much use. They were given at spare moments in the sacristy, standing up, hurriedly, between a baptism and a burial; or else the curé, if he had not to go out, sent for his pupil after the *Angelus*. They went up to his room and settled down; the flies and moths fluttered round the candle. It was close, the child fell asleep and the good man, beginning to doze with his hands on his stomach, was soon snoring with his mouth wide open. On other occasions, when Monsieur le Curé, on his way back after administering the viaticum to some sick person in the neighborhood, caught sight of Charles playing about the fields, he called him, lectured him for a quarter of an hour, and took advantage of the occasion to make him conjugate his verb at the foot of a tree. The rain interrupted them or an acquaintance passed. All the same he was always pleased with him, and even said the "young man" had a very good memory.

Charles could not go on like this. Madame Bovary took strong steps. Ashamed, or rather tired out, Monsieur Bovary gave in without a struggle, and they waited one year longer, so that the lad should take his first communion.

Six months more passed, and the year after Charles was finally sent to school at Rouen, whither his father took him towards the end of October, at the time of the St. Romain fair.

It would now be impossible for any of us to remember anything about him. He was a youth of even temperament, who played in playtime, worked in school-hours, was attentive in class, slept well in the dormitory, and ate well in the refectory. He had *in loco parentis* a wholesale ironmonger in the Rue Ganterie, who took him out once a month on Sundays after his shop was shut, sent him for a walk on the quay to look at the boats, and then brought him back to college at seven o'clock before supper. Every Thursday evening he wrote a long letter to his mother with red ink and three wafers; then he went over his history note-books, or read an old volume of "Anarchasis" that was knocking about the study. When we went for walks he talked to the servant who, like himself, came from the country.

By dint of hard work he kept always about the middle of the class; once even he got a certificate in natural history. But at the end of his third year his parents withdrew him from the school to make him study medicine, convinced that he could even take his degree by himself.

His mother chose a room for him on the fourth floor of a dyer's she knew, overlooking the Eau-de-Robec. She made arrangements for his board, got him furniture, a table and two chairs, sent home for an old cherry-tree bedstead, and bought besides a small cast-iron stove with the supply of wood that was to warm the poor child. Then at the end of a week she departed, after a thousand injunctions to be good, now that he was going to be left to himself.

The syllabus that he read on the notice-board stunned him: lectures on anatomy, lectures on pathology, lectures on physiology, lectures on pharmacy, lectures on botany and clinical medicine, and therapeutics, without counting hygiene and materia medica —all names of whose etymologies he was ignorant, and that were to him as so many doors to sanctuaries filled with magnificent darkness.

He understood nothing of it all; it was all very well to listen — he did not follow. Still he worked; he had bound note-books, he attended all the courses, never missed a single lecture. He did his little daily task like a mill-horse, who goes round and round with his eyes bandaged, not knowing what work he is doing.

To spare him expense his mother sent him every week by the carrier a piece of veal baked in the oven, on which he lunched when he came back from the hospital, while he sat kicking his feet against the wall. After this he had to run off to lectures, to the operation-room, to the hospital, and return to his home at the other end of the town. In the evening, after the poor dinner of his landlord, he went back to his room and set to work again in his wet clothes, that smoked as he sat in front of the hot stove.

On the fine summer evenings, at the time when the close streets are empty, when the servants are playing shuttlecock at the doors, he opened his window and leaned out. The river, that makes of this quarter of Rouen a wretched little Venice, flowed beneath him, between the bridges and the railings, yellow, violet, or blue. Working men, kneeling on the banks, washed their bare arms in the water. On poles projecting from the attics, skeins of cotton were drying in the air. Opposite, beyond the roofs, spread the pure heaven with the red sun setting. How pleasant it must be at home! How fresh under the beech-tree! And he expanded his nostrils to breathe in the sweet odors of the country which did not reach him.

He grew thin, his figure became taller, his face took a saddened look that made it almost interesting. Naturally, through indifference, he abandoned all the resolutions he had made. Once he missed a lecture; the next day all the lectures; and, enjoying his idleness, little by little he gave up work altogether. He got into the habit of going to the public-house, and had a passion for dominoes. To shut himself up every evening in the dirty public room, to push about on marble tables the small sheep-bones with black dots, seemed to him a fine proof of his freedom, which raised him in his own esteem. It was beginning to see life, the sweetness of stolen pleasures; and when he entered, he put his hand on the door-handle with a joy almost sensual. Then many things hidden within him come out; he learnt couplets by heart and sang them to his boon companions, became enthusiastic about Béranger, learnt how to make punch, and, finally, how to make love.

Thanks to these preparatory labors, he failed completely in his examination for an ordinary degree. He was expected home the same night to celebrate his success. He started on foot, stopped at the beginning of the village, sent for his mother, and told her all. She excused him, threw the blame of his failure on the injustice of the examiners, encouraged him a little, and took upon herself to set matters straight. It was only five years later that Monsieur Bovary knew the truth; it was old then, and he accepted it. Moreover, he could not believe that a man born of him could be a fool.

So Charles set to work again and crammed for his examination, ceaselessly learning all the old questions by heart. He passed pretty well. What a happy day for his mother! They gave a grand dinner.

Where should he go to practise? To Tostes, where there was only one old doctor. For a long time Madame Bovary had been on the look-out for his death, and the old fellow had barely been packed off when Charles was installed, opposite his place, as his successor.

But it was not everything to have brought up a son, to have had him taught medicine, and discovered Tostes, where he could practise it; he must have a wife. She found him one — the widow of a bailiff at

Dieppe, who was forty-five and had an income of twelve hundred francs. Though she was ugly, as dry as a bone, her face with as many pimples as the spring has buds, Madame Dubuc had no lack of suitors. To attain her ends Madame Bovary had to oust them all, and she even succeeded in very cleverly baffling the intrigues of a pork-butcher backed up by the priests.

Charles had seen in marriage the advent of an easier life, thinking he would be more free to do as he liked with himself and his money. But his wife was master; he had to say this and not say that in company, to fast every Friday, dress as she liked, harass at her bidding those patients who did not pay. She opened his letters, watched his comings and goings, and listened at the partition-wall when women came to consult him in his surgery.

She must have her chocolate every morning, attentions without end. She constantly complained of her nerves, her chest, her liver. The noise of footsteps made her ill; when people left her, solitude became odious to her; if they came back, it was doubtless to see her die. When Charles returned in the evening, she stretched forth two long thin arms from beneath the sheets, put them round his neck, and having made him sit down on the edge of the bed, began to talk to him of her troubles: he was neglecting her, he loved another. She had been warned she would be unhappy; and she ended by asking him for a dose of medicine and a little more love.

II.

A GOOD PATIENT.

NE night toward eleven o'clock they were awakened by the noise of a horse pulling up outside their door. The servant opened the garret-window and parleyed for some time with a man in the street below. He came for the doctor, had a letter for him. Nastasie came downstairs shivering and undid the bars and bolts one after the other. The man left his horse, and, fo'lowing the servant, suddenly came in behind her. He pulled out from his wool cap with grey top-knots a letter wrapped up in a rag and presented it gingerly to Charles, who rested his elbow on the pillow to read it. Nastasie, standing near the bed, held the light. Madame in modesty had turned to the wall and showed only her back.

This letter, sealed with a small seal in blue wax, begged Monsieur Bovary to come immediately to the farm of the Bertaux to set a broken leg. Now from Tostes to the Bertaux was a good eighteen miles across country by way of Longueville and Saint-Victor. It was a dark night; Madame Bovary junior was afraid of accidents for her husband. So it was decided the stable-boy should go on first; Charles would start three hours later when the moon rose. A boy was to be sent to meet him, and show him the way to the farm, and open the gates for him.

Towards four o'clock in the morning, Charles, well wrapped up in his cloak, set out for the Bertaux. Still sleepy from the warmth of his bed, he let himself be lulled by the quiet trot of his horse. When it stopped of its own accord in front of those holes surrounded with thorns that are dug on the margin of furrows, Charles awoke with a start, suddenly remembered the broken leg, and tried to call to mind all the fractures he knew. The rain had stopped, day was breaking, and on the branches of the leafless trees birds roosted motionless, their little feathers bristling in the cold morning wind. The flat country stretched as far as eye could see, and the tufts of trees round the farms at long intervals seemed like dark violet stains on the vast gray surface, that on the horizon faded into the gloom of the sky. Charles from time to time opened his eyes, his mind grew weary, and sleep coming upon him, he soon fell into a doze wherein his recent sensations blending with memories, he became conscious of a double self, at once student and married man, lying in his bed as but now, and crossing the operation theater as of old. The warm smell of poultices mingled in his brain with the fresh odor of dew; he heard the iron rings rattling along the curtain-rods of the bed, and saw his wife sleeping. As he passed Vassonville he came upon a boy sitting on the grass at the edge of a ditch.

"Are you the doctor?" asked the child.

And on Charles's answer he took his wooden shoes in his hands and ran on in front of him.

The general practitioner, riding along, gathered from his guide's talk that Monsieur Rouault must be one of the well-to-do farmers. He had broken his leg the evening before on his way home from a Twelfth-night feast at a neighbor's. His wife had been dead for two years. There was only his daughter, who helped him to keep house, with him.

The ruts were becoming deeper; they were approaching the Bertaux. The little lad, slipping through a hole in the hedge, disappeared; then he came back to the end of a courtyard to open the gate. The horse slipped on the wet grass; Charles had to stoop to pass under the branches. The watchdogs in their kennels barked, dragging at their chains. As he entered the Bertaux the horse took fright and stumbled.

It was a substantial-looking farm. In the stables, over the top of the open doors, one could see great cart-horses quietly feeding from new racks. Right along the outbuildings extended a large dunghill, from which manure liquid oozed, while amidst fowls and turkeys five or six peacocks, a luxury in Chauchois farmyards, were foraging on the top of it. The sheepfold was long, the barn high, with walls smooth as your hand. Under the cartshed were two large carts and four ploughs, with their whips, shafts, and harnesses complete, whose fleeces of blue wool were getting soiled by the fine dust that fell from the granaries. The courtyard sloped upwards, planted with trees set out symmetrically, and the chattering noise of a flock of geese was heard near the pond.

A young woman in a blue merino dress with three flounces came to the threshold of the door to receive Monsieur Bovary, whom she led to the kitchen, where a large fire was blazing. The servants' breakfast was boiling beside it in small pots of all sizes. Some damp clothes were drying inside the chimney-corner. The shovel, tongs, and the nozzle of the bellows, all of colossal size, shone like polished steel, while along the walls hung many pots and pans in which the clear flame of the hearth, mingling with the first rays of the sun coming in through the window, was mirrored fitfully.

Charles went up to the first floor to see the patient. He found him in his bed, sweating under his bed-clothes, having thrown his cotton nightcap far away from him. He was a fat little man of fifty, with white skin and blue eyes, the fore part of his head was bald, and he wore ear-rings. Near him on a chair stood a large decanter of brandy, whence he poured himself out a little from time to time to keep up his spirits; but as soon as he caught sight of the doctor his elation subsided, and instead of swearing, as he had been doing for the last twelve hours, he began to groan feebly.

The fracture was a simple one, without any kind of complication. Charles could not have hoped for an easier case. Then calling to mind the devices of his masters at the bedside of patients, he comforted the sufferer with all sorts of kindly remarks, those caresses of the surgeon that are like the oil they put on bistouries. In order to make some splints a bundle of laths was brought up from the cart-house. Charles selected one, cut it into two pieces and planed it with a fragment of window-pane, while the servant tore up sheets to make bandages, and Mademoiselle Emma tried to sew some pads. As she was a long time before she found her workcase, her father

grew impatient; she did not answer, but as she sewed she pricked her fingers, which she then put to her mouth to suck. Charles was much surprised at the whiteness of her nails. They were shiny, delicate at the tips, more polished than the ivory of Dieppe, and almond-shaped. Yet her hand was not beautiful, perhaps not white enough, and a little hard at the knuckles; besides, it was too long, with no soft inflections in the outlines. Her real beauty was in her eyes. Although brown, they seemed black because of the lashes, and her look came at you frankly, with a candid boldness.

The bandaging over, the doctor was invited by Monsieur Rouault himself to "pick a bit" before he left.

Charles went down into the room on the ground-floor. Knives and forks and silver goblets were laid for two on a little table at the foot of a huge bed that had a canopy of printed cotton with figures representing Turks. There was an odor of iris-root and damp sheets that escaped from a large oak chest opposite the window. On the floor in corners were sacks of flour stuck upright in rows. These were the overflow from the neighboring granary, to which three stone steps led. By way of decoration for the apartment, hanging to a nail in the middle of the wall, whose green paint had scaled off from the effects of saltpeter, was a crayon head of Minerva in a gold frame, underneath which was written in Gothic letters "To dear Papa."

First they spoke of the patient, then of the weather, of the great cold, of the wolves that infested the fields at night. Mademoiselle Rouault did not at all like the country, especially now that she had to look after the farm almost alone. As the room was chilly, she shivered as she ate. This showed something of her full lips, that she had a habit of biting when silent.

Her neck stood out from a white turned-down collar. Her hair, whose two black folds seemed each of a single piece, so smooth were they, was parted in the middle by a delicate line that curved slightly with the curve of the head; and, just showing the tip of the ear, it was joined behind in a thick chignon, with a wavy movement at the temples that the country doctor saw now for the first time in his life. The upper part of her cheek was rose-colored. She had, like a man, thrust in between two buttons of her bodice a tortoise-shell eyeglass.

When Charles, after bidding farewell to old Rouault, returned to the room before leaving, he found her standing, her forehead against the window, looking into the garden, where the bean props had been knocked down by the wind. She turned round.

"Are you looking for anything?" she asked.

"My whip, if you please," he answered.

He began rummaging on the bed, behind the doors, under the chairs. It had fallen to the floor, between the sacks and the wall. Mademoiselle Emma saw it, and bent over the flour sacks. Charles, out of politeness, made a dash also, and as he stretched out his arm, at the same moment felt his breast brush against the back of the young girl bending beneath him. She drew herself up, scarlet, and looked at him over her shoulder as she handed him his whip.

Instead of returning to the Bertaux in three days as he had promised, he went back the very next

day, than regularly twice a week, without counting
the visits he paid now and then as if by accident.

Everything, moreover, went well; the patient pro-
gressed favorably; and when, at the end of forty-six
days, old Rouault was seen trying to walk alone in
his "den," Monsieur Bovary began to be looked upon
as a man of great capacity. Old Rouault said that he
could not have been cured better by the first doctor
of Yvetot, or even of Rouen.

As to Charles, he did not stay to ask himself why
it was a pleasure to him to go to the Bertaux. Had
he done so, he would, no doubt, have attributed his
zeal to the importance of the case, or perhaps to the
money he hoped to make by it. Was it for this,
however, that his visits to the farm formed a de-
lightful exception to the meagre occupations of his
life? On these days he rose early, set off at a gallop, urging on his horse, then got down to wipe his
boots in the grass and put on black gloves before entering. He liked going into the courtyard, and noticing the gate turn against his shoulder, the cock crow
on the wall, the lads run to meet him. He liked the
granary and the stables; he liked old Rouault, who
pressed his hand and called him his savior; he liked
the small wooden shoes of Mademoiselle Emma on
the scoured flags of the kitchen — her high heels made
her a little taller; and when she walked in front of
him, the wooden soles springing up quickly struck
with a sharp sound against the leather of her boots.

She always reconducted him to the first step of
the stairs. When his horse had not yet been brought
round she stayed there. They had said "Good-bye;"
there was no more talking. The open air wrapped
her round, playing with the soft down on the back

of her neck, or blew to and fro on her hips her apron-strings, that fluttered like streamers. Once, during a thaw, the bark of the trees in the yard was oozing, the snow on the roofs of the out-buildings was melting; she stood on the threshold, and went to fetch her sunshade and opened it. The sunshade, of silk of the color of pigeons' breasts, through which the sun shone, lighted up with shifting hues the white skin of her face. She smiled under the tender warmth, and drops of water could be heard falling one by one on the stretched silk.

During the first period of Charles's visits to the Bertaux, Madame Bovary, junior, never failed to inquire after the invalid, and she had even chosen in the book that she kept on a system of double entry a clean blank page for Monsieur Rouault. But when she heard he had a daughter, she began to make inquiries, and she learnt that Mademoiselle Rouault, brought up at the Ursuline Convent, had received what is called "a good education;" and so knew dancing, geography, drawing, how to embroider and play the piano. That was the last straw.

"So it is for this," she said to herself, "that his face beams when he goes to see her, and that he puts on his new waistcoat at the risk of spoiling it with the rain. Ah! that woman! that woman!"

And she detested her instinctively. At first she solaced herself by allusions that Charles did not understand, then by casual observations that he let pass for fear of a storm, finally by open apostrophes to which he knew not what to answer. "Why did he go back to the Bertaux now that Monsieur Rouault was cured and that these folks hadn't paid yet? Ah! it was because a young lady was there, some one

who knew how to talk, to embroider, to be witty.
That was what he cared about; he wanted town
misses." And she went on:

"The daughter of old Rouault a town miss! Get
out! Their grandfather was a shepherd, and they
have a cousin who was almost had up at the assizes
for a nasty blow in a quarrel. It is not worth while
making such a fuss, or showing herself at church on
Sundays in a silk gown, like a countess. Besides, the
poor old chap, if it hadn't been for the colza last year,
would have had much ado to pay up his arrears."

For very weariness Charles left off going to the
Bertaux. Héloïse made him swear, his hand on the
prayer-book, that he would go there no more, after
much sobbing and many kisses, in a great outburst
of love. He obeyed then, but the strength of his desire protested against the servility of his conduct; and
he thought, with a kind of naïve hypocrisy, that this
interdict to see her gave him a sort of right to love
her. And then the widow was thin; she had long
teeth; wore in all weathers a little black shawl, the
edge of which hung down between her shoulder-
blades; her bony figure was sheathed in her clothes
as if they were a scabbard; they were too short,
and displayed her ankles with the laces of her large
boots crossed over gray stockings.

Charles's mother came to see them from time to
time, but after a few days the daughter-in-law seemed
to put her own edge on her, and then, like two knives,
they scarified him with their reflections and observations. It was wrong of him to eat so much. Why
did he always offer a glass of something to every one
who came? What obstinacy not to wear flannels!

In the spring it came about that a notary at Ingou-

ville, the holder of the widow Dubuc's property, one
fine day went off, taking with him all the money in
his office. Héloïse, it is true, still possessed, besides
a share in a boat valued at six thousand francs, her
house in the Rue St. François; and yet, with all this fortune that had been so trumpeted abroad, nothing, ex-
cepting perhaps a little furniture and a few clothes, had
appeared in the household. The matter had to be gone
into. The house at Dieppe was found to be eaten up
with mortgages to its foundations; what she had
placed with the notary God only knew, and her share
in the boat did not exceed one thousand crowns.
She had lied, the good lady! In his exasperation,
Monsieur Bovary the elder, smashing a chair on the
flags, accused his wife of having caused the misfortune of their son by harnessing him to such a har-
ridan, whose harness wasn't worth her hide. They
came to Tostes. Explanations followed. There were
scenes. Héloïse in tears, throwing her arms about
her husband, conjured him to defend her from his
parents. Charles tried to speak up for her. They
grew angry and left the house.

But the blow had struck home. A week after,
as she was hanging up some washing in her yard,
she was seized with a spitting of blood, and the next
day, while Charles had his back turned to her drawing the window-curtain, she said, "O God!" gave a
sigh and fainted. She was dead! What a surprise!

When all was over at the cemetery, Charles went
home. He found no one downstairs; he went up to
the first floor to their room; saw her dress still hanging at the foot of the alcove; then, leaning against
the writing-table, he stayed until the evening, buried
in a sorrowful reverie. She had loved him, after all!

III.

A LONELY WIDOWER.

NE morning old Rouault brought Charles the money for setting his leg — seventy-five francs in forty-sou pieces, and a turkey. He had heard of his loss, and consoled him as well as he could.

"I know what it is," said he, clapping him on the shoulder; "I've been through it. When I lost my dear departed, I went into the fields to be quite alone. I fell at the foot of a tree; I cried; I called on God; I talked nonsense to him. I wanted to be like the moles that I saw on the branches, their insides swarming with worms, dead, and an end of it. And when I thought that there were others at that very moment with their nice little wives holding them in their embrace, I struck great blows on the earth with my stick. I was pretty well mad with not eating; the very idea of going to a café disgusted me — you wouldn't believe it. Well, quite softly, one day following another, a spring on a winter, and an autumn after a summer, this wore away, piece by piece, crumb by crumb; it passed away, it is gone, I should say it has sunk; for something always remains at the bottom, as one would say — a

(23)

weight here, at one's heart. But since it is the lot of all of us, one must not give way altogether, and, because others have died, want to die too. You must pull yourself together, Monsieur Bovary. It will pass away. Come to see us; my daughter thinks of you now and again, d'ye know, and she says you are forgetting her. Spring will soon be here. We'll have some rabbit-shooting in the warrens to amuse you a bit."

Charles followed his advice. He went back to the Bertaux. He found all as he had left it, that is to say, as it was five months ago. The pear trees were already in blossom, and Farmer Rouault, on his legs again, came and went, making the farm more full of life.

Thinking it his duty to heap the greatest attention upon the doctor because of his sad position, he begged him not to take his hat off, spoke to him in an undertone as if he had been ill, and even pretended to be angry because nothing rather lighter had been prepared for him than for the others, such as a little clotted cream or stewed pears. He told stories. Charles found himself laughing, but the remembrance of his wife suddenly coming back to him depressed him. Coffee was brought in; he thought no more about her.

He thought less of her as he grew accustomed to living alone. The new delight of independence soon made his loneliness bearable. He could now change his meal-times, go in or out without explanation, and when he was very tired stretch himself full length on his bed. So he nursed and coddled himself and accepted the consolations that were offered him. On the other hand, the death of his wife had not served

him ill in his business, since for a month people had
been saying, "The poor young man! what a loss!"
His name had been talked about, his practice had
increased; and, moreover, he could go to the Bertaux just as he liked. He had an aimless hope, and
was vaguely happy; he thought himself better looking as he brushed his whiskers before the looking-
glass.

One day he got there about three o'clock. Everybody was in the fields. He went into the kitchen,
but did not at once catch sight of Emma; the outside
shutters were closed. Through the chinks of the
wood the sun sent across the flooring long fine rays
that were broken at the corners of the furniture and
trembled along the ceiling. Some flies on the table
were crawling up the glasses that had been used, and
buzzing as they drowned themselves in the dregs of
the cider. The daylight that came in by the chimney
made velvet of the soot at the back of the fireplace,
and touched with blue the cold cinders. Between the
window and the hearth Emma was sewing; she wore
no fichu; he could see small drops of perspiration on
her bare shoulders.

After the fashion of country folks she asked him to
have something to drink. He said no; she insisted
and at last laughingly offered to have a glass of liqueur
with him. So she went to fetch a bottle of curaçoa
from the cupboard, reached down two small glasses,
filled one to the brim, poured scarcely anything into
the other, and, after clinking their glasses, carried
hers to her mouth. As it was almost empty she
bent back to drink, her head thrown back, her lips
pouting, her neck on the strain. She laughed at getting none of it, while with the tip of her tongue

passing between her small teeth she licked drop by drop the bottom of her glass.

She sat down again and took up her work, a white cotton stocking she was darning. She worked with her head bent down; she did not speak, nor did Charles. The air coming in under the door blew a little dust over the flags; he watched it drift along, and heard nothing but the throbbing in his head and the faint clucking of a hen that had laid an egg in the yard. Emma from time to time cooled her cheeks with the palms of her hands, and cooled these again on the knobs of the huge fire-dogs.

She complained of suffering since the beginning of the season from giddiness; she asked if sea-baths would do her any good; she began talking of her convent, Charles of his school; words came to them. They went up into her bedroom. She showed him her old music-books, the little prizes she had won, and the oak-leaf crowns, left at the bottom of a cupboard. She spoke to him, too, of her mother, of the country, and even showed him the bed in the garden where, on the first Friday of every month, she gathered flowers to put on her mother's tomb. But their gardeners had understood nothing about it; servants were so careless. She would have dearly liked, if only for the winter, to live in town, although the length of the fine days made the country perhaps even more wearisome in the summer. And, according to what she was saying, her voice was clear, sharp, or, on a sudden, all languor, lingering out in modulations that ended almost in murmurs as she spoke to herself; now joyous, opening big, naïve eyes, then with her eyelids half closed, her look full of boredom, her thoughts wandering.

Going home at night, Charles went over her words, one by one, trying to recall them, to fill out their sense, that he might piece out the life she had lived before he knew her. But he never saw her in his thoughts other than he had seen her the first time, or as he had just left her. Then he asked himself what would become of her — if she would be married, and to whom? Alas! old Rouault was rich, and she! — so beautiful! But Emma's face always rose before his eyes, and a monotone, like the humming of a top, sounded in his ears, "If you should marry, after all! if you should marry!" At night he could not sleep; his throat was parched; he was athirst. He got up to drink from the water-bottle and opened the window. The night was covered with stars, a warm wind blowing in the distance; the dogs were barking. He turned his head toward the Bertaux.

Thinking that, after all, he should lose nothing, Charles promised himself to ask her in marriage as soon as occasion offered, but each time such occasion did offer the fear of not finding the right words sealed his lips.

Old Rouault would not have been sorry to be rid of his daughter, who was of no use to him in the house. In his heart he excused her, thinking her too clever for farming, a calling under the ban of Heaven, since one never saw a millionaire in it. Far from having made a fortune by it, the good man was losing every year; for if he was good in bargaining, in which he enjoyed the dodges of the trade, on the other hand, agriculture properly so called, and the internal management of the farm, suited him less than most people. He did not willingly take his hands out of his pockets, and did not spare expense in all that concerned himself, liking to eat well, to have good fires, and to sleep well. He liked old cider, under-done legs of mutton, *glorias** well beaten up. He took his meals in the kitchen alone, opposite the fire, on a little table brought to him all ready laid, as on the stage.

When, therefore, he perceived that Charles's cheeks grew red if near his daughter, which meant that he would propose for her one of these days, he chewed the cud of the matter beforehand. He certainly thought him a little meagre, and not quite the son-in-law he would have liked, but he was said to be well-conducted, economical, very learned, and no doubt would not make too many difficulties about the dowry. Now, as old Rouault would soon be forced to sell twenty-two acres of "his property," as he owed a good deal to the mason, to the harness-maker, and as the shaft of the cider-press wanted re-newing, "If he asks for her," he said to himself, "I'll give her to him."

At Michaelmas Charles went to spend three days at the Bertaux. The last had passed like the others, in procrastinating from hour to hour. Old Rouault was seeing him off; they were walking along the road full of ruts; they were about to part. This was the time. Charles gave himself as far as to the corner of the hedge, and at last, when past it:

"Monsieur Rouault," he murmured, "I should like to say something to you."

They stopped. Charles was silent.

"Well, tell me your story. Don't I know all about it?" said old Rouault, laughing softly.

---

* A mixture of coffee and spirits. — TRANS.

"Monsieur Rouault—Monsieur Rouault," stammered Charles.

"I ask nothing better," the farmer went on. "Although, no doubt, the little one is of my mind, still we must ask her opinion. So you get off — I'll go back home. If it is 'yes,' you needn't return because of all the people about, and besides it would upset her too much. But so that you mayn't be eating your heart, I'll open wide the outer shutter of the window against the wall; you can see it from the back by leaning over the hedge."

And he went off.

Charles fastened his horse to a tree; he ran into the road and waited. Half-an-hour passed, then he counted nineteen minutes by his watch. Suddenly a noise was heard against the wall; the shutter had been thrown back; the hook was still swinging.

The next day by nine o'clock he was at the farm. Emma blushed as he entered, and she gave a little forced laugh to keep herself in countenance. Old Rouault embraced his future son-in-law. The discussion of money matters was put off; moreover, there was plenty of time before them, as the marriage could not decently take place till Charles was out of mourning, that is to say, about the spring of the next year.

The winter passed waiting for this. Mademoiselle Rouault was busy with her trousseau. Part of it was ordered at Rouen, and she made herself chemises and nightcaps after fashion-plates that she borrowed. When Charles visited the farmer, the preparations for the wedding were talked over; they wondered in what room they should have dinner; they dreamed of the number of dishes that would be wanted, and what should be the entrées.

Emma would, on the contrary, have preferred to have a midnight wedding with torches, but old Rouault could not understand such an idea. So there was a wedding at which forty-three persons were present, at which they remained sixteen hours at table, began again the next day, and to some extent on the days following.

CONSOLATION.

THE guests arrived early in carriages, in one-horse chaises, two-wheeled cars, old open gigs, wagonettes with leather hoods, and the young people from the nearer villages in carts, in which they stood up in rows, holding on to the sides so as not to fall, going at a trot and well shaken up. Some came from a distance of thirty miles, from Goderville, from Normanville, and from Cany. All the relatives of both families had been invited, quarrels between friends arranged, acquaintances long since lost sight of written to.

From time to time one heard the crack of a whip behind the hedge; then the gates opened, a chaise entered. Galloping up to the foot of the steps, it stopped short and emptied its load. They got down from all sides, rubbing knees and stretching arms. The ladies wearing bonnets, had on dresses in the town fashion, gold watch chains, pelerines with the ends tucked into belts, or little colored fichus fastened down behind with a pin, that left the back of the neck bare. The lads, dressed like their papas, seemed uncomfortable in their new clothes (many that day

(31)

handselled their first pair of boots), and by their sides, speaking never a word, wearing the white dress of their first communion lengthened for the occasion, were some big girls of fourteen or sixteen, cousins or elder sisters no doubt, rubicund, bewildered, their hair greasy with rose-pomade, and very much afraid of soiling their gloves. As there were not enough stable-boys to unharness all the carriages, the gentlemen turned up their sleeves and set about it themselves. According to their different social positions, they wore tail-coats, overcoats, shooting-jackets, cutaway-coats: fine tail-coats, redolent of family respectability, that came out of the wardrobe only on state occasions; overcoats with long tails flapping in the wind and round capes and pockets like sacks; shooting-jackets of coarse cloth, usually worn with a cap with a brass-bound peak; very short cutaway-coats with two small buttons in the back, close together like a pair of eyes, the tails of which seemed cut out of one piece by a carpenter's hatchet. Some, too (but these, you may be sure, would sit at the bottom of the table), wore their best blouses — that is to say, with collars turned down to the shoulders, the back gathered into small plaits and the waist fastened very far down with a worked belt.

And the shirts stood out from the chests like cuirasses! Every one had just had his hair cut; ears stood out from the heads; they had been close-shaven; a few, even, who had had to get up before daybreak, and not been able to see to shave, had diagonal gashes under their noses or cuts the size of a three-franc piece along the jaws, which the fresh air *en route* had inflamed, so that the great, white, beaming faces were mottled here and there with red dabs.

The *mairie* was a mile and a half from the farm, and they went thither on foot, returning in the same way after the ceremony in the church. The procession, first united like one long colored scarf that undulated across the fields, along the narrow path winding amid the green corn, soon lengthened out, and broke up in different groups that loitered to talk. The fiddler walked in front with his violin, gay with ribbons at its pegs. Then came the married pair, the relations, the friends, all following pell-mell; the children stayed behind amusing themselves plucking the bell-flowers from oat-ears, or playing among themselves unseen. Emma's skirt, too long, trailed a little on the ground; from time to time she stopped to pull it up, and then delicately, with her gloved hands, she picked off the coarse grass and the thistle-downs, while Charles, empty handed, waited till she had finished. Old Rouault, with a new silk hat and the cuffs of his black coat covering his hands up to the nails, gave his arm to Madame Bovary, senior. As to Monsieur Bovary senior, who, heartily despising all these folk, had come simply in a frock-coat of military cut with one row of buttons — he was passing compliments of the bar to a fair young peasant. She bowed, blushed, and did not know what to say. The other wedding guests talked of their business or played tricks behind each other's backs, egging one another on in advance to be jolly. Those who listened could always catch the squeaking of the fiddler, who went on playing across the fields. When he saw that the rest were far behind he stopped to take breath, slowly rosined his bow, so that the strings should sound more shrilly, then set off again, by turns lowering and raising his neck, the better to mark time for himself. The noise of the instrument drove the little birds far away.

The table was laid under the cart-shed. On it were four sirloins, six chicken fricassées, stewed veal, three legs of mutton, and in the middle a fine roast sucking-pig, flanked by four chitterlings with sorrel. At the corners were decanters of brandy. Sweet bottled-cider frothed round the corks, and all the glasses had been filled to the brim with wine before-hand. Large dishes of yellow cream, that trembled with the least shake of the table, had designed on their smooth surface the initials of the newly wedded pair in nonpareil arabesques. A confectioner of Yvetot had been intrusted with the tarts and sweets. As he had only just set up in the place, he had taken great trouble, and at dessert he himself brought in a set dish that evoked loud cries of wonderment. To begin with, at its base was a square of blue card-board, representing a temple with porticoes, colonnades, and stucco statuettes all round, and in the niches were constellations of gilt paper stars; on the second stage was a dungeon of Savoy cake, surrounded by many fortifications in candied angelica, almonds, raisins, and quarters of oranges; and finally, on the upper layer was a green field with rocks set in lakes of jam, nutshell boats, and a small Cupid balancing himself in a chocolate swing, whose two uprights ended in real roses for balls at the top.

Until night they ate. When any of them were too tired of sitting, they went out for a stroll in the yard, or for a game with corks in the granary, and then returned to table. Toward the finish some went to sleep and snored. But with the coffee every one woke up. Then they began songs, showed off tricks, raised heavy weights, performed feats with their fingers, then tried lifting carts on their shoulders, made broad jokes, kissed the women. At night when they left, the horses, stuffed up to the nostrils with oats, could hardly be got into the shafts; they kicked, reared, the harness broke, their masters laughed or swore; and all night in the light of the moon along country roads there were runaway carts at full gallop plunging into the ditches, jumping over yard after yard of stones, clambering up the hills, with women leaning out from the tilt to catch hold of the reins.

Those who stayed at the Bertaux spent the night drinking in the kitchen. The children had fallen asleep under the seats.

The bride had begged her father to be spared the usual marriage pleasantries. However, a fishmonger, one of their cousins (who had even brought a pair of soles for his wedding present), began to squirt water from his mouth through the keyhole, when old Rouault came up just in time to stop him, and explain to him that the distinguished position of his son-in-law would not allow of such liberties. The cousin all the same did not give in to these reasons readily. In his heart he accused old Rouault of being proud, and he joined four or five other guests in a corner, who having, through mere chance, been several times running served with the worst helps of meat, also were of opinion they had been badly used, and were whispering about their host, and with covered hints hoping he would ruin himself.

Madame Bovary, senior, had not opened her mouth all day. She had been consulted neither as to the dress of her daughter-in-law nor as to the arrangement of the feast; she went to bed early. Her husband, instead of following her, sent to Saint-Victor for some cigars, and smoked till daybreak, drinking kirsch-punch, a mixture unknown to the company. This added greatly to the consideration in which he was held.

Charles, who was not of a facetious turn, did not shine at the wedding. He answered feebly to the puns, *doubles entendres*, compliments, and chaff that it was felt a duty to let off at him as soon as the soup appeared.

The next day, on the other hand, he seemed another man. It was he who might rather have been taken for the virgin of the evening before, whilst the bride gave no sign that revealed anything. The shrewdest did not know what to make of it, and they looked at her when she passed near them with an unbounded concentration of mind. But Charles concealed nothing. He called her "my wife," *tutoyéd* her, asked for her of every one, looked for her everywhere, and often he dragged her into the yards, where he could be seen from afar, among the trees, putting his arm round her waist, and walking half-bending over her, ruffling the chemisette of her bodice with his head.

Two days after the wedding the married pair left. Charles, on account of his patients, could not be away longer. Old Rouault had them driven back in his cart, and himself accompanied them as far as Vassonville. Here he embraced his daughter for the last time, got down, and went his way. When he had gone about a hundred paces he stopped, and as he saw the cart disappearing, its wheels turning in the dust, he gave a deep sigh. Then he remembered his wedding, the old times, the first pregnancy

of his wife; he, too, had been very happy the day
when he had taken her from her father to his home,
and had carried her off on a pillion, trotting through
the snow, for it was near Christmas-time, and the
country was all white. She held him by one arm, her
basket hanging from the other; the wind blew the
long lace of her Cauchois head-dress so that it sometimes flapped across his mouth, and when he turned
his head he saw near him, on his shoulder, her little
rosy face, smiling silently under the gold bands of
her cap. To warm her hands she put them from
time to time in his breast. How long ago it all was!
Their son would have been thirty by now. Then he
looked back and saw nothing on the road. He felt
dreary as an empty house; and tender memories
mingling with the sad thoughts in his brain, addled
by the fumes of the feast, he felt inclined for a moment to take a turn towards the church. As he was
afraid, however, that this sight would make him yet
more sad, he went directly home.

Monsieur and Madame Charles arrived at Tostes
about six o'clock. The neighbors came to the windows to see their doctor's new wife.

The old servant presented herself, curtsied to her,
apologised for not having dinner ready, and suggested
that madame, in the meantime, should look over her
house.

V.

THE NEW MÉNAGE.

THE brick front was just in a line with the street, or rather the road. Behind the door hung a cloak with a small collar, a bridle, and a black leather cap, and on the floor, in a corner, were a pair of leggings, still covered with dry mud. On the right was the one apartment that was both dining and sitting room. A canary-yellow paper, relieved at the top by a garland of pale flowers, was puckered everywhere over the badly-stretched canvas; white calico curtains with a red border hung crosswise the length of the window; and on the narrow mantelpiece a clock with a head of Hippocrates shone resplendent between two plate candlesticks under oval shades. On the other side of the passage was Charles's consulting-room, a little room about six paces wide, with a table, three chairs, and an office-chair. Volumes of the "Dictionary of Medical Science," uncut, but the binding rather the worse for the successive sales through which they had gone, occupied almost alone the six shelves of a deal bookcase. The smell of melted butter penetrated the thin walls when he saw patients, just as in the kitchen one could hear

(38)

the people coughing in the consulting-room and re-
counting their whole histories. Then, opening on the
yard, where the stable was, came a large dilapidated
room with a stove, now used as a wood-house, cellar, and pantry, full of old rubbish, of empty casks,
agricultural implements past service, and a mass of
dusty things whose use it was impossible to guess.

The garden, longer than wide, ran between two
mud walls with espaliered apricots, to a hawthorn
hedge that separated it from the field. In the middle
was a slate sundial on a brick pedestal; four flower-
beds with eglantines surrounded symmetrically the
more useful kitchen-garden bed. At the bottom, under the spruce bushes, was a curé in plaster reading
his breviary.

Emma went upstairs. The first room was not furnished, but in the second, which was their bedroom,
was a mahogany bedstead in an alcove with red
drapery. A shell-box adorned the chest of drawers,
and on the secretary near the window a bouquet of
orange blossoms tied with white satin ribbons stood
in a bottle. It was a bride's bouquet; it was the
other one's. She, looked at it. Charles noticed it; he
took it and carried it up to the attic, while Emma,
seated in an armchair (they were putting her things
down around her) thought of her bridal flowers
packed up in a bandbox, and wondered, dreaming,
what would be done with them if she were to die.

During the first days she occupied herself in thinking about changes in the house. She took the shades
off the candlesticks, had new wall-paper put up, the
staircase repainted, and seats made in the garden
round the sundial; she even inquired how she could
get a basin with a jet fountain and fishes. Finally,

her husband, knowing that she liked to drive out, picked up a second-hand dogcart, which, with new lamps and a splash-board in striped leather, looked almost like a tilbury.

He was happy then, and without a care in the world. A meal together, a walk in the evening on the highroad, a gesture of her hands over her hair, the sight of her straw hat hanging from the window-fastener, and many another thing in which Charles had never dreamed of pleasure, now made up the endless round of his happiness. In bed, in the morning, by her side, on the pillow, he watched the sunlight sinking into the down on her fair cheek, half hidden by the lappets of her nightcap. Seen thus closely, her eyes looked to him enlarged, especially when, on waking up, she opened and shut them rapidly many times. Black in the shade, dark blue in broad daylight, they had, as it were, depths of different colors, that, darker in the center, grew paler toward the surface of the eye. His own eyes lost themselves in these depths; he saw himself in miniature down to the shoulders, with his handkerchief round his head and the top of his shirt open. He rose. She came to the window to see him off, and stayed leaning on the sill between two pots of geranium, clad in her dressing-gown hanging loosely about her. Charles in the street buckled his spurs, his foot on the mounting stone, while she talked to him from above, picking with her mouth some scrap of flower or leaf that she blew out at him. Then this, eddying, floating, described semicircles in the air like a bird, and was caught before it reached the ground in the ill-groomed mane of the old white mare standing motionless at the door. Charles from horseback threw her a kiss; she answered with a nod; she shut the window, and he set off. And then along the highroad, spreading out its long ribbon of dust, along the deep lanes that the trees bent over as in arbors, along paths where the corn reached to the knees, with the sun on his back and the morning air in his nostrils, his heart full of the joys of the past night, his mind at rest, his flesh at ease, he went on, re-chewing his happiness, like those who after dinner taste again the truffles which they are digesting.

Until now what good had he had of his life? His time at school, when he remained shut up within the high walls, alone, in the midst of companions richer than he or cleverer at their work, who laughed at his accent, who jeered at his clothes, and whose mothers came to the school with cakes in their muffs? Or later, when he studied medicine, and never had his purse full enough to treat some little work-girl who would have become his mistress? Afterwards, he had lived fourteen months with the widow, whose feet in bed were cold as icicles. But now he had for life this beautiful woman whom he adored. For him the universe did not extend beyond the circumference of her petticoat, and he reproached himself with not loving her. He wanted to see her again; he turned back quickly, ran up the stairs with a beating heart. Emma, in her room, was dressing; he came up on tiptoe, kissed her back; she gave a cry.

He could not keep from continually touching her comb, her rings, her fichu; sometimes he gave her great sounding kisses with all his mouth on her cheeks, or else little kisses in a row all along her bare arm from the tip of her fingers up to her shoulder, and she put him away half-smiling, half-vexed, as you do a child who hangs about you.

Before marriage she thought herself in love; but the happiness that should have followed this love not having come, she must, she thought, have been mistaken. And Emma tried to find out what one meant exactly in life by the words *felicity, passion, rapture,* that had seemed to her so beautiful in books.

VI.

A Maiden's Yearnings.

SHE had read "Paul and Virginia," and she had dreamed of the little bamboo-house, the nigger Domingo, the dog Fidèle, but above all the sweet friendship of some dear little brother, who seeks red fruit for you on trees taller than steeples, or who runs barefoot over the sand, bringing you a bird's nest.

When she was thirteen, her father himself took her to town to place her in the convent. They stopped at an inn in the St. Gervais quarter, where, at their supper, they used painted plates that set forth the story of Mademoiselle de la Vallière. The explanatory legends, chipped here and there by the scratching of knives, all glorified religion, the tendernesses of the heart, and the pomps of court.

Far from being bored at first at the convent, she took pleasure in the society of the good sisters who, to amuse her, took her to the chapel, which one entered from the refectory by a long corridor. She played very little during recreation hours, knew her catechism well, and it was she who always answered Monsieur le Vicaire's difficult questions. Living thus, without ever leaving the warm atmosphere of the class-rooms, and amid these pale-faced women wearing rosaries with brass crosses, she was softly lulled by the mystic languor exhaled in the perfumes of the altar, the freshness of the holy water, and the lights of the tapers. Instead of attending to mass, she looked at the pious vignettes with their azure borders in her book, and she loved the sick lamb, the sacred heart pierced with sharp arrows, or the poor Jesus sinking beneath the cross he carries. She tried, by way of mortification, to eat nothing a whole day. She puzzled her head to find some vow to fulfill.

When she went to confession, she invented little sins in order that she might stay there longer, kneeling in the shadow, her hands joined, her face against the grating beneath the whispering of the priest. The comparisons of betrothed, husband, celestial lover, and eternal marriage, that recur in sermons, stirred within her soul depths of unexpected sweetness.

In the evening, before prayers, there was some religious reading in the study. On week-nights it was some abstract of sacred history or the Lectures of the Abbé Frayssinous, and on Sundays passages from the "Génie du Christianisme," as a recreation. How she listened at first to the sonorous lamentations of its romantic melancholies re-echoing through the world and eternity! If her childhood had been spent in the shop-parlor of some business quarter, she might perhaps have opened her heart to those lyrical invasions of Nature, which usually come to us only through translation in books. But she knew the country too well; she knew the lowing of cattle, the milking, the plow. Accustomed to calm aspects of life, she turned, on the contrary, to those of excitement. She loved the sea only for the sake of its storms, and the green fields only when broken up by ruins. She wanted to get some personal profit out of things, and she rejected as useless all that did not contribute to the immediate desires of her heart, being of a temperament more sentimental than artistic, looking for emotions, not landscapes.

At the convent there was an old maid who came for a week each month to mend the linen. Patronized by the clergy, because she belonged to an ancient family of noblemen ruined by the Revolution, she dined in the refectory at the table of the good sisters, and after the meal had a bit of chat with them before going back to her work. The girls often slipped out from the study to go and see her. She knew by heart the love-songs of the last century, and sang them in a low voice as she stitched away. She told stories, gave them news, went errands in the town, and on the sly lent the big girls some novel, that she always carried in the pockets of her apron, and of which the good lady herself swallowed long chapters in the intervals of her work. They were all love, lovers, sweethearts, persecuted ladies fainting in lonely pavilions, postilions killed at every stage, horses ridden to death on every page, somber forests, heartaches, vows, sobs, tears and kisses, little skiffs by moonlight, nightingales in shady groves, "gentlemen" brave as lions, gentle as lambs, virtuous as no one ever was, always well dressed, and weeping like fountains. For six months, then, Emma, at fifteen years of age, made her hands dirty with books from old lending libraries. With Walter Scott, later on, she fell in love with historical events, dreamed of old chests, guardrooms and minstrels. She would have liked to live in some old manor-house, like those long-waisted châtelaines who, in the shade of pointed arches, spent their days leaning on the stone, chin in hand, watching a cavalier with white plume galloping on his black horse from the distant fields. At this time she had a cult for Mary Stuart and enthusiastic veneration for illustrious or unhappy women. Joan of Arc, Héloïse, Agnès Sorel, the beautiful Ferronnière, and Clémence Isaure stood out to her like comets in the dark immensity of heaven, where also were seen, lost in shadow and all unconnected, St. Louis with his oak, the dying Bayard, some cruelties of Louis XI, a little of St. Bartholomew's, the plume of the Béarnais, and always the remembrance of the plates painted in honor of Louis XIV.

In the music-class, in the ballads she sang, there was nothing but little angels with golden wings, madonnas, lagunes, gondoliers;—mild compositions that allowed her to catch a glimpse athwart the obscurity of style and the weakness of the music of the attractive phantasmagoria of sentimental realities. Some of her companions brought "keepsakes" given them as New Year's gifts to the convent. These had to be hidden; it was quite an undertaking; they were read in the dormitory. Delicately handling the beautiful satin bindings, Emma looked with dazzled eyes at the names of the unknown authors, who had signed their verses for the most part as counts or viscounts.

She trembled as she blew back the tissue paper over the engraving and saw it folded in two and fall gently against the page. Here behind the balustrade of a balcony was a young man in a short cloak, holding in his arms a young girl in a white dress wearing an alms-bag at her belt; or there were nameless portraits of English ladies with fair curls, who looked at you from under their round straw hats with their large clear eyes. Some there were lounging in their carriages, gliding through parks, a greyhound bounding along in front of the equipage, driven at a trot by two small postilions in white breeches. Others, dreaming on sofas with an open letter, gazed at the moon through a slightly open window half draped by a black curtain. The naïve ones, a tear on their cheeks, were kissing doves through the bars of a Gothic cage, or, smiling, their heads on one side, were plucking the leaves of a marguerite with their taper fingers, that curved at the tips like peakèd shoes. And you too were there, Sultans with long pipes, reclining beneath arbors in the arms of Bayadères; Djiaours, Turkish sabers, Greek caps; and you especially, pale landscapes of dithyrambic lands, that often show us at once palm-trees and firs, tigers on the right, a lion to the left, Tartar minarets on the horizon; the whole framed by a very neat virgin forest, and with a great perpendicular sunbeam trembling in the water, where, standing out in relief like white excoriations on a steel-grey ground, swans are swimming about.

And the shade of the argand lamp fastened to the wall above Emma's head lighted up all these pictures of the world, that passed before her one by one in the silence of the dormitory, to the distant noise of some belated carriage rolling over the Boulevards.

When her mother died she cried much the first few days. She had a funeral picture made with the hair of the deceased, and, in a letter sent to the Bertaux full of sad reflections on life, she asked to be buried some day in the same grave. The goodman thought she must be ill, and came to see her. Emma was secretly pleased that she had reached at a first attempt the rare ideal of pale lives, never attained by mediocre hearts. She let herself glide along with Lamartine meanderings, listened to harps on lakes, to all the songs of dying swans, to the falling of the leaves, the pure virgins ascending to heaven, and the voice of the Eternal discoursing down the valleys. She wearied of it, would not confess it, continued from habit, and at last was surprised to feel herself soothed, and with no more sadness at heart than wrinkles on her brow.

The good nuns, who had been so sure of her vocation, perceived with great astonishment that Mademoiselle Rouault seemed to be slipping from them. They had indeed been so lavish to her of prayers, retreats, novenas, and sermons, they had so often preached the respect due to saints and martyrs, and given so much good advice as to the modesty of the body and the salvation of her soul, that she did as tightly reined horses: she pulled up short and the bit slipped from her teeth. This nature, positive in the midst of its enthusiasms, that had loved the church for the sake of the flowers, and music for the words of the songs, and literature for its passional stimulus, rebelled against the mysteries of faith as it grew irritated by discipline, a thing antipathetic to her constitution. When her father took her from school, no one was sorry to see her go. The Lady Superior even thought that she had latterly been somewhat irreverent to the community.

Emma at home once more, first took pleasure in looking after the servants, then grew disgusted with the country and missed her convent. When Charles came to the Bertaux for the first time, she thought herself quite disillusioned, with nothing more to learn, and nothing more to feel.

But the uneasiness of her new position, or perhaps the disturbance caused by the presence of this man, had sufficed to make her believe that she at last felt that wondrous passion which, till then, like a great bird with rose-colored wings, had hung in the splendor of the skies of poesy; and now she could not think that the calm in which she lived was the happiness she had dreamed.

1   G. F.—4

VII.

DISILLUSION.

SHE thought sometimes that, after all, this was the happiest time of her life—the honeymoon, as people called it. To taste the full sweetness of it, it would have been necessary doubtless to fly to those lands with sonorous names where the days after marriage are full of laziness most suave. In post-chaises behind blue silken curtains to ride slowly up steep roads, listening to the song of the postilion re-echoed by the mountains, along with the bells of goats and the muffled sound of a waterfall; at sunset on the shores of gulfs to breathe in the perfume of lemon-trees; then in the evening on the villa-terraces above, hand in hand to look at the stars, making plans for the future. It seemed to her that certain places on earth must bring happiness, as a plant peculiar to the soil, that cannot thrive elsewhere. Why could not she lean over balconies in Swiss châlets, or enshrine her melancholy in a Scotch cottage, with a husband dressed in a black velvet coat with long tails, and thin shoes, a pointed hat and frills?

Perhaps she would have liked to confide all these things to some one. But how tell an undefinable uneasiness, variable as the clouds, unstable as the

(50)

winds? Words failed her—the opportunity, the courage.

If Charles had but wished it, if he had guessed it, if his look had but once met her thought, it seemed to her that a sudden plenty would have gone out from her heart, as the fruit falls from a tree when shaken by a hand. But as the intimacy of their life became deeper, the greater became the gulf that separated her from him.

Charles's conversation was commonplace as a street pavement, and every one's ideas trooped through it in their everyday garb, without exciting emotion, laughter, or thought. He had never had the curiosity, he said, while he lived at Rouen, to go to the theatre to see the actors from Paris. He could neither swim, nor fence, nor shoot, and one day he could not explain some term of horsemanship to her that she had come across in a novel.

A man, on the contrary, should he not know everything, excel in manifold activities, initiate you into the energies of passion, the refinements of life, all mysteries? But this one taught nothing, knew nothing, wished nothing. He thought her happy; and she resented this easy calm, this serene heaviness, the very happiness she gave him.

Sometimes she would draw; and it was great amusement to Charles to stand there bolt upright and watch her bend over her cardboard, with eyes half-closed the better to see her work, or rolling, between her fingers, little bread-pellets. As to the piano, the more quickly her fingers glided over it the more he wondered. She struck the notes with aplomb, and ran from top to bottom of the keyboard without a break. Thus shaken up, the old instrument, whose strings buzzed, could be heard at the other end of the village when the window was open, and often the bailiff's clerk, passing along the highroad bareheaded and in list slippers, stopped to listen, his sheet of paper in his hand.

Emma, on the other hand, knew how to look after her house. She sent the patients' accounts in wellphrased letters that had no suggestion of a bill. When they had a neighbor to dinner on Sundays, she managed to have some dainty dish — piled up pyramids of green-gages on vine leaves, served up preserves turned out into plates — and even spoke of buying fingerglasses for dessert. From all this, much consideration was extended to Bovary.

Charles finished by rising in his own esteem for possessing such a wife. He showed with pride in the sitting-room two small pencil sketches by her that he had had framed in very large frames, and hung up against the wall-paper by long green cords. People returning from mass saw him at his door in his wool-work slippers.

He came home late — at ten o'clock, at midnight sometimes. Then he asked for something to eat, and as the servant had gone to bed, Emma waited, on him. He took off his coat to dine more at his ease. He told her, one after the other, the people he had met, the villages where he had been, the prescriptions he had written, and, well pleased with himself, he finished the remainder of the boiled beef and onions, picked pieces off the cheese, munched an apple, emptied his water-bottle, and then went to bed, and lay on his back and snored.

As he had been for a time accustomed to wear nightcaps, his handkerchief would not keep down over his ears, so that his hair in the morning was all tumbled pell-mell about his face and whitened with the feathers of the pillow, whose strings came untied during the night. He always wore thick boots that had two long creases over the instep running obliquely towards the ankle, while the rest of the upper continued in a straight line as if stretched on a wooden foot. He said that was "quite good enough for the country."

His mother approved of his economy, for she came to see him as formerly when there had been some violent scene at her place; and yet Madame Bovary senior seemed prejudiced against her daughter-in-law. She thought "her ways too fine for their position;" the wood, the sugar, and the candles disappeared as at "a grand establishment," and the amount of firing in the kitchen would have been enough for twenty-five courses. She put her linen in order for her in the presses, and taught her to keep an eye on the butcher when he brought the meat. Emma put up with these lessons. Madame Bovary was lavish of them; and the words "daughter" and "mother" were exchanged all day long, accompanied by little quiverings of the lips, each one uttering gentle words in a voice trembling with anger.

In Madame Dubuc's time the old woman felt that she was still the favorite; but now the love of Charles for Emma seemed to her a desertion from her tenderness, an encroachment upon what was hers, and she watched her son's happiness in sad silence, as a ruined man looks through the windows at people dining in his old house. She recalled to him as remembrances her troubles and her sacrifices, and, comparing these with Emma's negligence, came to the conclusion that it was not reasonable to adore her so exclusively.

Charles knew not what to answer: he respected his mother, and he loved his wife infinitely; he considered the judgment of the one infallible, and yet he thought the conduct of the other irreproachable. When Madame Bovary had gone he tried timidly and in the same terms to hazard one or two of the more anodyne observations he had heard from his mamma. Emma proved to him with a word that he was mistaken, and sent him off to his patients.

And yet, in accord with theories she believed right, she desired to make herself in love with him. By moonlight in the garden she recited all the passionate rhymes she knew by heart, and, sighing, sang to him many melancholy adagios; but she found herself as calm after this as before, and Charles seemed no more amorous and no more moved.

When she had thus for a while struck the flint on her heart without getting a spark, incapable, moreover, of understanding what she did not experience as of believing anything that did not present itself in conventional forms, she persuaded herself without difficulty that Charles's passion was nothing very exorbitant. His outbursts became regular; he embraced her at certain fixed times. It was one habit among other habits, and, like a dessert, looked forward to after the monotony of dinner.

A gamekeeper, cured by the doctor of inflammation of the lungs, had given madame a little Italian greyhound; she took her out walking, for she went out sometimes in order to be alone for a moment, and not to see before her eyes the eternal garden and the dusty road. She went as far as the beeches of Banneville, near the deserted pavilion which forms an angle of the wall on the side of the country. Amid the vegetation of the ditch there are long reeds with leaves that cut.

She began by looking round her to see if nothing had changed since last she had been there. She found again in the same places the foxgloves and wallflowers, the beds of nettles growing round the big stones, and the patches of lichen along the three windows, whose shutters, always closed, were rotting away on their rusty iron bars. Her thoughts, aimless at first, wandered at random, like her greyhound, who ran round and round in the fields, yelping after the yellow butterflies, chasing the shrew-mice, or nibbling the poppies on the edge of a cornfield. Then gradually her ideas took definite shape, and, sitting on the grass that she dug up with little prods of her sunshade, Emma repeated to herself, "Good heavens! why did I marry?"

She asked herself if by some other chance combination it would not have been possible to meet another man; and she tried to imagine what would have been these unrealized events, this different life, this unknown husband. All, surely, could not be like this one. He might have been handsome, witty, distinguished, attractive, such as, no doubt, her old companions of the convent had married. What were they doing now? In town, with the noise of the streets, the buzz of the theaters, and the lights of the ball-room, they were living lives where the heart expands, the senses bourgeon out. But she—her life was cold as a garret whose dormer-window looks on the north, and ennui, the silent spider, was weaving its web in the darkness in every corner of her heart. She recalled the prize-days, when she mounted the platform to receive her little crowns, with her hair in long plaits.

In her white frock and open prunella shoes she had a pretty way, and when she went back to her seat, the gentlemen bent over her to congratulate her; the courtyard was full of carriages; farewells were called to her through their windows; the music-master with his violin-case bowed in passing by. How far off all this! How far away!

She called Djali, took her between her knees, and smoothed the long, delicate head, saying, "Come, kiss mistress; you have no troubles."

Then noting the melancholy face of the graceful animal, who yawned slowly, she softened, and comparing her to herself, spoke to her aloud as to somebody in trouble whom one is consoling.

Occasionally there came gusts of wind, breezes from the sea rolling in one sweep over the whole plateau of the Caux country, which brought even to these fields a salt freshness. The rushes, close to the ground, whistled; the branches trembled in a swift rustling, while their summits, ceaselessly swaying, kept up a deep murmur. Emma drew her shawl round her shoulders and rose.

In the avenue a green light dimmed by the leaves lighted the short moss that crackled softly beneath her feet. The sun was setting; the sky showed red between the branches, and the trunks of the trees, uniform, and planted in a straight line, seemed a brown colonnade standing out against a background of gold. A fear took hold of her; she called Djali, and hurriedly retu.ned to Tostes by the highroad, threw herself into an armchair, and for the rest of the evening did not speak.

But towards the end of September something extraordinary fell upon her life; she was invited by the Marquis d'Andervilliers to Vaubyessard.

Secretary of State under the Restoration, the Marquis, anxious to re-enter political life, set about preparing for his candidature to the Chamber of Deputies long beforehand. In the winter he distributed a great deal of wood, and in the Conseil Général always enthusiastically demanded new roads for his arrondissement. During the dog-days he had suffered from an abscess, which Charles had cured as if by miracle by giving a timely little touch with the lancet. The steward sent to Tostes to pay for the operation reported in the evening that he had seen some superb cherries in the doctor's little garden. Now cherry-trees did not thrive at Vaubyessard; the Marquis asked Bovary for some slips; made it his business to thank him personally; saw Emma; thought she had a pretty figure, and that she did not bow like a peasant; so that he did not think he was going beyond the bounds of condescension, nor, on the other hand, making a mistake, in inviting the young couple.

One Wednesday at three o'clock, Monsieur and Madame Bovary, seated in their dog-cart, set out for Vaubyessard, with a great trunk strapped on behind and a bonnet-box in front on the apron. Besides these Charles held a bandbox between his knees.

They arrived at nightfall, just as the lamps in the park were being lighted to show the carriage-drive.

VIII.

THE château, a modern building in Italian style, with two projecting wings and three flights of steps, lay at the foot of an immense green-sward, on which some cows were grazing among groups of large trees set out at regular intervals, while large beds of arbutus, rhododendron, syringas, and guelder roses bulged out their irregular clusters of green along the curve of the gravel path. A river flowed under a bridge; through the mist one could distinguish buildings with thatched roofs scattered over the field bordered by two gently-sloping well-timbered hillocks, and in the background amid the trees rose in two parallel lines the coach-houses and stables, all that was left of the ruined old château.

Charles's dog-cart pulled up before the middle flight of steps; servants appeared; the Marquis came forward, and offering his arm to the doctor's wife, conducted her to the vestibule.

It was paved with marble slabs, was very lofty, and the sound of footsteps and that of voices re-echoed through it as in a church. Opposite rose a straight staircase, and on the left a gallery overlooking the garden led to the billiard-room, through whose door one could hear the click of the ivory balls. As she crossed it to go to the drawing-room, Emma saw standing round the table men with grave faces, their chins resting on high cravats. They all wore orders, and smiled silently as they made their strokes. On the dark wainscoting of the walls large gold frames bore at the bottom names written in black letters. She read:

"Jean-Antoine d'Andervilliers d'Yverbonville, Count de la Vaubyessard and Baron de la Fresnaye, killed at the battle of Coutras on the 20th of October 1587."

And on another:

"Jean-Antoine-Henry-Guy d'Andervilliers de la Vaubyessard, Admiral of France and Chevalier of the Order of St. Michael, wounded at the battle of the Hougue-Saint-Vaast on the 29th of May 1692; died at Vaubyessard on the 23rd of January 1693."

One could hardly make out those that followed, for the light of the lamps lowered over the green cloth threw a dim shadow round the room. Burnishing the horizontal pictures, it broke up against these in delicate lines where there were cracks in the varnish, and from all these great black squares framed in with gold stood out here and there some lighter portion of the painting — a pale brow, two eyes that looked at you, perukes flowing over and powdering red-coated shoulders, or the buckle of a garter above a well-rounded calf.

The Marquis opened the drawing-room door; one of the ladies (the Marchioness herself) came to meet Emma. She made her sit down by her on an ottoman, and began talking to her as amicably as if she had known her a long time. She was about forty years old, with fine shoulders, a hook nose, a drawling voice, and on this evening she wore over her brown hair a simple guipure fichu that fell in a point at the back. A fair young woman was by her side in a high-backed chair, and gentlemen with flowers in their buttonholes were talking to ladies round the fire.

At seven dinner was served. The men, who were in the majority, sat down at the first table in the vestibule; the ladies at the second in the dining-room with the Marquis and Marchioness.

Emma, on entering, felt herself wrapped round by the warm air, a blending of the perfume of flowers and of the fine linen, of the fumes of the viands, and the odor of the truffles. The silver dish-covers reflected the lighted wax candles in the candelabra, the cut crystal covered with light steam reflected pale rays from one to the other; bouquets were placed in a row the whole length of the table; and in the large-bordered plates each napkin, arranged after the fashion of a bishop's miter, held between its two gaping folds a small oval-shaped roll. The red claws of lobsters hung over the dishes; rich fruit in open baskets was piled up on moss; there were quails in their plumage; smoke was rising; and in silk stockings, knee-breeches, white cravat, and frilled shirt, the steward, grave as a judge, offered ready-carved dishes between the shoulders of the guests, and with a touch of the spoon gave the piece chosen. On the large stove of porcelain inlaid with copper baguettes the statue of a woman, draped to the chin, gazed motionless on the room full of life.

Madame Bovary noticed that many ladies had not put their gloves in their glasses.

But at the upper end of the table, alone among all those women, bent over his full plate, with his napkin tied round his neck like a child, an old man sat eating, letting drops of gravy drip from his mouth. His eyes were bloodshot, and he wore a little queue tied with a black ribbon. He was the Marquis's father-in-law, the old Duke de Laverdière, once on a time favorite of the Count d'Artois, in the days of the Vaudreuil hunting-parties at the Marquis de Conflans', and had been, it was said, the lover of Queen Marie Antoinette, between Monsieur de Coigny and Monsieur de Lauzun. He had lived a life of noisy debauch, full of duels, bets, elopements; he had squandered his fortune and frightened all his family. A servant behind his chair named aloud to him in his ear the dishes that he pointed to, stammering, and constantly Emma's eyes turned involuntarily to this old man with hanging lips, as to something extraordinary. He had lived at court and slept in the bed of queens!

Iced champagne was poured out. Emma shivered all over as she felt it cold in her mouth. She had never seen pomegranates nor tasted pine-apples. The powdered sugar even seemed to her whiter and finer than elsewhere.

The ladies afterward went to their rooms to prepare for the ball.

Emma made her toilet with the fastidious care of an actress on her début. She did her hair according to the directions of the hairdresser, and put on the barège dress spread out upon the bed. Charles's trousers were tight across the belly.

"My trouser-straps will be rather awkward for dancing," he said.

"Dancing?" repeated Emma.

"Yes!"

"Why, you must be mad! They would make fun of you; keep your place. Besides, it is more becoming for a doctor," she added.

Charles was silent. He walked up and down waiting for Emma to finish dressing.

He saw her from behind in the glass between two lights. Her black eyes seemed blacker than ever. Her hair, undulating toward the ears, shone with a blue luster; a rose in her chignon trembled on its mobile stalk, with artificial dewdrops on the tips of the leaves. She wore a gown of pale saffron trimmed with three bouquets of pompon roses mixed with green.

Charles came and kissed her on her shoulder.

"Let me alone!" she said; "you are tumbling me."

One could hear the flourish of the violin and the notes of a horn. She went downstairs restraining herself from running.

Dancing had begun. Guests were arriving. There was some crushing. She sat down on a form near the door.

The quadrille over, the floor was occupied by groups of men standing up and talking and servants in livery bearing large trays. Along the line of seated women painted fans were fluttering, bouquets half-hid smiling faces, and gold-stoppered scent-bottles were turned in partly-closed hands, whose white gloves outlined the nails and tightened on the flesh at the wrists. Lace trimmings, diamond brooches, medallion bracelets trembled on bodices, gleamed on breasts, clinked on bare arms. The hair, well smoothed over the temples and knotted at the nape, bore crowns, or bunches, or sprays of myosotis, jasmine, pomegranate blossoms, ears of corn, and cornflowers. Calmly seated in their places, mothers with forbidding countenances were wearing red turbans.

Emma's heart beat rather faster when, her partner holding her by the tips of the fingers, she took her place in a line with the dancers, and waited for the first note to start. But her emotion soon vanished, and, swaying to the rhythm of the orchestra, she glided forward with slight movements of the neck. A smile rose to her lips at certain delicate phrases of the violin, that sometimes played alone while the other instruments were silent; one could hear the clear clink of the louis-d'or that were being thrown down upon the card-tables in the next room; then all struck in again, the cornet-à-piston uttered its sonorous note, feet marked time, skirts swelled and rustled, hands touched and parted; the same eyes falling before you met yours again.

A few men (some fifteen or so), of twenty-five to forty, scattered here and there among the dancers or talking at the doorways, distinguished themselves from the crowd by a certain air of breeding, whatever their differences in age, dress, or face.

Their clothes, better made, seemed of finer cloth, and their hair, brought forward in curls towards the temples, glossy with more delicate pomades. They had the complexion of wealth,—that clear complexion that is heightened by the pallor of porcelain, the shimmer of satin, the veneer of old furniture, and that an ordered regimen of exquisite nurture maintains at its best. Their necks moved easily in their low cravats, their long whiskers fell over their turned-down collars, they wiped their lips upon handkerchiefs, with embroidered initials, that gave forth a subtle perfume. Those who were beginning to grow old had an air of youth, while there was something mature in the faces of the young. In their unconcerned looks was the calm of passions daily satiated, and through all their gentleness of manner pierced that peculiar brutality, the result of a command of half-easy things, in which force is exercised and vanity amused—the management of thoroughbred horses and the society of loose women.

A few steps from Emma a gentleman in a blue coat was talking of Italy with a pale young woman wearing a parure of pearls.

They were praising the breadth of the columns of St. Peter's, Tivoli, Vesuvius, Castellamare, and Cassines, the roses of Genoa, the Coliseum by moonlight. With her other ear Emma was listening to a conversation full of words she did not understand. A circle gathered round a very young man who the week before had beaten "Miss Arabella" and "Romulus," and won two thousand louis jumping a ditch in England. One complained that his racehorses were growing fat; another of the printers' errors that had disfigured the name of his horse.

The atmosphere of the ball was heavy; the lamps were growing dim. Guests were flocking to the billiard-room. A servant got upon a chair and broke the window-panes. At the crash of the glass Madame Bovary turned her head and saw in the garden the faces of peasants pressed against the window looking in at them. Then the memory of the Bertaux came back to her. She saw the farm again, the muddy pond, her father in a blouse under the apple-trees, and she saw herself again as formerly, skimming with her finger the cream off the milk-pans in the dairy. But in the refulgence of the present hour her past life, so distinct until then, faded away completely, and she almost doubted having lived it. She was there; beyond the ball was only shadow overspreading all the rest. She was just eating a maraschino ice that she held with her left hand in a silver-gilt cup, her eyes half-closed, and the spoon between her teeth.

A lady near her dropped her fan. A gentleman was passing.

"Would you be so good," said the lady, "as to pick up my fan that has fallen behind the sofa?"

The gentleman bowed, and as he moved to stretch out his arm, Emma saw the hand of the young woman throw something white, folded in a triangle, into his hat. The gentleman picking up the fan, offered it to the lady respectfully; she thanked him with an inclination of the head, and began smelling her bouquet.

After supper, where were plenty of Spanish and Rhine wines, soups *à la bisque* and *au lait d'amandes*, puddings *à la Trafalgar*, and all sorts of cold meats with jellies that trembled in the dishes, the carriages one after the other began to drive off. Raising the corner of the muslin curtain, one could see the light of their lanterns glimmering through the darkness. The seats began to empty, some card-players were still left; the musicians were cooling the tips of their fingers on their tongues. Charles was half asleep, his back propped against a door.

At three o'clock the cotillion began. Emma did not know how to waltz. Every one was waltzing,

1 G. F.—5

Mademoiselle d'Andervilliers herself and the Marquis;
only the guests staying at the castle were still there,
about a dozen persons.

One of the waltzers, however, who was familiarly
called Viscount, and whose low cut waistcoat seemed
moulded to his chest, came a second time to ask
Madame Bovary to dance, assuring her that he would
guide her, and that she would get through it very
well.

They began slowly, then went more rapidly.
They turned; all around them was turning — the
lamps, the furniture, the wainscoting, the floor, like
a disc on a pivot. On passing near the doors the
bottom of Emma's dress caught against his trousers.
Their legs commingled; he looked down at her; she
raised her eyes to his. A torpor seized her; she
stopped. They started again, and with a more rapid
movement; the Viscount, dragging her along, disappeared with her to the end of the gallery, where,
panting, she almost fell, and for a moment rested her
head upon his breast. And then, still turning, but
more slowly, he guided her back to her seat. She
leant back against the wall and covered her eyes
with her hands.

When she opened them again, in the middle of
the drawing-room three waltzers were kneeling before a lady sitting on a stool. She chose the Viscount, and the violin struck up once more.

Every one looked at them. They passed and re-
passed, she with rigid body, her chin bent down,
and he always in the same pose, his figure curved,
his elbow rounded, his chin thrown forward. That
woman knew how to waltz! They kept up a long
time, and tired out all the others.

Then they talked a few moments longer, and after the good-nights, or rather good-mornings, the guests of the château retired to bed.

Charles dragged himself up by the balusters. His knees were going up into his body. He had spent five consecutive hours standing bolt upright at the card-tables, watching them play whist, without understanding anything about it, and it was with a deep sigh of relief that he pulled off his boots.

Emma threw a shawl over her shoulders, opened the window, and leant out.

The night was dark; some drops of rain were falling. She breathed in the damp wind that refreshed her eyelids. The music of the ball was still murmuring in her ears, and she tried to keep herself awake in order to prolong the illusion of this luxurious life that she would soon have to give up.

Day began to break. She looked long at the windows of the château, trying to guess which were the rooms of all those she had noticed the evening before. She would fain have known their lives, have penetrated, blended with them. But she was shivering with cold. She undressed, and cowered down between the sheets against Charles, who was asleep.

There were a great many people to luncheon. The repast lasted ten minutes; no liqueurs were served, which astonished the doctor. Next, Mademoiselle d'Andervilliers collected some pieces of roll in a small basket to take them to the swans on the ornamental waters, and they went to walk in the hot-houses, where strange plants, bristling with hairs, rose in pyramids under hanging vases, whence, as from over-filled nests of serpents, fell long green cords interlacing. The orangery, which was at the other end, led

by a covered way to the outhouses of the château.
The Marquis, to amuse the young woman, took her
to see the stables. Above the basket-shaped racks
porcelain slabs bore the names of the horses in black
letters. Each animal in its stall whisked its tail when
any one went near and said "Tchk! tchk!" The
boards of the harness-room shone like the flooring of
a drawing-room. The carriage harness was piled up
in the middle against two twisted columns, and the
bits, the whips, the spurs, the curbs, were ranged in
a line all along the wall.

Charles, meanwhile, went to ask a groom to put
his horse to. The dog-cart was brought to the foot
of the steps, and all the parcels being crammed in,
the Bovarys paid their respects to the Marquis and
Marchioness and set out again for Tostes.

Emma watched the turning wheels in silence.
Charles, on the extreme edge of the seat, held the
reins with his two arms wide apart, and the little
horse ambled along in the shafts that were too big for
him. The loose reins hanging over his crupper were
wet with foam, and the box fastened on behind the
chaise gave great regular bumps against it.

They were on the heights of Thibourville when
suddenly some horsemen with cigars between their
lips passed, laughing. Emma thought she recognized
the Viscount, turned back, and caught on the horizon
only the movement of the heads rising or falling with
the unequal cadence of the trot or gallop.

A mile farther on they had to stop to mend with
some string the traces that had broken.

But Charles, giving a last look to the harness, saw
something on the ground between the horse's legs,
and he picked up a cigar-case with a green silk bor-

der and blazoned in the center like the door of a carriage.

"There are even two cigars in it," said he; "they'll do for this evening after dinner."

"Why, do you smoke?" she asked.

"Sometimes, when I get a chance."

He put his find in his pocket and whipped up the nag.

When they reached home the dinner was not ready. Madame lost her temper. Nastasie answered rudely.

"Leave the room!" said Emma. "You are forgetting yourself. I give you warning."

For dinner there was onion soup and a piece of veal with sorrel. Charles, seated opposite Emma, rubbed his hands gleefully.

"How good it is to be at home again!"

Nastasie could be heard crying. He was rather fond of the poor girl. She had formerly, during the wearisome time of his widowerhood, kept him company many an evening. She had been his first patient, his oldest acquaintance in the place.

"Have you given her warning for good?" he asked at last.

"Yes. Who is to prevent me?" she replied.

Then they warmed themselves in the kitchen while their room was being made ready. Charles began to smoke. He smoked with his lips protruded, spitting every moment, recoiling at every puff.

"You'll make yourself ill," she said scornfully.

He put down his cigar and ran to swallow a glass of cold water at the pump. Emma seizing hold of the cigar-case threw it quickly to the back of the cupboard.

The next day was a long one. She walked about her little garden, up and down the same walks, stopping before the beds, before the espalier, before the plaster curate, looking with amazement at all these things of once-on-a-time that she knew so well. How far off the ball seemed already! What was it that thus set so far asunder the morning of the day before yesterday and the evening of to-day? Her journey to Vaubyessard had made a hole in her life, like one of those great crevasses that a storm will sometimes make in one night in mountains. Still she was resigned. She devoutly put away in her closets her beautiful dress, down to the satin shoes whose soles were yellowed with the slippery wax of the dancing floor. Her heart was like these. In its friction against wealth something had come over it that could not be effaced.

The memory of this ball, then, became an occupation for Emma. Whenever the Wednesday came round she said to herself as she awoke, "Ah! I was there a week — a fortnight — three weeks ago." And little by little the faces grew confused in her remembrance. She forgot the tune of the quadrilles; she no longer saw the liveries and appointments so distinctly; some details escaped her, but the regret remained with her.

IX.

IDLE DREAMS.

FTEN when Charles was out she took from the cupboard, between the folds of the linen where she had left it, the green silk cigar-case. She looked at it, opened it, and even smelt the odor of the lining — a mixture of verbena and tobacco. Whose was it? The Viscount's? Perhaps it was a present from his mistress. It had been embroidered on some rosewood frame, a pretty little thing, hidden from all eyes, that had occupied many hours, and over which had fallen the soft curls of the pensive worker. A breath of love had passed over the stitches on the canvas; each prick of the needle had fixed there a hope or a memory, and all those interwoven threads of silk were but the continuity of the same silent passion. And then one morning the Viscount had taken it away with him. Of what had they spoken when it lay upon the wide-manteled chimneys between flower-vases and Pompadour clocks? She was at Tostes; he was at Paris now, far away! What was this Paris like? What a vague name! She repeated it in a low voice, for the mere pleasure of it; it rang in her ears like a great cathedral bell; it shone before her eyes, even on the labels of her pomade-pots.

At night, when the carriers passed under her windows in their carts singing the "Marjolaine," she awoke, and listened to the noise of the iron-bound wheels, which, as they gained the country road, was soon deadened by the soil. "They will be there to-morrow!" she said to herself.

And she followed them in thought up and down the hills, traversing villages, gliding along the high-roads by the light of the stars. At the end of some indefinite distance there was always a confused spot, into which her dream died.

She bought a plan of Paris, and with the tip of her finger on the map she walked about the capital. She went up the boulevards, stopping at every turning, between the lines of the streets, in front of the white squares that represented the houses. At last she would close the lids of her weary eyes, and see in the darkness the gas jets flaring in the wind and the steps of carriages lowered with much noise before the peristyles of theatres.   ·

She took in "La Corbeille," a lady's journal, and the "Sylphe des Salons." She devoured, without skipping a word, all the accounts of first nights, races, and soirées, took an interest in the début of a singer, in the opening of a new shop. She knew the latest fashions, the addresses of the best tailors, the days of the Bois and the Opera. In Eugène Suë she studied descriptions of furniture; she read Balzac and George Sand, seeking in them imaginary satisfaction for her own desires. Even at table she had her book by her, and turned over the pages while Charles ate and talked to her. The memory of the Viscount always returned

as she read. Between him and the imaginary personages she made comparisons. But the circle of which
he was the centre gradually widened round him, and
the aureole that he bore, fading from his form, broad-
ened out beyond, lighting up her other dreams.

Paris, more vague than the ocean, glimmered before
Emma's eyes in an atmosphere of vermilion. The
many lives that stirred amid this tumult were, however, divided into parts, classed as distinct pictures.
Emma perceived only two or three that hid from her
all the rest, and in themselves represented all humanity. The world of ambassadors moved over polished
floors in drawing-rooms lined with mirrors, round
oval tables covered with velvet and gold-fringed cloths.
There were skirts with trains; deep mysteries, anguish hidden beneath smiles. Then came the society
of the duchesses; all were pale; all got up at four
o'clock; the women, poor angels, wore English point
on their petticoats; and the men, unappreciated gen-
iuses under a frivolous outward seeming, rode horses
to death at pleasure parties, spent the summer season
at Baden, and towards the forties married heiresses.
In the private rooms of restaurants, where one sups
after midnight by the light of wax candles, laughed
the motley crowd of men of letters and actresses. They
were prodigal as kings, full of ideal, ambitious, fantastic frenzy. This was an existence outside that of all
others, between heaven and earth, in the midst of
storms, having something of the sublime. For the
rest of the world it was lost, with no particular place,
and as if non-existent. The nearer things were, moreover, the more her thoughts turned away from them.
All her immediate surroundings, the wearisome country, the middle-class imbeciles, the mediocrity of

existence, seemed to her exceptional, a peculiar chance that had caught hold of her, while beyond stretched as far as eye could see an immense land of joys and of passions. She confused in her desire the sensualities of luxury with the delights of the heart, elegance of manners with delicacy of sentiment. Did not love, like Indian plants, need a special soil, a particular temperature? Sighs by moonlight, long embraces, tears flowing over yielded hands, all the fevers of the flesh and the languors of tenderness could not be separated from the balconies of great castles full of indolence, from boudoirs with silken curtains and thick carpets, well-filled flower-stands, a bed on a raised daïs, nor from the flashing of precious stones and the shoulder-knots of liveries.

The lad from the posting-house, who came to groom the mare every morning, passed through the passage with his heavy wooden shoes; there were holes in his blouse; his feet were bare in list slippers. And this was the groom in knee-breeches with whom she had to be content! His work done, he did not come back again all day, for Charles on his return put up his horse himself, unsaddled him and put on the halter, while the servant-girl brought a bundle of straw and threw it as best she could into the manger.

To replace Nastasie (who left Tostes shedding torrents of tears) Emma took into her service a young girl of fourteen, an orphan with a sweet face. She forbade her wearing cotton caps, taught her to address her in the third person, to bring a glass of water on a plate, to knock before coming into a room, to iron, starch, and to dress her,— tried to make a lady's-maid of her. The new servant obeyed without a murmur, so as not to be sent away; and, as madame usually left the key in the sideboard, Félicité every evening took a small supply of sugar that she ate alone in her bed after she had said her prayers.

Sometimes in the afternoon she went to chat with the postilions. Madame was in her room upstairs. She wore an open dressing-gown, that showed between the shawl facings of her bodice a pleated chemisette with three gold buttons. Her belt was a corded girdle with great tassels, and her small garnet-colored slippers had a large knot of ribbon that fell over her instep. She had bought herself a blotting-book, writing-case, pen-holder, and envelopes, although she had no one to write to; she dusted her what-not, looked at herself in the glass, picked up a book, and then, dreaming between the lines, let it drop on her knees. She longed to travel or to go back to her convent. She wished at the same time to die and to live in Paris.

Charles in snow and rain trotted across country. He ate omelettes on farmhouse tables, poked his arm into damp beds, received the tepid spurt of blood-lettings in his face, listened to death-rattles, examined basins, turned over a good deal of dirty linen; but every evening he found a blazing fire, his dinner ready, easy-chairs, and a well-dressed woman, charming with an odor of freshness, though no one could say whence the perfume came, or if it were not her skin that made odorous her chemise.

She charmed him by numerous attentions; now it was some new way of arranging paper sconces for the candles, a flounce that she altered on her gown, or an extraordinary name for some very simple dish that the servant had spoilt, but that Charles swallowed with pleasure to the last mouthful. At Rouen she saw some ladies who wore a bunch of charms on their watch-chains; she bought some charms. She wanted for her mantelpiece two large blue glass vases, and some time after an ivory *nécessaire* with a silver-gilt thimble. The less Charles understood these refinements the more they seduced him. They added something to the pleasure of the senses and to the comfort of his fireside. It was like a golden dust sanding all along the narrow path of his life.

He was well, looked well; his reputation was firmly established. The country-folk loved him because he was not proud. He petted the children, never went to the public-house, and, moreover, his morals inspired confidence. He was specially successful with catarrhs and chest complaints. Being much afraid of killing his patients, Charles, in fact, prescribed only sedatives, from time to time an emetic, a footbath, or leeches. It was not that he was afraid of surgery; he bled people copiously like horses, and for the taking out of teeth he had the "devil's own wrist."

Finally, to keep up with the times, he took in "La Ruche Médicale," a new journal whose prospectus had been sent him. He read it a little after dinner, but in about five minutes, the warmth of the room added to the effect of his dinner sent him to sleep; and he sat there, his chin on his two hands and his hair spreading like a mane to the foot of the lamp. Emma looked at him and shrugged her shoulders. Why, at least, was not her husband one of those men of taciturn passions who work at their books all night, and at last, when about sixty, the age when rheumatism sets in, wear a string of orders on their ill-fitting black coats? She could have wished this name of Bovary, which was hers, had been illustrious, to see it displayed at the booksellers', repeated in the newspapers, known to all France. But Charles had no ambition. An Yvetot doctor whom he had lately met in consultation had somewhat humiliated him at the very bedside of the patient, before the assembled relatives. When, in the evening, Charles told her this anecdote, Emma inveighed loudly against his colleague. Charles was much touched. He kissed her forehead with a tear in his eyes. But she was angered with shame; she felt a wild desire to strike him; she went to open the window in the passage and breathed in the fresh air to calm herself.

"What a man! what a man!" she said in a low voice, biting her lips.

Besides, she was becoming more irritated with him. As he grew older his manner grew heavier; at dessert he cut the corks of the empty bottles; after eating he cleaned his teeth with his tongue; in taking soup he made a gurgling noise with every spoonful; and, as he was getting fatter, the puffed-out cheeks seemed to push the eyes, always small, up to the temples.

Sometimes Emma tucked the red borders of his under-vest into his waistcoat, rearranged his cravat, and threw away the soiled gloves he was going to put on; and this was not, as he fancied, for himself; it was for herself, by a diffusion of egotism, of nervous irritation. Sometimes, too, she told him of what she had read, such as a passage in a novel, of a new play, or an anecdote of the "upper ten" that she had seen in a feuilleton; for, after all, Charles was something, an ever-open ear, an ever-ready approbation. She confided many a thing to her greyhound. She would have done so to the logs in the fireplace or to the pendulum of the clock.

At bottom of her heart, however, she was waiting for something to happen. Like shipwrecked sailors, she turned despairing eyes upon the solitude of her life, seeking afar off some white sail in the mists of the horizon. She did not know what this chance would be, what wind would bring it her, toward what shore it would drive her, if it would be a shallop or a three-decker, laden with anguish or full of bliss to the port-holes. But each morning, as she awoke, she hoped it would come that day; she listened to every sound, sprang up with a start, wondered that it did not come; then at sunset, always more saddened, she longed for the morrow.

Spring came round. With the first warm weather, when the pear-trees began to blossom, she suffered from dyspnœa.

From the beginning of July she counted how many weeks there were to October, thinking that perhaps the Marquis d'Andervilliers would give another ball at Vaubyessard. But all September passed without letters or visits.

After the ennui of this disappointment her heart once more remained empty, and then the same series of days recommenced. So now they would thus follow one another, always the same, immovable, and bringing nothing. Other lives, however flat, had at least the chance of some event. One adventure sometimes brought with it infinite consequences, and the scene changed. But nothing happened to her; God had willed it so! The future was a dark corridor, with its door at the end shut fast.

She gave up music. What was the good of playing? Who would hear her? Since she could never, in a velvet gown with short sleeves, striking with her light fingers the ivory keys of an Erard at a concert, feel the murmur of ecstasy envelop her like a breeze, it was not worth while boring herself with practising. Her drawing cardboard and her embroidery she left in the cupboard. What was the good? what was the good? Sewing irritated her. "I have read everything," she said to herself. And she sat there making the tongs red-hot, or looked at the rain falling.

How sad she was on Sundays when vespers sounded! She listened with dull attention to each stroke of the cracked bell. A cat slowly walking over some roof put up his back in the pale rays of the sun. The wind on the highroad blew up clouds of dust. Afar off a dog sometimes howled; and the bell, keeping time, continued its monotonous ringing that died away over the fields.

But the people came out from church. The women in waxed clogs, the peasants in new blouses, the little bareheaded children skipping along in front of them, all were going home. And till nightfall, five or six men, always the same, stayed playing at corks in front of the large door of the inn.

The winter was severe. The windows every morning were covered with rime, and the light shining through them, dim as through ground-glass, sometimes did not change the whole day long. At four o'clock the lamp had to be lighted.

On fine days she went down into the garden. The dew had left on the cabbages a silver lace with long transparent threads spreading from one to the other. No birds were to be heard; everything seemed asleep, the espalier covered with straw, and the vine, like a great sick serpent under the coping of the wall, along which, on drawing near, one saw the many-footed woodlice crawling. Under the spruce by the hedgerow, the curé in the three-cornered hat reading his breviary had lost his right foot, and the very plaster, scaling off with the frost, had left white scabs on his face.

Then she went up again, shut her door, put on coals, and fainting with the heat of the hearth, felt her boredom weigh more heavily than ever. She would have liked to go down and talk to the servant, but a sense of shame restrained her.

Every day at the same time the schoolmaster in a black skull-cap opened the shutters of his house, and the rural policeman, wearing his sabre over his blouse, passed by. Night and morning the post-horses, three by three, crossed the street to water at the pond. From time to time the bell of a public-house door rang, and when it was windy one could hear the little brass basins that served as signs for the hairdresser's shop creaking on their two rods. This shop had as decoration an old engraving of a fashion-plate stuck against a window-pane and the wax bust of a woman with yellow hair. He, too, the hairdresser, lamented his wasted calling, his hopeless future, and dreaming of some shop in a big town — at Rouen, for example, overlooking the harbor, near the theater — he walked up and down all day from the mairie to the church, sombre, and waiting for customers. When Madame Bovary looked up, she always saw him there, like a sentinel on duty, with his skull-cap over his ears and his waistcoat of lasting.

Sometimes in the afternoon, outside the window of her room, the head of a man appeared, a swarthy head with black whiskers, smiling slowly, with a

broad, gentle smile that showed his white teeth. A
waltz immediately began, and on the organ, in a little
drawing-room, dancers the size of a finger, women
in pink turbans, Tyrolians in jackets, monkeys in
frock-coats, gentlemen in knee-breeches, turned and
turned between the sofas, the consoles, multiplied in
the bits of looking-glass held together at their corners
by a piece of gold paper. The man turned his handle, looking to the right and left, and up at the windows. Now and again, while he shot out a long
squirt of brown saliva against the milestone, with his
knee he raised his instrument, whose hard straps tired
his shoulder; and now, doleful and drawling, or gay
and hurried, the music escaped from the box, dron-
ing through a curtain of pink taffeta under a brass
claw in arabesque. They were airs played in other
places at the theaters, sung in drawing-rooms, danced
to at night under lighted lustres, echoes of the world
that reached even to Emma. Endless sarabands ran
through her head, and, like an Indian dancing-girl on
the flowers of a carpet, her thoughts leaped with the
notes, swung from dream to dream, from sadness to
sadness. When the man had caught some coppers in
his cap, he drew down an old cover of blue cloth,
hitched his organ on to his back, and went off with
a heavy tread. She watched him going.

But it was above all the meal-times that were unbearable to her, in this small room on the ground-
floor, with its smoking stove, its creaking door, the
walls that sweated, the damp flags; all the bitterness
of life seemed served up on her plate, and with the
smoke of the boiled beef arose from her secret
soul whiffs of sickliness. Charles was a slow eater;
she played with a few nuts, or, leaning on her elbow,

1 G. F.—6

amused herself with drawing lines along the oil-cloth table-cover with the point of her knife.

She now let everything in her household take care of itself, and Madame Bovary senior, when she came to spend part of Lent at Tostes, was much surprised at the change. She who was formerly so careful, so dainty, now passed whole days without dressing, wore gray cotton stockings, and burnt tallow candles. She kept saying they must be economical since they were not rich, adding that she was very contented, very happy, that Tostes pleased her very much, with other speeches that closed the mouth of her mother-in-law. Besides, Emma no longer seemed inclined to follow her advice; once even, Madame Bovary having thought fit to maintain that mistresses ought to keep an eye on the religion of their servants, she had answered with so angry a look and so cold a smile that the good woman did not mention it again.

Emma was growing *difficile*, capricious. She ordered dishes for herself, then she did not touch them; one day drank only pure milk, and the next cups of tea by the dozen. Often she persisted in not going out, then, stifling, threw open the windows and put on light frocks. After she had well scolded her servant, she gave her presents or sent her out to see the neighbors, just as she sometimes threw beggars all the silver in her purse, although she was by no means tender-hearted or easily accessible to the feelings of others, like most country-bred people, who always retain in their souls something of the horny hardness of the paternal hands.

Toward the end of February old Rouault, in memory of his cure, himself brought his son-in-law a superb turkey, and stayed three days at Tostes. Charles

being with his patients, Emma kept him company.
He smoked in the room, spat on the fire-dogs, talked
farming, calves, cows, poultry, and municipal council,
so that when he left she closed the door on him with
a feeling of satisfaction that surprised even herself.
Moreover, she no longer concealed her contempt for
anything or anybody, and at times she set herself to
express singular opinions, finding fault with that
which others approved, and approving things perverse
and immoral, all which made her husband open his
eyes widely.

Would this misery last forever? Would she never
issue from it? Yet she was as good as all the women
who were living happily. She had seen duchesses at
Vaubyessard with clumsier waists and commoner
ways, and she execrated the injustice of God. She
leant her head against the walls to weep; she envied
lives of stir; longed for masked balls, for violent
pleasures, with all the wildness, that she did not
know, but that these must surely yield.

She grew pale and suffered from palpitations of
the heart. Charles prescribed valerian and camphor
baths. Everything that was tried only seemed to irri-
tate her the more.

On certain days she chattered with feverish rapid-
ity, and this over-excitement was suddenly followed
by a state of torpor, in which she remained without speaking, without moving. What then revived
her was pouring a bottle of eau-de-cologne over her
arms.

As she was constantly complaining about Tostes,
Charles fancied that her illness was no doubt due to
some local cause, and fixing on this idea, began to
think seriously of setting up elsewhere.

From that moment she drank vinegar, contracted a sharp little cough, and completely lost her appetite.

It cost Charles much to give up Tostes after living there four years and when he was "beginning to get on there." Yet if it must be! He took her to Rouen to see his old master. It was a nervous complaint: change of air was needed.

After looking about him on this side and on that, Charles learnt that in the Neufchâtel arrondissement there was a considerable market-town called Yonville-l'Abbaye, whose doctor, a Polish refugee, had decamped a week before. Then he wrote to the chemist of the place to ask the number of the population, the distance from the nearest doctor, what his predecessor had made a year, and so forth; and the answer being satisfactory, he made up his mind to move towards the spring, if Emma's health did not improve.

One day when, in view of her departure, she was tidying a drawer, something pricked her finger. It was a wire of her wedding-bouquet. The orange blossoms were yellow with dust and the silver-bordered satin ribbons frayed at the edges. She threw it into the fire. It flared up more quickly than dry straw. Then it was like a red bush in the cinders, slowly devoured. She watched it burn. The little pasteboard berries burst, the wire twisted, the gold lace melted; and the shrivelled paper corollas, fluttering like black butterflies at the back of the stove, at last flew up the chimney.

When they left Tostes in the month of March, Madame Bovary was pregnant.

PART II.

I.

A New Field.

YONVILLE-L'ABBAYE (so called from an old Capuchin abbey of which not even the ruins remain) is a market-town twenty-four miles from Rouen, between the Abbeville and Beauvais roads, at the foot of a valley watered by the Rieule, a little river that runs into the Andelle after turning three water-mills near its mouth, where there are a few trout that the lads amuse themselves by fishing for on Sundays.

We leave the highroad at La Boissière and keep straight on to the top of the Leux hill, whence the valley is seen. The river that runs through it makes of it, as it were, two regions with distinct physiognomies,—all on the left is pasture land, all on the right arable. The meadow stretches under a bulge of low hills to join at the back with the pasture land of the Bray country, while on the eastern side, the plain, gently rising, broadens out, showing as far as eye can follow its blond cornfields. The water, flowing by the grass, divides with a white line the color of the

(85)

roads and of the plains, and the country is like a great unfolded mantle with a green velvet cape bordered with a fringe of silver.

Before us, on the verge of the horizon, lie the oaks of the forest of Argueil, with the steeps of the Saint-Jean hills scarred from top to bottom with red irregular lines; they are rain-tracks, and these brick-tones standing out in narrow streaks against the gray color of the mountain are due to the quantity of iron springs that flow beyond in the neighboring country.

Here we are on the confines of Normandy, Picardy, and the Île-de-France, a bastard land, whose language is without accent as its landscape is without character. It is there that they make the worst Neufchâtel cheeses of all the arrondissement; and, on the other hand, farming is costly because so much manure is needed to enrich this friable soil full of sand and flints.

Up to 1835 there was no practicable road for getting to Yonville, but about this time a cross-road was made which joins that of Abbeville to that of Amiens, and is occasionally used by the Rouen wagoners on their way to Flanders. Yonville-l'Abbaye has remained stationary in spite of its "new outlet." Instead of improving the soil, they persist in keeping up the pasture lands, however depreciated they may be in value, and the lazy borough, growing away from the plain, has naturally spread riverwards. It is seen from afar sprawling along the banks like a cowherd taking a siesta by the water-side.

At the foot of the hill beyond the bridge begins a roadway, planted with young aspens, that leads in a straight line to the first houses in the place. These,

fenced in by hedges, are in the middle of courtyards
full of straggling buildings, wine-presses, cart-sheds,
and distilleries scattered under thick trees, with lad-
ders, poles, or scythes hung on to the branches. The
thatched roofs, like fur caps drawn over eyes, reach
down over about a third of the low windows, whose
coarse convex glasses have knots in the middle like
the bottoms of bottles. Against the plaster wall, diag-
onally crossed by black joists, a meagre pear-tree
sometimes leans, and the ground floors have at their
door a small swing-gate, to keep out the chicks that
come pilfering crumbs of bread steeped in cider on
the threshold. But the courtyards grow narrower,
the houses closer together, and the fences disappear;
a bundle of ferns swings under a window from the
end of a broomstick; there is a blacksmith's forge
and then a wheelwright's, with two or three new
carts outside that partly block up the way. Then
across an open space appears a white house beyond
a grass mound ornamented by a Cupid, his finger
on his lips; two brass vases are at each end of a
flight of steps; scutcheons * blaze upon the door. It
is the notary's house, and the finest in the place.

The church is on the other side of the street, twenty
paces farther down, at the entrance of the square.
The little cemetery that surrounds it, closed in by a
wall breast-high, is so full of graves that the old stones,
level with the ground, form a continuous pavement,
on which the grass of itself has marked out regular
green squares. The church was rebuilt during the last
years of the reign of Charles X. The wooden roof is

---

* The *panonceaux* that have to be hung over the doors of
notaries. — TRANS.

beginning to rot from the top, and here and there has black hollows in its blue color. Over the door. where the organ should be, is a loft for the men, with a spiral staircase that reverberates under their wooden shoes.

The daylight coming through the plain glass windows falls obliquely upon the pews ranged along the walls, which are adorned here and there with a straw mat bearing beneath it the words in large letters, "Monsieur So-and-so's pew." And at the spot where the building narrows, the confessional forms a pendant to a statuette of the Virgin, clothed in a satin robe, coifed with a tulle veil sprinkled with silver stars, and with red cheeks, like an idol of the Sandwich Islands; and, finally, a copy of the "Holy Family, presented by the Minister of the Interior," overlooking the high altar, between four candlesticks, closes in the perspective. The choir stalls, of deal wood, have been left unpainted.

The market, that is to say, a tiled roof supported by some twenty posts, occupies of itself about half the public square of Yonville. The town hall, constructed "from the designs of a Paris architect," is a sort of Greek temple that forms the corner next to the chemist's shop. On the ground floor are three Ionic columns, and on the first floor a semicircular gallery, while the dome that crowns it is occupied by a Gallic cock, resting one foot upon the "Charte" and holding in the other the scales of Justice.

But that which most attracts the eye is, opposite the Lion d'Or inn, the chemist's shop of Monsieur Homais. In the evening especially its argand lamp is lighted, and the red and green jars that embellish his shop-front throw far across the street their two streams of color; then across them, as if in Bengal lights, is seen the shadow of the chemist leaning over his desk. His house from top to bottom is placarded with inscriptions written in large hand, round hand, printed hand: "Vichy, Seltzer, Barège waters, blood purifiers, Raspail patent medicine, Arabian racahout, Darcet lozenges, Regnault paste, trusses, baths, hygienic chocolate," &c. And the signboard, which takes up all the breadth of the shop, bears in gold letters, "Homais, Chemist." Then at the back of the shop, behind the great scales fixed to the counter, the word "Laboratory" appears on a scroll above a glass door, which about half-way up once more repeats "Homais" in gold letters on a black ground.

Beyond this there is nothing to see at Yonville. The street (the only one) a gunshot in length, and flanked by a few shops on either side, stops short at the turn of the highroad. If it is left on the right hand and the foot of the Saint-Jean hills followed, the cemetery is soon reached.

At the time of the cholera, in order to enlarge this, a piece of wall was pulled down, and three acres of land by its side purchased; but all the new portion is almost tenantless; the tombs, as heretofore, continue to crowd together toward the gate. The keeper, who is at once gravedigger and church beadle (thus making a double profit out of the parish corpses), has taken advantage of the unused plot of ground to plant potatoes there. From year to year, however, his small field grows smaller, and when there is an epidemic, he does not know whether to rejoice at the deaths or regret the burials.

"You live on the dead, Lestiboudois!" the curé at last said to him one day. This grim remark made him reflect; it checked him for some time; but to this day he carries on the cultivation of his little tubers, and even maintains stoutly that they grow naturally.

Since the events about to be narrated, nothing in fact has changed at Yonville. The tin tricolor flag still swings at the top of the church-steeple; the two chintz streamers still flutter in the wind from the linendraper's; the chemist's fœtuses, like lumps of white amadou, rot more and more in their turbid alcohol, and above the big door of the inn the old golden lion, faded by rain, still shows passers-by its poodle mane.

On the evening when the Bovarys were to arrive at Yonville, Widow Lefrançois, the landlady of this inn, was so very busy that she sweated great drops as she moved her saucepans. To-morrow was market-day. The meat had to be cut beforehand, the fowls drawn, the soup and coffee made. Moreover, she had the boarders' meals to see to, and that of the doctor, his wife, and their servant; the billiardroom was echoing with bursts of laughter; three millers in the small parlor were calling for brandy; the wood was blazing, the brazen pan was hissing, and on the long kitchen table, amid the quarters of raw mutton, rose piles of plates that rattled with the shaking of the block on which the spinach was being chopped. From the poultry-yard was heard the screaming of the fowls which the servant was chasing in order to wring their necks.

A man slightly marked with small-pox, in green leather slippers, and wearing a velvet cap with a gold tassel, was warming his back at the chimney. His face expressed nothing but self-satisfaction, and he appeared to take life as calmly as the goldfinch suspended over his head in its wicker cage: this was the chemist.

"Artémise!" shouted the landlady, "chop some wood, fill the water bottles, bring some brandy, look sharp! If only I knew what dessert to offer the guests you are expecting! Good heavens! Those furniture-movers are beginning their racket in the billiard-room again; and their van has been left before the front door! The 'Hirondelle' might run into it when it draws up. Call Polyte and tell him to put it up. Only to think, Monsieur Homais, that since morning they have had about fifteen games, and drunk eight jars of cider! Why, they'll tear my cloth for me," she went on, looking at them from a distance, her strainer in her hand.

"That wouldn't be much of a loss," replied Monsieur Homais. "You would buy another."

"Another billiard-table!" exclaimed the widow.

"Since that one is coming to pieces, Madame Lefrançois. I tell you again you are doing yourself harm, much harm! And besides, players now want narrow pockets and heavy cues. Hazards aren't played now; everything is changed! One must keep pace with the times! Just look at Tellier!"

The hostess reddened with vexation. The chemist went on:

"You may say what you like; his table is better than yours; and if one were to think, for example, of getting up a patriotic pool for Poland or the sufferers from the Lyons floods"—

"It isn't beggars like him that'll frighten us," interrupted the landlady, shrugging her fat shoulders. "Come, come, Monsieur Homais; as long as the

'Lion d'Or' exists people will come to it. We've feathered our nest; while one of these days you'll find the 'Café Français' closed with a big placard on the shutters. Change my billiard-table!" she went on, speaking to herself, "the table that comes in so handy for folding the washing, and on which, in the hunting season, I have slept six visitors! But that dawdler, Hivert, doesn't come!"

"Are you waiting for him for your gentlemen's dinner?"

"Wait for him! And what about Monsieur Binet? As the clock strikes six you'll see him come in, for he hasn't his equal under the sun for punctuality. He must always have his seat in the small parlor. He'd rather die than dine anywhere else. And so squeamish as he is, and so particular about the cider! Not like Monsieur Léon; he sometimes comes at seven, or even half-past, and he doesn't so much as look at what he eats. Such a nice young man! Never speaks a rough word!"

"Well, you see, there's a great difference between an educated man and an old carabineer who is now a tax-collector."

Six o'clock struck. Binet came in.

He wore a blue frock-coat falling in a straight line round his thin body, and his leather cap, with its lappets knotted over the top of his head with string, showed under the turned-up peak a bald forehead, flattened by the constant wearing of a helmet. He wore a black cloth waistcoat, a hair collar, gray trousers, and, all the year round, well-blacked boots, that had two parallel swellings due to the sticking out of his big toes. Not a hair stood out from the regular line of fair whiskers, which encircling his jaws, framed, after the fashion of a garden border, his long, wan face, whose eyes were small and the nose hooked. Clever at all games of cards, a good hunter, and writing a fine hand, he had at home a lathe, and amused himself by turning napkin-rings, with which he filled up his house, with the jealousy of an artist and the egotism of a bourgeois.

He went to the small parlor, but the three millers had to be got out first, and during the whole time necessary for laying the cloth, Binet remained silent in his place near the stove. Then he shut the door and took off his cap in his usual way.

"It isn't with saying civil things that he'll wear out his tongue," said the chemist, as soon as he was alone with the landlady.

"He never talks more," she replied. "Last week two travelers in the cloth line were here — such clever chaps, who told such jokes in the evening, that I fairly cried with laughing; and he stood there like a dab fish and never said a word."

"Yes," observed the chemist; "no imagination, no sallies, nothing that makes the society man."

"Yet they say he has parts," objected the land-lady.

"Parts!" replied Monsieur Homais; "he parts! In his own line it is possible," he added in a calmer tone. And he went on —

"Ah! that a merchant, who has large connections, a juris-consult, a doctor, a chemist, should be thus absent-minded, that they should become whimsical or even peevish, I can understand; such cases are cited in history. But at least it is because they are think-ing of something. Myself, for example, how often has it happened to me to look on the bureau for my pen to write a label, and to find, after all, that I had put it behind my ear?"

Madame Lefrançois just then went to the door to see if the "Hirondelle" were not coming. She started. A man dressed in black suddenly came into the kitchen. By the last gleam of the twilight one could see that his face was rubicund and his form athletic.

"What can I do for you, Monsieur le Curé?" asked the landlady, as she reached down from the chimney one of the copper candlesticks placed with their candles in a row. "Will you take something? A thimbleful of *cassis*? A glass of wine?"

The priest declined very politely. He had come for his umbrella, that he had forgotten the other day at the Ernemont convent, and after asking Madame Lefrançois to have it sent to him at the presbytery in the evening, he left for the church, from which the Angelus was ringing.

When the chemist no longer heard the noise of his boots along the square, he thought the priest's behavior just now very unbecoming. This refusal to take any refreshment seemed to him the most odious hypocrisy; all priests tippled on the sly, and were trying to bring back the days of the tithe.

The landlady took up the defense of her curé.

"Besides, he could double up four men like you over his knee. Last year he helped our people to bring in the straw; he carried as many as six trusses at once, he is so strong."

"Bravo!" said the chemist. "Now just send your daughters to confess to fellows with such a temperament! I, if I were the Government, I'd have the priests bled once a month. Yes, Madame Lafrançois, every month—a good phlebotomy, in the interests of the police and morals."

"Be quiet, Monsieur Homais. You are an infidel; you've no religion."

The chemist answered: "I have a religion, my religion, and I even have more than all these others with their mummeries and their juggling. I adore God, on the contrary. I believe in the Supreme Being, in a Creator, whatever he may be. I care little who has placed us here below to fulfil our duties as citizens and fathers of families; but I don't need to go to church to kiss silver plates, and fatten, out of my pocket, a lot of good-for-nothings who live better than we do. For one can know him as well in a wood, in a field, or even contemplating the eternal vault like the ancients. My God! mine is the God of Socrates, of Franklin, of Voltaire, and Béranger! I am for the profession of faith of the 'Savoyard Vicar,' and the immortal principles of '89! And I can't admit of an old boy of a God who takes walks in his garden with a cane in his hand, who lodges his friends in the belly of whales, dies uttering a cry, and rises again at the end of three days; things absurd in themselves, and completely opposed, moreover, to all physical laws, which proves to us, by the way, that priests have always wallowed in torpid ignorance, in which they would fain engulf the people with them."

He ceased looking round for an audience, for in his bubbling over the chemist had, for a moment fancied himself in the midst of the town council. But the landlady no longer heeded him; she was listening to a distant rolling. One could distinguish the noise of a carriage mingled with the clattering of loose horseshoes that beat against the ground, and at last the "Hirondelle" stopped at the door.

It was a yellow box on two large wheels, that, reaching to the tilt, prevented travelers from seeing the road and soiled their shoulders. The small panes of the narrow windows rattled in their sashes when the coach was closed, and retained here and there patches of mud amid the old layers of dust, that not even storms of rain had altogether washed away. It was drawn by three horses, the first a leader, and when it came down-hill its bottom jolted against the ground.

Some of the inhabitants of Yonville came out into the square; they all spoke at once, asking for news, for explanations, for hampers. Hivert did not know whom to answer. It was he who did the errands of the place in town. He went to the shops and brought back rolls of leather for the shoemaker, old iron for the farrier, a barrel of herrings for his mistress, caps from the milliner's, locks from the hairdresser's, and all along the road on his return journey he distributed his parcels, which he threw, standing upright on his seat and shouting at the top of his voice, over the enclosures of the yards.

An accident had delayed him. Madame Bovary's greyhound had run across the field. They had whistled for him a quarter of an hour; Hivert had even gone back a mile and a half expecting every moment to catch sight of her; but it had been necessary to go on. Emma had wept, grown angry; she had accused Charles of this misfortune. Monsieur Lheureux, a draper, who happened to be in the coach with her, had tried to console her by a number of examples of lost dogs recognizing their masters at the end of long

years. One, he said, had been told of who had come
back to Paris from Constantinople. Another had gone
one hundred and fifty miles in a straight line, and
swam four rivers; and his own father had possessed
a poodle, which, after twelve years of absence, had
all of a sudden jumped on his back in the street as
he was going to dine in town.

G. F.—7

II.

NEW FRIENDS.

EMMA got out first, then Félicité, Monsieur Lheureux, and a nurse, and they had to wake up Charles in his corner, where he had slept soundly since night set in.

Homais introduced himself; he offered his homages to Madame and his respects to Monsieur; said he was charmed to have been able to render them some slight service, and added with a cordial air that he had ventured to invite himself, his wife being away.

When Madame Bovary was in the kitchen she went up to the chimney. With the tips of her fingers she caught her dress at the knee, and having thus pulled it up to her ankle, held out her foot in its black boot to the fire above the revolving leg of mutton. The flame lit up the whole of her, penetrating with a crude light the woof of her gown, the fine pores of her fair skin, and even her eyelids, which she blinked now and again. A great red glow passed over her with the blowing of the wind through the half-open door. On the other side of the chimney a young man with fair hair watched her silently.

As he was a good deal bored at Yonville, where he was a clerk at the notary's, Monsieur Guillaumin,

(98)

Monsieur Léon Dupuis (it was he who was the second *habitué* of the "Lion d'Or") frequently put back his dinner-hour in the hope that some traveler might come to the inn, with whom he could chat in the evening. On the days when his work was done early, he had, for want of something else to do, to come punctually, and endure from soup to cheese a *tête-à-tête* with Binet. It was therefore with delight that he accepted the landlady's suggestion that he should dine in company with the newcomers, and they passed into the large parlor where Madame Lefrançois, for the purpose of showing off, had had the table laid for four.

Homais asked to be allowed to keep on his skull-cap, for fear of coryza; then turning to his neighbor—

"Madame is no doubt a little fatigued; one gets jolted so abominably in our 'Hirondelle.'"

"That is true," replied Emma; "but moving about always amuses me. I like change of place."

"It is so tedious," sighed the clerk, "to be always riveted to the same places."

"If you were like me," said Charles, "constantly obliged to be in the saddle"—

"But," Léon went on, addressing himself to Madame Bovary, "nothing, it seems to me, is more pleasant—when one can," he added.

"Moreover," said the chemist, "the practice of medicine is not very hard work in our part of the world, for the state of our roads allows us the use of gigs, and generally, as the farmers are well off, they pay pretty well. We have, medically speaking, besides the ordinary cases of enteritis, bronchitis, bilious affections, etc., now and then a few intermittent fevers at harvest-time; but on the whole, little of

a serious nature, nothing special to note, unless it be
a great deal of scrofula, due, no doubt, to the deplorable hygienic conditions of our peasant dwellings.
Ah! you will find many prejudices to combat, Monsieur Bovary, much obstinacy of routine, with which
all the efforts of your science will daily come into
collision; for people still have recourse to novenas, to
relics, to the priest, rather than come straight to the
doctor or the chemist. The climate, however, is not,
truth to tell, bad, and we even have a few nono-
genarians in our parish. The thermometer (I have
made some observations) falls in winter to 4 degrees,
and in the hottest season rises to 25 or 30 degrees Centigrade at the outside, which gives us 24 degrees Réaumur as the maximum, or otherwise 54 degrees
Fahrenheit (English scale), not more. And, as a
matter of fact, we are sheltered from the north winds
by the forest of Argueil on the one side, from the
west winds by the St. Jean range on the other; and
this heat, moreover, which, on account of the aqueous
vapors given off by the river and the considerable
number of cattle in the fields, which, as you know,
exhale much ammonia, that is to say, nitrogen, hydrogen, and oxygen (no, nitrogen and hydrogen
alone), and which sucking up into itself the humus
from the ground, mixing together all those different
emanations, unites them into a stack, so to say, and
combining with the electricity diffused through the
atmosphere, when there is any, might in the long
run, as in tropical countries, engender insalubrious
miasmata,—this heat, I say, finds itself perfectly tempered on the side whence it comes, or rather whence
it should come—that is to say, the southern side—
by the south-eastern winds, which, having cooled

themselves passing over the Seine, reach us sometimes all at once, like breezes from Russia."

"At any rate, you have some walks in the neighborhood?" continued Madame Bovary, speaking to the young man.

"Oh, very few," he answered. "There is a place they call La Pâture, on the top of the hill, on the edge of the forest. Sometimes, on Sundays, I go and stay there with a book, watching the sunset."

"I think there is nothing so admirable as sunsets," she resumed; "but especially by the side of the sea."

"Oh, I adore the sea!" said Monsieur Léon.

"And then, does it not seem to you," continued Madame Bovary, "that the mind travels more freely on this limitless expanse, the contemplation of which elevates the soul, gives ideas of the infinite, the ideal?"

"It is the same with mountainous landscapes," continued Léon. "A cousin of mine who traveled in Switzerland last year told me that one could not picture to oneself the poetry of the lakes, the charm of the waterfalls, the gigantic effect of the glaciers. One sees pines of incredible size across torrents, cottages suspended over precipices, and, a thousand feet below one, whole valleys when the clouds open. Such spectacles must stir to enthusiasm, incline to prayer, to ecstasy; and I no longer marvel at that celebrated musician who, the better to inspire his imagination, was in the habit of playing the piano before some imposing site."

"You play?" she asked.

"No, but I am very fond of music," he replied.

"Ah! don't you listen to him, Madame Bovary," interrupted Homais, bending over his plate. "That's

sheer modesty. Why, my dear fellow, the other day
in your room you were singing 'L'Ange Gardien'
ravishingly. I heard you from the laboratory. You
gave it like an actor."

Léon, in fact, lodged at the chemist's, where he
had a small room on the second floor, overlooking the
Place. He blushed at the compliment of his landlord,
who had already turned to the doctor, and was enu-
merating to him, one after the other, all the principal
inhabitants of Yonville. He was telling anecdotes,
giving information; the fortune of the notary was not
known exactly, and "there was the Tuvache household," who made a good deal of show.

Emma continued, "And what music do you pre-
fer?"

"Oh, German music; that which makes you
dream."

"Have you been to the opera?"

"Not yet; but I shall go next year, when I am
living at Paris to finish reading for the bar."

"As I had the honor of putting it to your husband," said the chemist, "with regard to this poor
Yanoda who has run away, you will find yourself,
thanks to his extravagance, in the possession of one
of the most comfortable houses of Yonville. Its
greatest convenience for a doctor is a door giving on
the Walk, where one can go in and out unseen.
Moreover, it contains everything that is agreeable in
a household—a laundry, kitchen with offices, sitting-
room, fruit-room, etc. He was a gay dog, who didn't
care what he spent. At the end of the garden, by
the side of the water, he had an arbor built just for
the purpose of drinking beer in summer; and if madame is fond of gardening she will be able"—

"My wife doesn't care about it," said Charles; "although she has been advised to take exercise, she prefers always sitting in her room reading."

"Like me," replied Léon. "And indeed, what is better than to sit by one's fireside in the evening with a book, while the wind beats against the window and the lamp is burning?"

"What, indeed?" she said, fixing her large black eyes wide open upon him.

"One thinks of nothing," he continued; "the hours slip by. Motionless we traverse countries we fancy we see, and your thought, blending with the fiction, playing with the details, follows the outline of the adventures. It mingles with the characters, and it seems as if it were yourself palpitating beneath their costumes."

"That is true! that is true!" she said.

"Has it ever happened to you" Léon went on, "to come across some vague idea of one's own in a book, some dim image that comes back to you from afar, and as the completest expression of your own slightest sentiment?"

"I have experienced it," she replied.

"That is the reason why," he said, "I especially love the poets. I think verse more tender than prose, and that it moves far more easily to tears."

"Still in the long run it is tiring," continued Emma. "Now I, on the contrary, adore stories that rush breathlessly along, that frighten one. I detest commonplace heroes and moderate sentiments, such as there are in nature."

"In fact," observed the clerk, "these works, not touching the heart, it seems to me, the true end of art. It is so sweet, amid all the disenchantments of life, to be able to dwell in thought upon noble characters, pure affections, and pictures of happiness. For myself, living here far from the world, this is my one distraction; but Yonville affords so few resources."

"Like Tostes, no doubt," replied Emma; "and so I always subscribed to a lending library."

"If madame will do me the honor of making use of it," said the chemist, who had just caught the last words, "I have at her disposal a library composed of the best authors, Voltaire, Rousseau, Delille, Walter Scott, the 'Echo des Feuilletons;' and in addition I receive various periodicals, among them the 'Fanal de Rouen' daily, having the advantage to be its correspondent for the districts of Buchy, Forges, Neufchâtel, Yonville and vicinity."

For two hours and a half they had been at table; for the servant Artémise, carelessly dragging her old list slippers over the flags, brought one plate after the other, forgot everything, and constantly left the door of the billiard-room half open, so that it beat against the wall with its hooks.

Unconsciously, Léon, while talking, had placed his foot on one of the bars of the chair on which Madame Bovary was sitting. She wore a small blue silk necktie, that kept up like a ruff a gauffered cambric collar, and with the movements of her head the lower part of her face gently sunk into the linen or came out from it. Thus, side by side, while Charles and the chemist chatted, they entered into one of those vague conversations where the hazard of all that is said brings you back to the fixed center of a common sympathy. The Paris theaters, titles of novels, new quadrilles, and the world they did not know;

Tostes, where she had lived, and Yonville, where they were; they examined all, talked of everything till to the end of dinner.

When coffee was served Félicité went away to get ready the room in the new house, and the guests soon raised the siege. Madame Lefrançois was asleep near the cinders, while the stable-boy, lantern in hand, was waiting to show Monsieur and Madame Bovary the way home. Bits of straw stuck in his red hair, and he limped with his left leg. When he had taken in his other hand the curé's umbrella, they started.

The town was asleep; the pillars of the market threw great shadows; the earth was all gray as on a summer's night. But as the doctor's house was only some fifty paces from the inn, they had to say good-night almost immediately, and the company dispersed.

As soon as she entered the passage, Emma felt the cold of the plaster fall about her shoulders like damp linen. The walls were new and the wooden stairs creaked. In their bedroom, on the first floor, a whitish light passed through the curtainless windows. She could catch glimpses of tree-tops, and beyond, the fields, half-drowned in the fog that lay reeking in the moonlight along the course of the river. In the middle of the room, pell-mell, were scattered drawers, bottles, curtain-rods, gilt poles, with mattresses on the chairs and basins on the floor,—the two men who had brought the furniture had left everything about carelessly.

This was the fourth time that she had slept in a strange place. The first was the day of her going to the convent; the second. of her arrival at Tostes; the third, at Vaubyessard; and this was the fourth. And each one had marked, as it were, the inauguration of a new phase in her life. She did not believe that things could present themselves in the same way in different places, and since the portion of her life lived had been bad, no doubt that which remained to be lived would be better.

III.

ADDED CARES.

T HE next day, as she was getting up, she saw the clerk on the Place. She had on a dressing-gown. He looked up and bowed. She nodded quickly and reclosed the window.

Léon waited all day for six o'clock in the evening to come, but on going to the inn, he found no one but Monsieur Binet, already at table. The dinner of the evening before had been a considerable event for him; he had never till then talked for two hours consecutively to a "lady." How then had he been able to explain, and in such language, the number of things that he could not have said so well before? He was usually shy, and maintained that reserve which partakes at once of modesty and dissimulation. At Yonville he was considered "well-bred." He listened to the arguments of the older people, and did not seem hot about politics — a remarkable thing for a young man. Then he had some accomplishments; he painted in water-colors, could read the key of G, and readily talked literature after dinner when he did not play cards. Monsieur Homais respected him for his education; Madame Homais liked him for his good-nature, for he often took the little Homaises into

(107)

the garden—little brats who were always dirty, very much spoiled, and somewhat lymphatic, like their mother. Besides the servant to look after them, they had Justin, the chemist's apprentice, a second cousin of Monsieur Homais, who had been taken into the house from charity, and who was useful at the same time as a servant.

The chemist proved the best of neighbors. He gave Madame Bovary information as to the tradespeople, sent expressly for his own cider merchant, tasted the drink himself, and saw that the casks were properly placed in the cellar; he explained how to set about getting in a supply of butter cheap, and made an arrangement with Lestiboudois, the sacristan, who, besides his sacerdotal and funereal functions, looked after the principal gardens at Yonville by the hour or the year, according to the taste of the customers.

The need of looking after others was not the only thing that urged the chemist to such obsequious cordiality; there was a plan underneath it all.

He had infringed the law of the 19th Ventôse, year xi., article 1, which forbade all persons not having a diploma to practice medicine; so that, after certain anonymous denunciations, Homais had been summoned to Rouen to see the procureur of the king in his own private room; the magistrate receiving him standing up, ermine on shoulder and cap on head. It was in the morning, before the court opened. In the corridors one heard the heavy boots of the gendarmes walking past, and like a far-off noise great locks that were shut. The chemist's ears tingled as if he were about to have an apoplectic stroke; he saw the depths of dungeons, his family in tears, his shop sold, all the jars dispersed; and he was obliged to enter a café and take a glass of rum and seltzer to recover his spirits.

Little by little the memory of this reprimand grew fainter, and he continued, as heretofore, to give ano-dyne consultations in his back-parlor. But the mayor resented it, his colleagues were jealous, everything was to be feared; gaining over Monsieur Bovary by his at-tentions was to earn his gratitude, and prevent his speaking out later, should he notice anything. So every morning Homais brought him "the paper," and often in the afternoon left his shop for a few moments to have a chat with the Doctor.

Charles was dull: patients did not come. He re-mained seated for hours without speaking, went into his consulting-room to sleep, or watched his wife sewing. Then for diversion he employed himself at home as a workman; he even tried to do up the attic with some paint which had been left behind by the painters. But money matters worried him. He had spent so much for repairs at Tostes, for madame's toilette, and for the moving, that the whole dowry, over three thousand crowns, had slipped away in two years. Then how many things had been spoilt or lost during their carriage from Tostes to Yonville, without counting the plaster curé, who, falling out of the coach at an over-severe jolt, had been dashed into a thou-sand fragments on the pavement of Quincampoix!

A pleasanter trouble came to distract him, namely, the pregnancy of his wife. As the time of her confine-ment approached he cherished her the more. It was another bond of the flesh establishing itself, and, as it were, a continued sentiment of a more complex union. When from afar he saw her languid walk, and her figure without stays turning softly on her hips; when opposite one another he looked at her at his ease, while she took tired poses in her armchair, then his happiness knew no bounds; he got up, embraced her, passed his hands over her face, called her little mamma, wanted to make her dance, and, half-laughing, half-crying, uttered all kinds of caressing pleasantries that came into his head. The idea of having begotten a child delighted him. Now he wanted nothing. He knew human life from end to end, and he sat down to it with serenity.

Emma at first felt a great astonishment; then was anxious to be delivered that she might know what it was to be a mother. But not being able to spend as much as she would have liked, to have a swing-bassinette with rose silk curtains, and embroidered caps, in a fit of bitterness she gave up looking after the trousseau, and ordered the whole of it from a village needlewoman, without choosing or discussing anything. Thus she did not amuse herself with those preparations that stimulate the tenderness of mothers, and so her affection was from the very outset, per-- haps, to some extent attenuated.

As Charles, however, spoke of the boy at every meal, she soon began to think of him more consecutively.

She hoped for a son; he would be strong and dark; she would call him George; and this idea of having a male child was like an expected revenge for all her impotence in the past. A man, at least, is free; he may travel over passions and over countries, overcome obstacles, taste of the most far-away pleasures. But a woman is always hampered. At once inert and flexible, she has against her the weakness of the flesh and legal dependence. Her will, like the veil of her bonnet, held by a string, flutters in every wind; there is always some desire that draws her, some conventionality that restrains.

She was confined on a Sunday at about six o'clock, as the sun was rising.

"It is a girl!" said Charles.

She turned her head away and fainted.

Madame Homais, as well as Madame Lefrançois of the Lion d'Or, almost immediately came running in to embrace her. The chemist, as a man of discretion, offered only a few provisional felicitations through the half-open door. He wished to see the child, and thought it well made.

While she was getting well she occupied herself much in seeking a name for her daughter. First she went over all those that have Italian endings, such as Clara, Louisa, Amanda, Atala; she liked Galsuinde very well, and Yseult or Léocadie still better. Charles wanted the child to be called after her mother; Emma opposed this. They ran over the calendar from end to end, and then consulted outsiders.

"Monsieur Léon," said the chemist, "with whom I was talking about it the other day, wonders you do not choose Madeleine. It is very much in fashion just now."

But Madame Bovary, senior, cried out loudly against this name of a sinner. As to Monsieur Homais, he had a preference for all those that recalled some great man, an illustrious fact, or a generous idea, and it was on this system that he baptized his four children. Thus Napoleon represented glory and Franklin liberty; Irma was perhaps a concession to romanticism, but Athalie was a homage to the greatest masterpiece of the French stage. For his philosophical convictions did not interfere with his artistic tastes; in him the thinker did not stifle the man of sentiment; he could make distinctions, make allowances for imagination and fanaticism. In this tragedy, for example, he found fault with the ideas, but admired the style; he detested the conception, but applauded all the details, and loathed the characters while he grew enthusiastic over their dialogue. When he read the fine passages he was transported, but when he thought that mummers would get something out of them for their show, he was disconsolate; and in this confusion of sentiments in which he was involved he would have liked at once to crown Racine with both his hands and argue with him for a good quarter of an hour.

At last Emma remembered that at the château of Vaubyessard she had heard the Marchioness call a young lady Berthe; from that moment this name was chosen; and as old Rouault could not come, Monsieur Homais was requested to stand godfather. His gifts were all products from his establishment, to wit: six boxes of jujubes, a whole jar of racahout, three cakes of marsh-mallow paste, and six sticks of sugar-candy, into the bargain, that he had come across in a cupboard. On the evening of the ceremony there was a grand dinner; the curé was present; there was much excitement. Monsieur Homais toward liqueur-time began singing "Le Dieu des bonnes gens." Monsieur Léon sang a barcarolle, and Madame Bovary, senior, who was godmother, a romance of the time of the Empire; finally, M. Bovary, senior, insisted on having the child brought down, and began baptizing it with a glass of champagne that he poured over its head. This mockery of the first of the sac-

raments made the Abbé Bournisien angry; old Bovary
replied by a quotation from "La Guerre des Dieux;"
the curé wished to leave; the ladies implored, Homais
interfered; and they succeeded in making the priest
sit down again, and he quietly went on with the
half-finished coffee in his saucer.

Monsieur Bovary, senior, stayed at Yonville a
month, dazzling the natives by a superb policeman's
cap with silver tassels that he wore in the morning
when he smoked his pipe in the square. Being also
in the habit of drinking a good deal of brandy, he
often sent the servant to the Lion d'Or to buy him a
bottle, which was put down to his son's account, and
to perfume his handkerchiefs he used up his daughter-
in-law's whole supply of eau-de-cologne.

The latter did not at all dislike his company. He
had knocked about the world, he talked about Berlin,
Vienna, and Strasbourg, of his soldier times, of the
mistresses he had had, the grand luncheons of which
he had partaken; then he was amiable, and sometimes even, either on the stairs or in the garden,
would seize hold of her waist, crying, "Charles, look
out for yourself."

Then Madame Bovary, senior, became alarmed for
her son's happiness, and fearing that her husband
might in the long run have an immoral influence
upon the ideas of the young woman, took care to
hurry their departure. Perhaps she had more serious
reasons for uneasiness. Monsieur Bovary was not the
man to respect anything.

One day Emma was suddenly seized with the desire to see her little girl, who had been put to nurse
with the carpenter's wife, and without looking at the
almanac to see whether the six weeks of the Virgin

were yet passed, she set out for the Rollets' house, situated at the extreme end of the village, between the highroad and the fields.

It was mid-day, the shutters of the houses were closed, and the slate roofs that glittered beneath the fierce light of the blue sky seemed to strike sparks from the crest of their gables. A heavy wind was blowing; Emma felt weak as she walked; the stones of the pavement hurt her; she was doubtful whether she would not go home again, or go in somewhere to rest.

At this moment Monsieur Léon came out from a neighboring door with a bundle of papers under his arm. He came to greet her, and stood in the shade in front of Lheureux's shop under the projecting gray awning.

Madame Bovary said she was going to see her baby, but that she was beginning to grow tired.

"If—" said Léon, not daring to go on.

"Have you any business to attend to?" she asked.

And on the clerk's answer, she begged him to accompany her. That same evening this was known in Yonville, and Madame Tuvache, the mayor's wife, declared in the presence of her servant that "Madame Bovary was compromising herself."

To get to the nurse's it was necessary to turn to the left on leaving the street, as if making for the cemetery, and to follow between little houses and yards a small path bordered with privet hedges. They were in bloom, and so were the speedwells, eglantines, thistles, and the sweetbriar that sprang up from the thickets. Through openings in the hedges one could see into the huts, some pig on a dung-heap, or tethered cows rubbing their horns against the trunks

of trees. The two, side by side, walked slowly, she
leaning upon him, and he restraining his pace, which
he regulated by hers; in front of them a swarm of
midges fluttered, buzzing in the warm air.

They recognized the house by an old walnut-tree
which shaded it. Low, and covered with brown
tiles, outside it hung, beneath the dormer-window of
the garret, a string of onions. Faggots upright against
a thorn fence surrounded a bed of lettuces, a few
square feet of lavender, and sweet peas strung on
sticks. Dirty water was running here and there on
the grass, and several indefinite rags, knitted stockings, a red calico jacket, and a large sheet of
coarse linen, were spread over the hedge. At the
noise of the gate the nurse appeared with a baby she
was suckling on one arm. With her other hand she
was pulling along a poor puny little fellow, his face
covered with scrofula, the son of a Rouen hosier,
whom his parents, too taken up with their business,
left in the country.

"Go in," she said; "your little one is there
asleep."

The room on the ground floor, the only one in
the dwelling, had at its farther end, against the wall,
a large bed without curtains, while a kneading-trough
took up the side by the window, one pane of which
was mended with a piece of blue paper. In the
corner behind the door, shining hobnailed shoes stood
in a row under the slab of the washstand, near a
bottle of oil with a feather stuck in its mouth; a
Matthieu Laensberg lay on the dusty mantelpiece amid
gun-flints, candle-ends, and bits of amadou. Finally,
the last luxury in the apartment was a "Fame"
blowing her trumpets, a picture cut out, no doubt,

from some perfumer's prospectus and nailed to the wall with six wooden shoe-pegs.

Emma's child was asleep in a wicker-cradle. She took it up in the wrapping that enveloped it and began singing softly as she rocked herself to and fro.

Léon walked up and down the room; it seemed strange to him to see this beautiful woman in her nankeen dress in the midst of all this poverty. Madame Bovary reddened; he turned away, thinking perhaps there had been an impertinent look in his eyes. Then she put back the baby girl, who had just vomited over her frock. The nurse at once came to dry her, protesting that it wouldn't show.

"She gives me other doses," she said; "I am always a-washing of her. If you would have the goodness to order Camus, the grocer, to let me have a little soap; it would really be more convenient for you, as I needn't trouble you then."

"Very well! very well!" said Emma. "Good morning, Madame Rollet," and she went out, wiping her shoes at the door.

The good woman accompanied her to the end of the garden, talking all the time of the trouble she had getting up of nights.

"I'm that worn out sometimes as I drop asleep on my chair. I'm sure you might at least give me just a pound of ground coffee; that'd last me a month, and I'd take it of a morning with some milk."

After submitting to her thanks, Madame Bovary left. She had gone a little way down the path when, at the sound of wooden shoes, she turned round. It was the nurse.

"What is it?"

Then the peasant woman, taking her aside behind an elm tree, began talking to her of her husband, who with his trade and six francs a year that the captain —

"Oh, be quick!" said Emma.

"Well," the nurse went on, heaving sighs between each word, "I'm afraid he'll be put out seeing me have coffee alone; you know men —"

"But you are to have some," Emma repeated; "I will give you some. You bother me!"

"Oh, dear! my poor, dear lady! you see, in consequence of his wounds he has terrible cramps in the chest. He even says that cider weakens him."

"Do make haste, Mère Rollet!"

"Well," the latter continued, making a curtsey, "if it weren't asking too much," and she curtsied once more, "if you would"— and her eyes begged —"a jar of brandy," she said at last, "and I'd rub your little one's feet with it; they're as tender as one's tongue."

Once rid of the nurse, Emma again took Monsieur Léon's arm. She walked fast for some time, then more slowly, and looking straight in front of her, her eyes rested on the shoulder of the young man, whose frock-coat had a black-velvet collar. His brown hair fell over it, straight and carefully arranged. She noticed his nails, which were longer than one wore them at Yonville. It was one of the clerk's chief occupations to trim them, and for this purpose he kept a special knife in his writing-desk.

They returned to Yonville by the water-side. In the warm season the bank, wider than at other times, showed to its foot the garden walls, whence a few steps led to the river. It flowed noiselessly, swift, and cold to the eye; long, thin grasses huddled to-gether in it as the current drove them, and spread themselves upon the limpid water like streaming hair; sometimes at the top of the reeds or on the leaf of a water-lily an insect with thin legs crawled or rested. The sun pierced with a ray the small blue bubbles of the waves that, breaking, followed each other; branchless old willows mirrored their gray backs in the water; beyond, all around, the meadows seemed empty. It was the dinner-hour at the farms, and the young woman and her companion heard nothing as they walked but the fall of their steps on the earth of the path, the words they spoke, and the sound of Emma's skirts rustling around her.

The walls of the gardens, with pieces of bottle on their coping, were as hot as the glass windows of a conservatory. Wallflowers had sprung up between the bricks, and with the tip of her open sunshade Madame Bovary, as she passed, made some of their faded flowers crumble into a yellow dust, or a spray of overhanging honeysuckle and clematis caught in its fringe and dangled for a moment over the silk.

They were talking of a troupe of Spanish dancers who were expected shortly at the Rouen theatre.

"Are you going?" she asked.

"If I can," he answered.

Had they nothing else to say to one another? Yet their eyes were full of more serious speech, and while they forced themselves to find trivial phrases, they felt the same languor stealing over them both. It was the whisper of the soul, deep, continuous, dominating that of their voices. Surprised with wonder at this strange sweetness, they did not think of speaking of the sensation or of seeking its cause.

Coming joys, like tropical shores, throw over the immensity before them their inborn softness, an odorous wind, and we are lulled by this intoxication without a thought of the horizon that we do not even know.

In one place the ground had been trodden down by the cattle; they had to step on large green stones put here and there in the mud. She often stopped a moment to look where to place her foot, and tottering on the stone that shook, her arms outspread, her form bent forward with a look of indecision, she would laugh, afraid of falling into the puddles of water.

When they arrived in front of her garden, Madame Bovary opened the little gate, ran up the steps and disappeared.

Léon returned to his office. His chief was away; he just glanced at the briefs, then cut himself a pen, and at last took up his hat and went out.

He went to La Pâture at the top of the Argueil hills at the beginning of the forest; he threw himself upon the ground under the pines and gazed at the sky through his fingers.

"How bored I am!" he said to himself, "how bored I am!"

He thought he was to be pitied for living in this village, with Homais for a friend and Monsieur Guillaumin for master. The latter, entirely absorbed by his business, wearing gold-rimmed spectacles and red whiskers over a white cravat, understood nothing of mental refinements, although he affected a stiff English manner, which in the beginning had impressed the clerk.

As to the chemist's spouse, she was the best wife in Normandy, gentle as a sheep, loving her children, her father, her mother, her cousins, weeping for others' woes, letting everything go in her household, and detesting corsets; but so slow of movement, such a bore to listen to, so common in appearance, and of such restricted conversation, that although she was thirty, he only twenty, although they slept in rooms next each other and he spoke to her daily, he never thought that she might be a woman for another, or that she possessed anything else of her sex than the gown.

And what else was there? Binet, a few shop-keepers, two or three publicans, the curé, and, finally, Monsieur Tuvache, the mayor, with his two sons, rich, crabbed, obtuse persons, who farmed their own lands and had feasts among themselves, bigoted to boot, and quite unbearable companions.

But from the general background of all these human faces Emma's stood out isolated and yet farthest off; for between her and him he seemed to see a vague abyss.

In the beginning he had called on her several times along with the druggist. Charles had not appeared particularly anxious to see him again, and Léon did not know what to do between his fear of being indiscreet and the desire for an intimacy that seemed almost impossible.

IV.

Silent Homage.

WHEN the first cold days set in Emma left her bedroom for the sitting-room, a long apartment with a low ceiling, in which there was on the mantelpiece a large bunch of coral spread out against the looking-glass. Seated in her arm-chair near the window, she could see the villagers pass along the pavement.

Twice a day Léon went from his office to the Lion d'Or. Emma could hear him coming from afar; she leant forward listening, and the young man glided past the curtain, always dressed in the same way, and without turning his head. But in the twilight, when, her chin resting on her left hand, she let the embroidery she had begun fall on her knees, she often shuddered at the apparition of this shadow suddenly gliding past. She would get up and order the table to be laid.

Monsieur Homais called at dinner-time. Skull-cap in hand, he came in on tiptoe, in order to disturb no one, always repeating the same phrase, "Good evening, everybody." Then, when he had taken his seat at table between the pair, he asked the doctor about his patients, and the latter consulted him as to the probability of their payment. Next they talked of what was in the paper. Homais by this hour knew it almost by heart, and he repeated it from end to end, with the reflections of the penny-a-liners, and all the stories of individual catastrophes that had occurred in France or abroad. But the subject becoming exhausted, he was not slow in throwing out some remarks on the dishes before him. Sometimes even, half-rising, he delicately pointed out to Madame the tenderest morsel, or turning to the servant, gave her some advice on the manipulation of stews and the hygiene of seasoning. He talked aroma, osmazome, juices, and gelatine in a bewildering manner. Moreover, Homais, with his head fuller of recipes than his shop of jars, excelled in making all kinds of preserves, vinegars, and sweet liqueurs; he knew also all the last inventions in economic stoves, together with the art of preserving cheeses and of curing sick wines.

At eight o'clock Justin came to fetch him to shut up the shop. Then Monsieur Homais gave him a sly look, especially if Félicité was there, for he had noticed that his apprentice was fond of the doctor's house.

"The young dog," he said, "is beginning to have ideas, and the devil take me if I don't believe he's in love with your servant!"

But a more serious fault with which he reproached Justin was his constantly listening to conversation. On Sunday, for example, one could not get him out of the drawing-room, whither Madame Homais had called him to fetch the children, who were falling asleep in the arm-chairs, and dragging down with their backs calico chair-covers that were too large.

Not many people came to these soirées at the chemist's, his scandal-mongering and political opinions having successively alienated various respectable persons from him. The clerk never failed to be there. As soon as he heard the bell he ran to meet Madame Bovary, took her shawl, and put away under the shop-counter the thick list shoes that she wore over her boots when there was snow.

First they played some hands at trente-et-un; next Monsieur Homais played écarté with Emma; Léon behind her gave her advice. Standing up with his hands on the back of her chair, he saw the teeth of her comb that bit into her chignon. With every movement that she made to throw her cards the right side of her bodice was drawn up. From her turned-up hair a dark color fell over her back, and growing gradually paler, lost itself little by little in the shade. Then her skirt fell on both sides of her chair, puffing out, full of folds, and reaching the floor. When Léon occasionally felt the sole of his boot resting on it, he drew back as if he had trodden upon some one.

When the game of cards was over, the druggist and the Doctor played dominoes, and Emma, changing her place, leant her elbow on the table, turning over the leaves of "L'Illustration." She had brought her ladies' journal with her. Léon sat down near her; they looked at the engravings together, and waited for each other at the bottom of the pages. She often begged him to read her the verses; Léon declaimed them in a languid voice, to which he carefully gave a dying fall in the love passages. But the noise of the dominoes annoyed him. Monsieur Homais was strong at the game; he could beat Charles and give him a double-six. Then, the three hundred finished, they both stretched themselves out in front of the fire, and were soon asleep. The fire was dying out in the cinders; the teapot was empty, Léon was still reading. Emma listened to him, mechanically turning round the lamp-shade, on the gauze of which were painted clowns in carriages, and tight-rope dancers with their balancing-poles. Léon stopped, pointing with a gesture to his sleeping audience; then they talked in low tones, and their conversation seemed the more sweet to them because it was unheard.

Thus a kind of bond was established between them, a constant commerce of books and of romances. Monsieur Bovary, little given to jealousy, did not trouble himself about it.

On his birthday he received a beautiful phrenological head, all marked with figures to the thorax, and painted blue. This was an attention of the clerk's. He showed him many others, even to doing errands for him at Rouen; and the book of a novelist having made the mania for cactuses fashionable, Léon bought some for Madame Bovary, bringing them back on his knees in the "Hirondelle," pricking his fingers with their stiff hairs.

She had a board with a balustrade fixed against her window to hold the pots. The clerk, too, had his small hanging garden; they saw each other tending their flowers at their windows.

Of the windows of the village there was one yet more often occupied; for on Sundays, from morning to night, and every morning when the weather was bright, one could see at the dormer-window of a garret the profile of Monsieur Binet bending over his lathe, whose monotonous humming could be heard at the Lion d'Or.

One evening on coming home Léon found in his room a rug in velvet and wool with leaves on a pale ground. He called Madame Homais, Monsieur Homais, Justin, the children, the cook; he spoke of it to his chief; every one wished to see this rug. Why did the doctor's wife give the clerk presents? It looked queer. They decided that she must be in love with him.

He made this seem likely, so ceaselessly did he talk of her charms and of her wit; so much so, that Binet once roughly answered him:

"What does it matter to me since I'm not in her set?"

He tortured himself to find out how he could make his declaration to her, and, always halting between the fear of displeasing her and the shame of being such a coward, he wept with discouragement and desire. Then he took energetic resolutions, wrote letters that he tore up, put it off to times that he again deferred. Often he set out with the determination to dare all; but this resolution soon deserted him in Emma's presence, and when Charles, dropping in, invited him to jump into his chaise to go with him to see some patient in the neighborhood, he at once accepted, bowed to madame, and went out. Her husband, was he not something belonging to her?

As to Emma, she did not ask herself whether she loved. Love, she thought, must come suddenly, with great outbursts and lightnings,—a hurricane of the skies, which falls upon life, revolutionizes it, roots up the will like a leaf, and sweeps the whole heart into the abyss. She did not know that on the terraces of houses lakes are formed when the pipes are choked, and she would thus have remained in her security when she suddenly discovered a rent in its wall.

V.

I T WAS a Sunday in February, an afternoon when the snow was falling.

They had all, Monsieur and Madame Bovary, Homais, and Monsieur Léon, gone to see a yarn-mill that was being built in the valley a mile and half from Yonville. The druggist had taken Napoleon and Athalie to give them some exercise, and Justin accompanied them, carrying the umbrellas on his shoulder.

Nothing, however, could be less curious than this curiosity. A great piece of waste ground, on which pell-mell, amid a mass of sand and stones, were a few brake-wheels, already rusty, surrounded by a quadrangular building pierced by a number of little windows. The building was unfinished; the sky could be seen through the joists of the roofing. Attached to the stop-plank of the gable a bunch of straw mixed with corn-ears fluttered its tricolored ribbons in the wind.

Homais was talking. He explained to the company the future importance of this establishment, computed the strength of the floorings, the thickness of the walls, and regretted extremely not having a yard-stick such as Monsieur Binet possessed for his own special use.

Emma, who had taken his arm, bent lightly against his shoulder, and she looked at the sun's disc shedding afar through the mist his pale splendor. She turned. Charles was there. His cap was drawn down over his eyebrows, and his two thick lips were trembling, which added a look of stupidity to his face; his very back, his calm back, was irritating to behold, and she saw written upon his coat all the platitude of the bearer.

While she was considering him thus, tasting in her irritation a sort of depraved pleasure, Léon made a step forward. The cold that made him pale seemed to add a more gentle languor to his face; between his cravat and his neck the somewhat loose collar of his shirt showed the skin; the lobe of his ear looked out from beneath a lock of hair, and his large blue eyes, raised to the clouds, seemed to Emma more limpid and more beautiful than those mountain-lakes where the heavens are mirrored.

"Wretched boy!" suddenly cried the chemist.

And he ran to his son, who had just precipitated himself into a heap of lime in order to whiten his boots. At the reproaches with which he was being overwhelmed Napoleon began to roar, while Justin dried his shoes with a wisp of straw. But a knife was wanted; Charles offered his.

"Ah!" she said to herself, "he carries a knife in his pocket like a peasant."

The hoar-frost was falling, and they turned back to Yonville.

In the evening Madame Bovary did not go to her neighbor's, and when Charles had left and she felt herself alone, the comparison recurred with the clearness of a sensation almost actual, and with that lengthening of perspective which memory gives to things. Looking from her bed at the clear fire that was burning, she still saw, as she had down there, Léon standing up with one hand bending his cane, and with the other holding Athalie, who was quietly sucking a piece of ice. She thought him charming; she could not tear herself away from him; she recalled his other attitudes on other days, the words he had spoken, the sound of his voice, his whole person; and she repeated, pouting out her lips as if for a kiss —

"Yes, charming! charming! Is he not in love?" she asked herself; "but with whom? With me?"

All the proofs arose before her at once; her heart leapt. The flame of the fire threw a joyous light upon the ceiling; she turned on her back, stretching out her arms.

Then began the eternal lamentation: "Oh, if Heaven had but willed it! And why not? What prevented it?"

When Charles came home at midnight, she seemed to have just awakened, and as he made a noise undressing, she complained of a headache, then asked carelessly what had happened that evening.

"Monsieur Léon," he said, "went to his room early."

She could not help smiling, and she fell asleep, her soul filled with a new delight.

The next day, at dusk, she received a visit from Monsieur Lheureux, the draper. He was a man of ability, was this shopkeeper. Born a Gascon but bred a Norman, he grafted upon his southern volubility the

cunning of the Cauchois. His fat, flabby, beardless face seemed dyed by a decoction of liquorice, and his white hair made even more vivid the keen brilliance of his small black eyes. No one knew what he had been formerly; a pedlar, said some, a banker at Routot, according to others. What was certain was, that he made complex calculations in his head that would have frightened Binet himself. Polite to obsequiousness, he always held himself with his back bent in the position of one who bows or who invites.

After leaving at the door his hat surrounded with crape, he put down a green bandbox on the table, and began by complaining to madame, with many civilities, that he should have remained till that day without gaining her confidence. A poor shop like his was not made to attract a "fashionable lady;" he emphasized the words; yet she had only to command, and he would undertake to provide her with anything she might wish, either in haberdashery or linen, millinery or fancy goods, for he went to town regularly four times a month. He was connected with the best houses. You could speak of him at the "Trois Frères," at the "Barbe d'Or," or at the "Grand Sauvage;" all these gentlemen knew him as well as the insides of their pockets. To-day, then, he had come to show madame, in passing, various articles he happened to have, thanks to the most rare opportunity. And he pulled out half-a-dozen embroidered collars from the box.

Madame Bovary examined them. "I do not require anything," she said.

Then Monsieur Lheureux delicately exhibited three Algerian scarves, several packets of English needles, a pair of straw slippers, and, finally, four eggcups in

cocoa-nut wood, carved in open-work by convicts.
Then, with both hands on the table, his neck stretched
out, his figure bent forward, open-mouthed, he watched
Emma's look, who was walking up and down undecided amid these goods. From time to time, as if to
remove some dust, he filliped with his nail the silk
of the scarves spread out at full length, and they
rustled with a little noise, making in the green twilight the gold spangles of their tissue scintillate like
little stars.

"How much are they?"

"A mere nothing," he replied, "a mere nothing.
But there's no hurry; whenever it's convenient. We
are not Jews."

She reflected for a few moments, and ended by
again declining Monsieur Lheureux's offer. He replied
quite unconcernedly:

"Very well. We shall understand each other by
and by. I have always got on with ladies — if I
didn't with my own!"

Emma smiled.

"I wanted to tell you," he went on good-naturedly,
after his joke, "that it isn't the money I should
trouble about. Why, I could give you some, if need
be."

She made a gesture of surprise.

"Ah!" said he quickly and in a low voice, "I
shouldn't have to go far to find you some, rely on
that."

And he began asking after Père Tellier, the pro-
prietor of the "Café Français," whom Monsieur Bovary was then attending.

"What's the matter with Père Tellier? He coughs
so that he shakes his whole house, and I'm afraid

he'll soon want a deal covering rather than a flannel vest. He was such a rake as a young man! That sort of people, madame, have not the least regularity; he's burnt up with brandy. Still it's sad, all the same, to see an acquaintance go off."

And while he fastened up his box he discoursed about the doctor's patients.

"It's the weather, no doubt," he said, looking frowningly at the floor, "that causes these illnesses. I, too, don't feel the thing. One of these days I shall even have to consult the doctor for a pain I have in my back. Well, good-bye, Madame Bovary. At your service; your very humble servant." And he closed the door gently.

Emma had her dinner served in her bedroom on a tray by the fireside; she was a long time over it; everything was well with her.

"How good I was!" she said to herself, thinking of the scarves.

She heard some steps on the stairs. It was Léon. She got up and took from the chest of drawers the first of a pile of dusters to be hemmed. When he came in she seemed very busy.

The conversation languished; Madame Bovary gave it up every few minutes, while he himself seemed quite embarrassed. Seated on a low chair near the fire, he turned round in his fingers the ivory thimble-case. She stitched on, or from time to time turned down the hem of the cloth with her nail. She did not speak; he was silent, captivated by her silence, as he would have been by her speech.

"Poor fellow!" she thought.

"How have I displeased her?" he asked himself.

At last, however, Léon said that he should have,

one of these days, to go to Rouen on some office business.

"Your music subscription is out; am I to renew it?"

"No," she replied.

"Why?"

"Because—"

And pursing her lips she slowly drew a long stitch of gray thread.

This work irritated Léon. It seemed to roughen the ends of her fingers. A gallant phrase came into his head, but he did not risk it.

"Then you are giving it up?" he went on.

"What?" she asked hurriedly. "Music? Ah! yes! Have I not my house to look after, my husband to attend to, a thousand things, in fact, many duties that must be considered first?"

She looked at the clock. Charles was late. Then she affected anxiety. Two or three times she even repeated, "He is so good!"

The clerk was fond of Monsieur Bovary. But this tenderness in his behalf astonished him unpleasantly; nevertheless he took up his praises, which he said every one was singing, especially the chemist.

"Ah! he is a good fellow," continued Emma.

"Certainly," replied the clerk.

And he began talking of Madame Homais, whose very untidy appearance generally made them laugh.

"What does it matter?" interrupted Emma. "A good housewife does not trouble about her appearance."

Then she relapsed into silence.

It was the same on the following days; her talk, her manners, everything changed. She took interest in the house-work, went to church regularly, and looked after her servant with more severity.

She took Berthe from nurse. When visitors called, Félicité brought her in, and Madame Bovary undressed her to show off her limbs. She declared she adored children; this was her consolation, her joy, her passion, and she accompanied her caresses with lyrical outbursts which would have reminded any one but the Yonville people of Sachette in "Nôtre Dame de Paris."

When Charles came home he found his slippers put to warm near the fire. His waistcoat now never wanted lining, nor his shirt buttons, and it was quite a pleasure to see in the cupboard the night-caps arranged in piles of the same height. She no longer grumbled as formerly at taking a turn in the garden; what he proposed was always done, although she did not understand the wishes to which she submitted without a murmur; and when Léon saw him by his fireside after dinner, his two hands on his stomach, his two feet on the fender, his cheeks red with feeding, his eyes moist with happiness, the child crawling along the carpet, and this woman with the slender waist who came behind his arm-chair to kiss his forehead:

"What madness!" he said to himself. "And how to reach her!"

And thus she seemed so virtuous and inaccessible to him that he lost all hope, even the faintest. But by this renunciation he placed her on an extraordinary pinnacle. To him she stood outside those fleshly attributes from which he had nothing to obtain, and in his heart she rose ever, and became farther removed from him after the magnificent manner of an apotheosis that is taking wing. It was one of those pure feelings that do not interfere with life, that are cultivated because they are rare, and whose loss would afflict more than their passion rejoices.

Emma grew thinner, her cheeks paler, her face longer. With her black hair, her large eyes, her aquiline nose, her birdlike walk, and always silent now, did she not seem to be passing through life scarcely touching it, and to bear on her brow the vague impress of some divine destiny? She was so sad and so calm, at once so gentle and so reserved, that near her one felt oneself seized by an icy charm, as we shudder in churches at the perfume of the flowers mingling with the cold of the marble. The others even did not escape from this seduction. The chemist said—

"She is a woman of great parts, who wouldn't be misplaced in a sub-prefecture."

The housewives admired her economy, the patients her politeness, the poor her charity.

But she was eaten up with desires, with rage, with hate. That dress with the narrow folds hid a distracted heart, of whose torment those chaste lips said nothing. She was in love with Léon, and sought solitude that she might with the more ease delight in his image. The sight of his form troubled the voluptuousness of this meditation. Emma thrilled at the sound of his step; then in his presence the emotion subsided, and afterwards there remained to her only an immense astonishment that ended in sorrow.

Léon did not know that when he left her in despair, she rose after he had gone to see him in the street. She concerned herself about his comings and goings; she watched his face; she invented quite a history to find an excuse for going to his room. The chemist's wife seemed happy to her to sleep under the same roof, and her thoughts constantly centred upon this house, like the "Lion d'Or" pigeons, who came there to dip their red feet and white wings in its gutters. But the more Emma recognized her love, the more she crushed it down, that it might not be evident, that she might make it less. She would have liked Léon to guess it, and she imagined chances, catastrophes that should facilitate this. What restrained her was, no doubt, idleness and fear, and a sense of shame also. She thought she had repulsed him too much, that the time was past, that all was lost. Then pride, the joy of being able to say to herself, "I am virtuous," and to look at herself in the glass taking resigned poses, consoled her a little for the sacrifice she believed she was making.

Then the lusts of the flesh, the longing for money, and the melancholy of passion, all blended themselves into one suffering, and instead of turning her thoughts from it, she clave to it the more, urging herself to pain, and seeking everywhere occasions for it. She was irritated by an ill-served dish or by a half-open door; bewailed the velvets she had not, the happiness she had missed, her too exalted dreams, her narrow home.

What exasperated her was that Charles did not seem to notice her anguish. His conviction that he was making her happy seemed to her an imbecile insult, and his sureness on this point ingratitude. For whose sake, then, was she virtuous? Was it not for him, the obstacle to all felicity, the cause of all misery, and, as it were, the sharp clasp of that complex strap that buckled her in on all sides?

On him alone, then, she concentrated all the various hatreds that resulted from her boredom, and every effort to diminish only augmented it; for this useless trouble was added to the other reasons for despair, and contributed still more to the separation between them. Her own gentleness to herself made her rebel against him. Domestic mediocrity drove her to lewd fancies, marriage tendernesses to adulterous desires. She would have liked Charles to beat her, that she might have a better right to hate him, to revenge herself upon him. She was surprised sometimes at the atrocious conjectures that came into her thoughts, and she had to go on smiling, to hear repeated to her at all hours that she was happy, to pretend to be happy, to let it be believed.

Yet she had loathing of this hypocrisy. She was seized with the temptation to flee somewhere with Léon to try a new life; but at once a vague chasm full of darkness opened within her soul.

"Besides, he no longer loves me," she thought. "What is to become of me? What help is to be hoped for, what consolation, what solace?"

She was left broken, breathless, inert, sobbing in a low voice, with flowing tears.

"Why don't you tell master?" the servant asked her when she came in during these crises.

"It is the nerves," said Emma. "Do not speak to him of it; it would worry him."

"Ah! yes," Félicité went on, "you are just like La Guérine, Père Guérin's daughter, the fisherman at Pollet, that I used to know at Dieppe before I came to you. She was so sad, so sad, that to see her standing upright on the threshold of her house, she seemed to you like a winding-sheet spread out before the door. Her illness, it appears, was a kind of fog that she had in her head, and the doctors could not do anything, nor the priest either. When she was taken too bad she went off quite alone to the sea-shore, so that the customs officer, going his rounds, often found her lying flat on her face, crying on the shingle. Then, after her marriage, it went off, they say."

"But with me," replied Emma, "it was after marriage that it began."

VI.

ONE evening when the window was open, and she, sitting by it, had been watching Lestiboudois, the beadle, trimming the box, she suddenly heard the Angelus ringing.

It was the beginning of April, when the primroses are in bloom, and a warm wind blows over the flower-beds newly turned, and the gardens, like women, seem to be getting ready for the summer fêtes. Through the bars of the arbor and away beyond, the river could be seen in the fields, meandering through the grass in wandering curves. The evening vapors rose between the leafless poplars, touching their outlines with a violet tint, paler and more transparent than a subtle gauze caught athwart their branches. In the distance cattle moved about; neither their steps nor their lowing could be heard; and the bell, still ringing through the air, kept up its peaceful lamentation.

With this repeated tinkling the thoughts of the young woman lost themselves in old memories of her youth and school-days. She remembered the great candlesticks that rose above the vases full of flowers on the altar, and the tabernacle with its small columns. She would have liked to be once more lost in the long line of white veils, marked off here and there by the stiff black hoods of the good sisters bending over their prie-Dieu. At mass on Sundays, when she looked up, she saw the gentle face of the Virgin amid the blue smoke of the rising incense. Then she was moved; she felt herself weak and quite deserted, like the down of a bird whirled by the tempest, and it was unconsciously that she went towards the church, inclined to no matter what devotions, so that her soul was absorbed and all existence lost in it.

On the Place she met Lestiboudois on his way back, for, in order not to shorten his day's labor, he preferred interrupting his work, then beginning it again, so that he rang the Angelus to suit his own convenience. Besides, the ringing over a little earlier warned the lads of catechism hour.

Already a few who had arrived were playing marbles on the stones of the cemetery. Others, astride the wall, swung their legs, kicking with their clogs the large nettles growing between the little enclosure and the newest graves. This was the only green spot. All the rest was but stones, always covered with a fine powder, despite the vestry-broom.

The children in list shoes ran about there as if it were an enclosure made for them. The shouts of their voices could be heard through the humming of the bell. This grew less and less with the swinging of the great rope that, hanging from the top of the belfry, dragged its end on the ground. Swallows flitted to and fro uttering little cries, cut the air with the edge of their wings, and swiftly returned to their yellow nests under the tiles of the coping. At the end of the church a lamp was burning, the wick of a night-light in a glass hung up. Its light from a distance looked like a white stain trembling in the oil. A long ray of the sun fell across the nave and seemed to darken the lower sides and the corners.

"Where is the curé?" asked Madame Bovary of one of the lads, who was amusing himself by shaking a swivel in a hole too large for it.

"He is just coming," he answered.

And in fact the door of the presbytery grated; Abbé Bournisien appeared; the children, pell-mell, fled into the church.

"These young scamps!" murmured the priest, "always the same!" Then, picking up a catechism all in rags that he had struck with his foot, "They respect nothing!" But as soon as he caught sight of Madame Bovary, "Excuse me," he said; "I did not recognize you."

He thrust the catechism into his pocket, and stopped short, balancing the heavy vestry key between his two fingers.

The light of the setting sun that fell full upon his face paled the lasting of his cassock, shiny at the elbows, ravelled at the hem. Grease and tobacco stains followed along his broad chest the lines of the buttons, and grew more numerous the farther they were from his neckcloth, in which the massive folds of his red chin rested; this was dotted with yellow spots, that disappeared beneath the coarse hair of his greyish beard. He had just dined, and was breathing noisily.

"How are you?" he added.

"Not well," replied Emma; "I am ill."

"Well, and so am I," answered the priest. "These first warm days weaken one most remarkably, don't they? But, after all, we are born to suffer, as St. Paul says. But what does Monsieur Bovary think of it?"

"He!" she said with a gesture of contempt.

"What!" replied the good fellow, quite astonished, "doesn't he prescribe something for you?"

"Ah!" said Emma, "it is no earthly remedy I need."

But the curé from time to time looked into the church, where the kneeling boys were shouldering one another, and tumbling over like packs of cards.

"I should like to know —" she went on.

"You look out, Riboudet," cried the priest in an angry voice; "I'll warm your ears, you imp!" Then turning to Emma. "He's Boudet the carpenter's son; his parents are well off, and let him do just as he pleases. Yet he could learn quickly if he would, for he is very sharp. And so sometimes for a joke I call him *Ri*boudet (like the road one takes to go to Ma-romme), and I even say '*Mon* Riboudet.' Ha! ha! '*Mont* Riboudet.' The other day I repeated that jest to Monsignor, and he laughed at it; he condescended to laugh at it. And how is Monsieur Bovary?"

She seemed not to hear him. And he went on:

"Always very busy, no doubt; for he and I are certainly the busiest people in the parish. But he is doctor of the body," he added with a thick laugh, "and I of the soul."

She fixed her pleading eyes upon the priest. "Yes," she said, "you solace all sorrows."

"Ah! don't talk to me of it, Madame Bovary. This morning I had to go to Bas-Diauville for a cow that was ill; they thought it was under a spell. All their cows, I don't know how it is—But pardon me! Longuemarre and Boudet! Bless me! will you leave off?"

And with a bound he ran into the church.

The boys were just then clustering round the large desk, climbing over the precentor's footstool, opening the missal; and others on tiptoe were just about to venture into the confessional. But the priest suddenly distributed a shower of cuffs among them. Seizing them by the collars of their coats, he lifted them from the ground, and deposited them on their knees on the stones of the choir, firmly, as if he meant planting them there.

"Yes," said he, when he returned to Emma, unfolding his large cotton handkerchief, one corner of which he put between his teeth, "farmers are much to be pitied."

"Others, too," she replied.

"Assuredly. Town-laborers, for example."

"It is not they—"

"Pardon! I've there known poor mothers of families, virtuous women, I assure you, real saints, who wanted even bread."

"But those," replied Emma, and the corners of her mouth twitched as she spoke, "those, Monsieur le Curé, who have bread and have no—"

"Fire in the winter," said the priest.

"Oh, what does that matter?"

"What! What does it matter? It seems to me that when one has firing and food—for, after all—"

"My God! my God!" she sighed.

"Do you feel unwell?" he asked, approaching her anxiously. "It is indigestion, no doubt? You must get home, Madame Bovary; drink a little tea, that will strengthen you, or else a glass of fresh water with a little moist sugar."

"Why?" And she looked like one awaking from a dream.

"Well, you see, you were putting your hand to your forehead. I thought you felt faint." Then, bethinking himself, "But you were asking me something? What was it? I really don't remember."

"I? Nothing! nothing!" repeated Emma.

And the glance she cast round her slowly fell upon the old man in the cassock. They looked at one another face to face without speaking.

"Then, Madame Bovary," he said at last, "excuse me, but duty first, you know; I must look after my good-for-nothings. The first communion will soon be upon us, and I fear we shall be behind after all. So after Ascension Day I keep them *recta* an extra hour every Wednesday. Poor children! One cannot lead them too soon into the path of the Lord, as, moreover, he has himself recommended us to do by the mouth of His Divine Son. Good health to you, madame; my respects to your husband."

And he went into the church making a genuflexion as soon as he reached the door.

Emma saw him disappear between the double row of forms, walking with heavy tread, his head a little bent over his shoulder, and with his two hands half-open behind him.

Then she turned on her heel with one movement, like a statue on a pivot, and went homewards. But the loud voice of the priest, the clear voices of the boys still reached her ears, and went on behind her.

"Are you a Christian?"

"Yes, I am a Christian?"

"What is a Christian?"

"He who, being baptized—baptized—baptized—"

She went up the steps of the staircase holding on to the banisters, and when she was in her room threw herself into an arm-chair.

The whitish light of the window-panes fell with soft undulations. The furniture in its place seemed to have become more immobile, and to lose itself in the shadow as in an ocean of darkness. The fire was out, the clock went on ticking, and Emma vaguely marvelled at this calm of all things while within herself was such tumult. But little Berthe was there, between the window and the work-table, tottering on her knitted shoes, and trying to come to her mother to catch hold of the ends of her apron-strings.

"Leave me alone," said the latter, putting her from her with her hand.

The little girl soon came up closer against her knees, and leaning on them with her arms, she looked up with her large blue eyes, while a small thread of pure saliva dribbled from her lips on to the silk apron.

"Leave me alone," repeated the young woman quite irritably.

Her face frightened the child, who began to scream.

"Will you leave me alone?" she said, pushing her with her elbow.

Berthe fell at the foot of the drawers against the brass handle, cutting against it her cheek, which began to bleed. Madame Bovary sprang to lift her up, broke the bell-rope, called for the servant with all her might, and she was just going to curse herself when Charles appeared. It was the dinner-hour; he had come home.

"Look, dear!" said Emma, in a calm voice, "the little one fell down while she was playing, and has hurt herself."

Charles reassured her; the case was not a serious one, and he went for some sticking plaster.

Madame Bovary did not go downstairs to the dining-room; she wished to remain alone to look after the child. Then, watching her sleep, the little anxiety she felt gradually wore off, and she seemed very stupid to herself, and very good to have been so worried just now at so little. Berthe, in fact, no longer sobbed. Her breathing now imperceptibly raised the cotton covering. Big tears lay in the corner of the half-closed eyelids, through whose lashes one could see two pale sunken pupils; the plaster stuck on her cheek drew the skin obliquely.

"It is very strange," thought Emma, "how ugly this child is!"

When at eleven o'clock Charles came back from the chemist's shop, whither he had gone after dinner to return the remainder of the sticking-plaster, he found his wife standing by the cradle.

"I assure you it's nothing," he said, kissing her on the forehead. "Don't worry, my poor darling; you will make yourself ill."

He had stayed a long time at the chemist's. Although he had not seemed much moved, Homais, nevertheless, had exerted himself to buoy him up, to "keep up his spirits." Then they had talked of the various dangers that threaten childhood, of the carelessness of servants. Madame Homais knew something of it, having still upon her chest the marks left by a basin full of soup that a cook had formerly dropped on her pinafore, and her good parents took no end of trouble for her. The knives were not sharpened, nor the floors waxed; there were iron gratings to the windows and strong bars across the fireplace; the little Homaises, in spite of their spirit, could not stir without some one watching them; at the slightest cold their father stuffed them with pectorals; and until they were turned four they all, without pity, had to wear wadded head-protectors. This, it is true, was a fancy of Madame Homais's; her husband was inwardly afflicted at it. Fearing the possible consequences of such compression to the intellectual organs, he even went so far as to say to her, "Do you want to make Caribs or Botocudos of them?"

Charles, however, had several times tried to interrupt the conversation. "I should like to speak to you," he had whispered in the clerk's ear, who went upstairs in front of him.

"Can he suspect anything?" Léon asked himself. His heart beat, and he racked his brain with surmises.

At last, Charles, having shut the door, asked him to see himself what would be the price at Rouen of a fine daguerreotype. It was a sentimental surprise he intended for his wife, a delicate attention—his portrait in a frock-coat. But he wanted first to know how much it would be. The inquiries would not put Monsieur Léon out, since he went to town almost every week.

Why? Monsieur Homais suspected some "young man's affair" at the bottom of it, an intrigue. But he was mistaken. Léon was after no love-making. He was sadder than ever, as Madame Lefrançois saw from the amount of food he left on his plate. To find out more about it she questioned the tax-collector.

Binet answered roughly that he wasn't paid by the police.

All the same, his companion seemed very strange to him, for Léon often threw himself back in his chair, and stretching out his arms, complained vaguely of life.

"It's because you don't take enough recreation," said the collector.

"What recreation?"

"If I were you I'd have a lathe."

"But I don't know how to turn," answered the clerk.

"Ah! that's true," said the other, rubbing his chin with an air of mingled contempt and satisfaction.

Léon was weary of loving without any result; moreover, he was beginning to feel that depression caused by the repetition of the same kind of life, when no interest inspires and no hope sustains it. He was so bored with Yonville and the Yonvillers, that the sight of certain persons, of certain houses, irritated him beyond endurance; and the chemist, good fellow though he was, was becoming absolutely unbearable to him. Yet the prospect of a new condition of life frightened as much as it seduced him.

This apprehension soon changed into impatience, and then Paris from afar sounded its fanfare of masked balls with the laugh of grisettes. As he was to finish reading there, why not set out at once? What prevented him? And he began making home preparations; he arranged his occupations beforehand. He furnished in his head an apartment. He would lead an artist's life there! He would take lessons on the guitar! He would have a dressing-gown, a Basque cap, blue velvet slippers! He even already was admiring two crossed foils over his chimney-piece, with a death's-head on the guitar above them.

The difficulty was the consent of his mother; nothing, however, seemed more reasonable. Even his employer advised him to go to some other chambers where he could advance more rapidly. Taking a middle course, then, Léon looked for some place as second clerk at Rouen; found none, and at last wrote his mother a long letter full of details, in which he set forth the reasons for going to live at Paris immediately. She consented.

He did not hurry. Every day for a month Hivert carried boxes, valises, parcels for him from Yonville to Rouen and from Rouen to Yonville; and when Léon had packed up his wardrobe, had his three arm-chairs restuffed, bought a stock of cravats, in a word, had made more preparations than for a voyage round the world, he put it off from week to week, until he received a second letter from his mother urging him to leave, since he wanted to pass his examination before the vacation.

When the moment for the farewells had come, Madame Homais wept, Justin sobbed; Homais, as a man of nerve, concealed his emotion; he wished to carry his friend's overcoat himself as far as the gate of the notary, who was taking Léon to Rouen in his carriage. The latter had just time to bid farewell to Monsieur Bovary.

When he reached the head of the stairs he stopped, he was so out of breath. On his coming in, Madame Bovary rose hurriedly.

"It is I again!" said Léon.

"I was sure of it!"

She bit her lips, and a rush of blood flowing under her skin made her red from the roots of her hair to the top of her collar. She remained standing, leaning with her shoulder against the wainscot.

"The doctor is not here?" he went on.

"He is out." She repeated, "He is out."

Then there was silence. They looked one at the other, and their thoughts, confounded in the same agony, clung close together like two throbbing breasts.

"I should like to kiss Berthe," said Léon.

Emma went down a few steps and called Félicité.

He threw one long look around him that took in the walls, the brackets, the fireplace, as if to penetrate everything, carry away everything. But she returned, and the servant brought Berthe, who was swinging a windmill roof downward at the end of a string. Léon kissed her several times on the neck.

"Good-bye, poor child! good-bye, dear little one! good-bye!"

And he gave her back to her mother.

"Take her away," she said.

They remained alone — Madame Bovary, her back turned, her face pressed against a window-pane; Léon held his cap in his hand, knocking it softly against his thigh.

"It is going to rain," said Emma.

"I have a cloak," he answered.

"Ah!"

She turned round, her chin lowered, her forehead bent forward. The light fell on it as on a piece of marble to the curve of the eyebrows, without one's being able to guess what Emma was seeing in the horizon or what she was thinking within herself.

"Well, good-bye," he sighed.

She raised her head with a quick movement.

"Yes, good-bye — go!"

They advanced toward each other; he held out his hand; she hesitated.

"In the English fashion, then," she said, giving her own hand wholly to him, and forcing a laugh.

Léon felt it between his fingers, and the very essence of all his being seemed to pass down into that moist palm. Then he opened his hand; their eyes met again, and he disappeared.

When he reached the market-place, he stopped and hid behind a pillar to look for the last time at this white house with the four green blinds. He thought he saw a shadow behind the window in the room; but the curtain, sliding along the pole as though no one were touching it, slowly opened its long oblique folds, that spread out with a single movement, and thus hung straight and motionless as a plaster wall. Léon set off running.

From afar he saw his employer's gig in the road, and by it a man in a coarse apron holding the horse. Homais and Monsieur Guillaumin were talking. They were waiting for him.

"Embrace me," said the chemist with tears in his eyes. "Here is your coat, my good friend. Mind the cold; take care of yourself; look after yourself."

"Come, Léon, jump in," said the notary.

Homais bent over the splash-board, and in a voice broken by sobs, uttered these three sad words:

"A pleasant journey!"

"Good-night," said Monsieur Guillaumin. "Give him his head."

They set out, and Homais went back.

*   *   *   *   *   *   *

Madame Bovary had opened her window overlooking the garden and watched the clouds. They were gathering round the sunset on the side of Rouen, and swiftly rolled back their black columns, behind which the great rays of the sun looked out like the golden arrows of a suspended trophy, while the rest of the empty heavens was white as porcelain. But a gust of wind bowed the poplars, and suddenly the rain fell; it pattered against the green leaves. Then the sun reappeared, the hens clucked, sparrows shook their wings in the damp thickets, and the pools of water on the gravel as they flowed away carried off the pink flowers of an acacia.

"Ah! how far off he must be already!" she thought.

Monsieur Homais, as usual, came at half-past six during dinner.

"Well," said he, "so we've sent off our young friend!"

"So it seems," replied the doctor. Then turning on his chair: "Any news at home?"

"Nothing much. Only my wife was a little moved this afternoon. You know women — a nothing upsets them, especially my wife. And we should be wrong to object to that, since their nervous organization is much more malleable than ours."

"Poor Léon!" said Charles. "How will he live at Paris? Will he get used to it?"

Madame Bovary sighed.

"Get along!" said the chemist, smacking his lips. "The outings at restaurants, the masked balls, the champagne — all that'll be jolly enough, I assure you."

"I don't think he'll go wrong," objected Bovary.

"Nor do I," said Monsieur Homais quickly; "although he'll have to do like the rest for fear of passing for a Jesuit. And you don't know what a life those dogs lead in the Latin Quarter with actresses. Besides, students are thought a great deal of at Paris. Provided they have a few accomplishments, they are received in the best society; there are even ladies of the Faubourg Saint-Germain who fall in love with them, which subsequently furnishes them opportunities for making very good matches."

"But," said the doctor, "I fear for him that down there—"

"You are right," interrupted the chemist; "that is the reverse of the medal. And one is constantly obliged to keep one's hand in one's pocket there. Thus, we will suppose you are in a public garden. An individual presents himself, well dressed, even wearing an order, whom any one would take for a diplomatist. He approaches you, he insinuates himself; offers you a pinch of snuff, or picks up your hat. Then you become more intimate; he takes you to a café, invites you to his country-house, introduces you, between two drinks, to all sorts of people; and three fourths of the time it's only to plunder your watch or lead you into some pernicious step."

"That is true," said Charles; "but I was thinking especially of illnesses—of typhoid fever, for example, that attacks students from the provinces."

Emma shuddered.

"Because of the change of regimen," continued the chemist, "and of the perturbation that results therefrom in the whole system. And then the water at Paris, don't you know! The dishes at restaurants, all the spiced food, end by heating the blood, and are not worth, whatever people may say of them, a good soup. For my own part, I have always preferred plain living; it is more healthful. So when I was studying pharmacy at Rouen, I boarded in a boarding-house; I dined with the professors."

And thus he went on, expounding his opinions generally and his personal likings, until Justin came to fetch him for a mulled egg that was wanted.

"Not a moment's peace!" he cried; "always at it! I can't go out for a minute! Like a plough-horse, I have always to be moiling and toiling. What drudgery!" Then, when he was at the door, "By the way, do you know the news?"

"What news?"

"That it is very likely," Homais went on, raising his eyebrows and assuming one of his most serious expressions, "that the agricultural meeting of the Seine-Inférieure will be held this year at Yonville-l'Abbaye. The rumor, at all events, is going the round. This morning the paper alluded to it. It would be of the utmost importance for our district. But we'll talk it over later on. I can see, thank you; Justin has the lantern."

VII.

A Woman's Whims.

THE next day was a dreary one for Emma. Every thing seemed to her enveloped in a black atmosphere floating confusedly over the exterior of things, and sorrow was engulphed within her soul with soft shrieks such as the winter wind makes in ruined castles. It was that reverie which we give to things that will not return, the lassitude that seizes you after everything done; that pain, in fine, that the interruption of every wonted movement, the sudden cessation of any prolonged vibration, brings on.

As on the return from Vaubyessard, when the quadrilles were running in her head, she was full of a gloomy melancholy, of a numb despair. Léon reappeared, taller, handsomer, more charming, more vague. Though separated from her, he had not left her; he was there, and the walls of the house seemed to hold his shadow. She could not detach her eyes from the carpet where he had walked, from those empty chairs where he had sat. The river still flowed on, and slowly drove its ripples along the slippery banks. They had often walked there to the murmur of the waves, over the moss-covered pebbles. How bright the sun had been! What happy

(154)

afternoons they had seen alone in the shade at the end of the garden! He read aloud, bareheaded, sitting on a footstool of dry sticks; the fresh wind of the meadow set trembling the leaves of the book and the nasturtiums of the arbor. Ah! he was gone, the only charm of her life, the only possible hope of joy. Why had she not seized this happiness when it came to her? Why not have kept hold of it with both hands, with both knees, when it was about to flee from her? And she cursed herself for not having loved Léon. She thirsted for his lips. The wish took possession of her to run after and rejoin him, throw herself into his arms and say to him, "It is I; I am yours." But Emma recoiled beforehand at the difficulties of the enterprise, and her desires, increased by regret, became only the more acute.

Henceforth the memory of Léon was the centre of her boredom; it burnt there more brightly than the fire travelers leave on the snow of a Russian steppe. She sprang towards him, she pressed against him, she stirred carefully the dying embers, sought all around her anything that could revive it; and the most distant reminiscences, like the most immediate occasions, what she experienced as well as what she imagined, her voluptuous desires that were unsatisfied, her projects of happiness that crackled in the wind like dead boughs, her sterile virtue, her lost hopes, the domestic tête-à-tête,—she gathered it all up, took everything, and made it all serve as fuel for her melancholy.

The flames, however, subsided, either because the supply had exhausted itself, or because it had been piled up too much. Love, little by little, was quelled by absence; regret stifled beneath habit; and this incendiary light that had empurpled her pale sky was overspread and faded by degrees. In the supineness of her conscience she even took her repugnance towards her husband for aspirations towards her lover, the burning of hate for the warmth of tenderness; but as the tempest still raged, and as passion burnt itself down to the very cinders, and no help came, no sun rose, there was night on all sides, and she was lost in the terrible cold that pierced her.

Then the evil days of Tostes began again. She thought herself now far more unhappy; for she had the experience of grief, with the certainty that it would not end.

A woman who had laid on herself such sacrifices could well allow herself certain whims. She bought a gothic prie-Dieu, and in a month spent fourteen francs on lemons for polishing her nails; she wrote to Rouen for a blue cashmere gown; she chose one of Lheureux's finest scarves, and wore it knotted round her waist over her dressing-gown; and, with closed blinds and a book in her hand, she lay stretched out on a couch in this garb.

She often changed her coiffure; she did her hair à la Chinoise, in flowing curls, in plaited coils; she parted it on one side and rolled it under like a man's.

She wished to learn Italian; she bought dictionaries, a grammar, and a supply of white paper. She tried serious reading, history, and philosophy. Sometimes in the night Charles woke up with a start, thinking he was being called to a patient. "I'm coming," he stammered; and it was the noise of a match Emma had struck to relight the lamp. But her reading fared like her pieces of embroidery, all of which, only just begun, filled her cupboard; she took it up, left it, passed on to other books.

She had attacks in which she could easily have been driven to commit any folly. She maintained one day, in opposition to her husband, that she could drink off a large glass of brandy, and. as Charles was stupid enough to dare her to, she swallowed the brandy to the last drop.

In spite of her vaporish airs (as the housewives of Yonville called them), Emma, all the same, never seemed gay, and usually she had at the corners of her mouth that immobile contraction that puckers the faces of old maids, and those of men whose ambition has failed. She was pale all over, white as a sheet; the skin of her nose was drawn at the nostrils, her eyes looked at you vaguely. After discovering three gray hairs on her temples, she talked much of her old age.

She often fainted. One day she even spat blood, and, as Charles fussed round her showing his anxiety—

"Bah!" she answered, "what does it matter?"

Charles fled to his study and wept there, both his elbows on the table, sitting in an arm-chair at his bureau under the phrenological head.

Then he wrote to his mother to beg her to come, and they had many long consultations together on the subject of Emma.

What should they decide? What was to be done since she rejected all medical treatment?

"Do you know what your wife wants?" replied Madame Bovary, senior. "She wants to be forced to occupy herself with some manual work. If she were obliged, like so many others, to earn her living, she wouldn't have these vapors, that come to her from a lot of ideas she stuffs into her head, and from the idleness in which she lives."

"Yet she is always busy," said Charles.

"Ah! always busy at what? Reading novels, bad books, works against religion, in which they mock at priests in speeches taken from Voltaire. But all that leads you far astray, my poor child. Any one who has no religion always ends by turning out badly."

So they decided to stop Emma from reading novels. The enterprise did not seem easy. The good lady undertook it. She was, when she passed through Rouen, to go herself to the lending-library and represent that Emma had discontinued her subscription. Would they not have a right to apply to the police if the librarian persisted all the same in his poisonous trade?

The farewells of mother and daughter-in-law were cold. During the three weeks that they had been together they had not exchanged half-a-dozen words apart from the inquiries and phrases when they met at table and in the evening before going to bed.

Madame Bovary left on a Wednesday, the market-day at Yonville.

The Place since morning had been blocked by a row of carts, which, on end and their shafts in the air, spread all along the line of houses from the church to the inn. On the other side there were canvas booths, where cotton checks, blankets, and woollen stockings were sold, together with harness for horses, and packets of blue ribbon, whose ends fluttered in the wind. The coarse hardware was spread out on the ground between pyramids of eggs and hampers of cheeses, from which sticky straw stuck out. Near the corn-machines clucking hens passed their necks through the bars of flat cages. The people, crowding in the same place and unwilling to move thence, sometimes threatened to smash the shop-front of the chemist. On Wednesdays his shop was never empty, and the people pushed in less to buy drugs than for consultations, so great was Homais's reputation in the neighboring villages. His robust aplomb had fascinated the rustics. They considered him a greater doctor than all the doctors.

Emma was leaning out at the window; she was often there. The window in the provinces replaces the theatre and the promenade, and she amused herself with watching the crowd of boors, when she saw a gentleman in a green velvet coat. He had on yellow gloves, although he wore heavy gaiters; he was coming towards the doctor's house, followed by a peasant walking with bent head and quite a thoughtful air.

"Can I see the doctor?" he asked Justin, who was talking on the doorsteps with Félicité, and, taking him for a servant of the house: "Tell him that Monsieur Rodolphe Boulanger of La Huchette is here."

It was not from territorial vanity that the new arrival added "of La Huchette" to his name, but to make himself the better known. La Huchette, in fact, was an estate near Yonville, where he had just bought the château and two farms that he cultivated himself, without, however, troubling very much about them. He lived as a bachelor, and was supposed to have at least fifteen thousand francs a year.

Charles came into the room. Monsieur Boulanger introduced his man, who wanted to be bled because he felt "a tingling all over."

"That'll purge me," he urged as an objection to all reasoning.

So Bovary ordered a bandage and a basin, and asked Justin to hold it. Then addressing the countryman, already pale—

"Don't be afraid, my lad."

"No, no, sir," said the other; "get on."

And with an air of bravado he held out his great arm. At the prick of the lancet the blood spurted out, splashing against the looking-glass.

"Hold the basin nearer," exclaimed Charles.

"Lor!" said the peasant, "one would swear it was a little fountain flowing. How red my blood is! That's a good sign isn't it?"

"Sometimes," answered the doctor, "one feels nothing at first, and then syncope sets in, and more especially with people of strong constitution like this man."

At these words the rustic let go the lancet-case he was twisting between his fingers. A shudder of his shoulders made the chair-back creak. His hat fell off.

"I thought as much," said Bovary, pressing his finger on the vein.

The basin was beginning to tremble in Justin's hands; his knees shook, he turned pale.

"Emma! Emma!" called Charles.

With one bound she came down the staircase.

"Some vinegar," he cried. "O dear! two at once!"

And in his emotion he could hardly put on the compress.

"It is nothing," said Monsieur Boulanger quietly, taking Justin in his arms. He seated him on the table with his back resting against the wall.

Madame Bovary began taking off his cravat. The strings of his shirt had got into a knot, and she was for some minutes moving her light fingers about the young fellow's neck. Then she poured some vinegar on her cambric handkerchief; she moistened his temples with little dabs, and then blew upon them softly. The ploughman revived, but Justin's syncope still lasted, and his eyeballs disappeared in their pale sclerotic like blue flowers in milk.

"We must hide this from him," said Charles.

Madame Bovary took the basin to put it under the table. With the movement she made in bending down, her skirt (it was a summer frock with four flounces, yellow, long in the waist and wide in the skirt) spread out around her on the flags of the room; and as Emma, stooping, staggered a little as she stretched out her arms, the stuff here and there gave with the inflections of her bust. Then she went to fetch a bottle of water, and she was melting some pieces of sugar when the chemist arrived. The servant had been to fetch him in the tumult. Seeing his pupil with his eyes open he drew a long breath; then going round him he looked at him from head to foot.

"Fool!" he said, "really a little fool! A fool in four letters! A phlebotomy's a big affair, isn't it! And a fellow who isn't afraid of anything; a kind of squirrel, just as he is who climbs to vertiginous heights to shake down nuts. Oh, yes! you just talk to me, boast about yourself! Here's a fine fitness for practising pharmacy later on; for under serious circumstances you may be called before the tribunals in order to enlighten the minds of the magistrates, and you would have to keep your head then, to reason, show yourself a man, or else pass for an imbecile."

Justin did not answer. The chemist went on—

"Who asked you to come? You are always pestering the doctor and madame. On Wednesday, moreover, your presence is indispensable to me. There are now twenty people in the shop. I left everything because of the interest I take in you. Come, get along! Sharp! Wait for me, and keep an eye on the jars."

When Justin, who was rearranging his dress, had gone, they talked for a little while about fainting-fits. Madame Bovary said she had never fainted.

"That is extraordinary for a lady," said Monsieur Boulanger; "but some people are very susceptible. Thus, in a duel, I have seen a second lose consciousness at the mere sound of the loading of pistols."

"For my part," said the chemist, "the sight of other people's blood doesn't affect me at all, but the mere thought of my own flowing would make me faint, if I reflected upon it too much."

Monsieur Boulanger, however, dismissed his servant, advising him to calm himself, since his fancy was over.

"It procured me the advantage of making your acquaintance," he added, and he looked at Emma as he said this. Then he put three francs on the corner of the table, bowed negligently, and went out.

He was soon on the other side of the river (this was his way back to La Huchette), and Emma saw him in the meadow, walking under the poplars, slackening his pace now and then as one who reflects.

"She is very pretty," he said to himself; "she is very pretty, this doctor's wife. Fine teeth, black eyes, a dainty foot, a figure like a Parisienne's. Where the devil does she come from? Wherever did this fat fellow pick her up?"

Monsieur Rodolphe Boulanger was thirty-four; he was of brutal temperament and intelligent perspicacity, having, moreover, had much to do with women, and knowing them well. This one had seemed pretty to him; so he was thinking about her and her husband.

"I think he is very stupid. She is tired of him, no doubt. He has dirty nails, and hasn't shaved for three days. While he is trotting after his patients, she sits there botching socks. And she gets bored! She would like to live in town and dance polkas every evening. Poor little woman! She is gaping after love like a carp after water on a kitchen-table. With three words of gallantry she'd adore one, I'm sure of it. She'd be tender, charming! Yes; but how get rid of her afterwards?"

Then the difficulties of love-making seen in the distance made him by contrast think of his mistress. She was an actress at Rouen, whom he kept; and when he had pondered over this image, with which, even in remembrance, he was satiated—

"Ah! Madame Bovary," he thought, "is much prettier, especially fresher. Virginie is decidedly beginning to grow fat. She is so finikin with her pleasures; and, besides, she has a mania for prawns."

The fields were empty, and around him Rodolphe heard only the regular beating of the grass striking against his boots, with the cry of the grasshopper hidden at a distance among the oats. He again saw

Emma in her room, dressed as he had seen her, and he undressed her.

"Oh, I will have her," he cried, striking a blow with his stick at a clod in front of him. And he at once began to consider the political part of the enterprise. He asked himself—

"Where shall we meet? By what means? We shall always be having the brat on our hands, and the servant, the neighbors, the husband, all sorts of worries. Pshaw! one would lose too much time over it."

Then he resumed, "She really has eyes that pierce one's heart like a gimlet. And that pale complexion' I adore pale women!"

When he reached the top of the Argueil hills he had made up his mind. "It's only finding the opportunities. Well, I will call in now and then. I'll send them venison, poultry; I'll have myself bled, if need be. We shall become friends; I'll invite them to my place. By Jove!" added he, "there's the agricultural show coming on. She'll be there. I shall see her. We'll begin boldly, for that's the surest way."

VIII.

A Village Festival.

AT LAST it came, the famous agricultural show. On the morning of the solemnity all the inhabitants at their doors were chatting over the preparations. The pediment of the townhall had been hung with garlands of ivy; a tent had been erected in a meadow for the banquet; and in the middle of the Place, in front of the church, a kind of bombarde was to announce the arrival of the prefect and the names of the successful farmers who had obtained prizes. The National Guard of Buchy (there was none at Yonville) had come to join the corps of firemen, of whom Binet was captain. On that day he wore a collar even higher than usual; and, tightly buttoned in his tunic, his figure was so stiff and motionless that the whole vital portion of his person seemed to have descended into his legs, which rose in a cadence of set steps with a single movement. As there was some rivalry between the tax-collector and the colonel, both, to show off their talents, drilled their men separately. One saw the red epaulettes and the black breastplates pass and repass alternately; there was no end to it, and it continually began again. There had never been such a display of pomp. Several citizens had washed down their houses the evening before; tricolored flags hung from half-open windows; all the public-houses were full; and in the lovely weather the starched caps, the golden crosses, and the colored neckerchiefs seemed whiter than snow, shone in the sun, and relieved with their motley colors the somber monotony of the frock-coats and blue smocks. The neighboring farmers' wives, when they got off their horses, pulled out a long pin that fastened round them their skirts, turned up for fear of mud; the husbands, on the contrary, in order to save their hats, kept their handkerchiefs round them, holding one corner between their teeth.

The crowd came into the main street from both ends of the village. People poured in from the lanes, the alleys, the houses; and from time to time one heard knockers banging against doors closing behind women with their gloves, who were going out to see the fête. What was most admired were two long lamp-stands covered with lanterns, that flanked a platform on which the authorities were to sit. Besides this there were against the four columns of the town-hall four kinds of poles, each bearing a small standard of greenish cloth, embellished with inscriptions in gold letters. On one was written, "To Commerce;" on the other, "To Agriculture;" on the third, "To Industry;" and on the fourth, "To the Fine Arts."

But the jubilation that brightened all faces seemed to darken that of Madame Lefrançois, the innkeeper. Standing on her kitchen-steps she muttered to herself, "What rubbish! what rubbish! With their canvas booth! Do they think the prefect will be glad to dine down there under a tent like a gipsy? They call all this fussing doing good to the place! Then it wasn't worth while sending to Neufchâtel for the keeper of a cookshop! And for whom? For cow-herds! tatterdemalions!"

The chemist was passing. He had on a frock-coat, nankeen trousers, beaver shoes, and, for a won-der, a hat with a low crown.

"Your servant! Excuse me, I am in a hurry."

And as the fat widow asked where he was going—

"It seems odd to you, doesn't it, to see me who am always more cooped up in my laboratory than the man's rat in his cheese, taking a holiday?"

"What cheese?" asked the landlady.

"Oh, nothing! nothing!" Homais continued. "I merely wished to convey to you, Madame Lefrançois, that I usually live at home like a recluse. To-day, however, considering the circumstances, it is neces-sary—"

"Oh, you're going down there!" she said con-temptuously.

"Yes, I am going," replied the chemist, aston-ished. "Am I not a member of the consulting com-mission?"

Mère Lefrançois looked at him for a few moments, and ended by saying with a smile:

"That's another pair of shoes! But what does agriculture matter to you? Do you understand any-thing about it?"

"Certainly I understand it, since I am a druggist, —that is to say, a chemist. And the object of chem-istry, Madame Lefrançois, being the knowledge of the reciprocal and molecular action of all natural bodies, it follows that agriculture is comprised within its domain. And, in fact, the composition of the manure, the fermentation of liquids, the analyses of gases, and the influence of miasmata, what, I ask you, is all this, if it isn't chemistry, pure and simple?"

The landlady did not answer. Homais went on:

"Do you think that to be an agriculturist it is necessary to have tilled the earth or fattened fowls oneself? It is necessary rather to know the composition of the substances in question — the geological strata, the atmospheric actions, the quality of the soil, the minerals, the waters, the density of the different bodies, their capillarity, and what not. And one must be master of all the principles of hygiene in order to direct, criticise the construction of buildings, the feeding of animals, the diet of the domestics. And, moreover, Madame Lefrançois, one must know botany, be able to distinguish between plants, you understand, which are the wholesome and those that are deleterious, which are unproductive and which nutritive, if it is well to pull them up here and re-sow them there, to propagate some, destroy others; in brief, one must keep pace with science by means of pamphlets and public papers, be always on the alert to find out improvements."

The landlady never took her eyes off the "Café Français," and the chemist went on:

"Would to God our agriculturists were chemists, or that at least they would pay more attention to the counsels of science. Thus, lately I myself wrote a considerable tract, a memoir of more than seventy-two pages, entitled, 'Cider, its Manufacture and its Effects, together with some New Reflections on this Subject,' that I sent to the Agricultural Society of Rouen, and which even procured me the honor of being received among its members — Section, Agriculture;

Class, Pomological. Well, if my work had been given to the public—" But the druggist stopped, Madame Lefrançois seemed so preoccupied.

"Just look at them!" she said. "It's past comprehension! Such a cookshop as that!" And with a shrug of the shoulders that stretched out over her breast the stitches of her knitted bodice, she pointed with both hands at her rival's inn, whence songs were heard issuing. "Well, it won't last long," she added; "it'll be over before a week."

Homais drew back with stupefaction. She came down three steps and whispered in his ear:

"What! you didn't know it? There'll be an execution in next week. It's Lheureux who is selling him up; he has killed him with bills."

"What a terrible catastrophe!" cried the chemist, who always found expressions in harmony with all imaginable circumstances.

Then the landlady began telling him this story, that she had heard from Theodore, Monsieur Guillaumin's servant, and although she detested Tellier, she blamed Lheureux. He was "a wheedler, a sneak."

"There!" she said. "Look at him! he is in the market; he is bowing to Madame Bovary, who's got on a green bonnet. Why, she's taking Monsieur Boulanger's arm."

"Madame Bovary!" exclaimed Homais. "I must go at once and pay her my respects. Perhaps she'd be very glad to have a seat in the enclosure under the peristyle." And, without heeding Madame Lefrançois, who was calling him back to tell him more about it, the druggist walked off rapidly with a smile on his lips, with straight knees, bowing exuberantly right and left, and taking up much room with the large tails of his frock-coat that fluttered behind him in the wind.

Rodolphe, having caught sight of him from afar, hurried on, but Madame Bovary lost her breath; so he walked more slowly, and, smiling at her, said in a rough tone:

"It's only to get away from that fat fellow, you know, the druggist." She pressed his elbow.

"What's the meaning of that?" he asked himself. And he looked at her out of the corner of his eyes.

Her profile was so calm that one could guess nothing from it. It stood out in the light from the oval of her bonnet, with pale ribbons on it like the leaves of reeds. Her eyes with their long curved lashes looked straight before her, and though wide open, they seemed slightly puckered by the cheek-bones, because of the blood pulsing gently under the delicate skin. A pink line ran along the partition between her nostrils. Her head leaned towards her shoulder, and the pearly tips of her white teeth were seen between her lips.

"Is she making fun of me?" thought Rodolphe.

Emma's gesture, however, had only been meant for a warning; for Monsieur Lheureux was accompanying them, and spoke now and again as if to enter into the conversation.

"What a superb day! Everybody is out! The wind is east!"

And neither Madame Bovary nor Rodolphe answered him, while at the slightest movement made by them he drew near, saying, "I beg your pardon!" and raised his hat.

When they reached the farrier's house, instead of following the road up to the fence, Rodolphe suddenly turned down a path, drawing with him Madame Bovary. He called out:

"Good evening, Monsieur Lheureux! See you again presently."

"How you got rid of him!" she said, laughing.

"Why," he went on, "allow oneself to be intruded upon by others? And as to-day I have the happiness of being with you——"

Emma blushed. He did not finish his sentence. Then he talked of the fine weather and of the pleasure of walking on the grass. A few daisies had sprung up again.

"Here are some pretty Easter daisies," he said, "and enough of them to furnish oracles to all the amorous maids in the place." He added, "Shall I pick some? What do you think?"

"Are you in love?" she asked, coughing a little.

"H'm, h'm! who knows?" answered Rodolphe.

The meadow began to fill, and the housewives hustled one with their great umbrellas, their baskets, and their babies. One had often to get out of the way of a long file of country folk, servant-maids with blue stockings, flat shoes, and silver rings, who smelled of milk when one passed close to them. They walked along holding one another by the hand, and thus they spread over the whole field from the row of open trees to the banquet tent. But this was the examination time, and the farmers one after the other entered a kind of enclosure formed by a long cord supported on sticks.

The beasts were there, their noses toward the cord, and making a confused line with their unequal rumps. Drowsy pigs were burrowing in the earth with their snouts, calves were bleating, lambs baaing; the cows, on knees folded in, were stretching their bellies on the grass, slowly chewing the cud, and blinking their heavy eyelids at the gnats that buzzed round them. Ploughmen with bare arms were holding by the halter prancing stallions that neighed with dilated nostrils, looking toward the mares. These stood quietly, stretching out their heads and flowing manes, while their foals rested in their shadow, or now and then came and sucked them. And above the long undulation of these crowded animals one saw some white mane rising in the wind like a wave, or some sharp horns sticking out, and the heads of men running about. Apart, outside the enclosure, a hundred paces off, was a large black bull, muzzled, with an iron ring in its nostrils, who moved no more than if he had been in bronze. A child in rags was holding him by a rope.

Between the two lines the committee-men were walking with heavy steps, examining each animal, then consulting one another in a low voice. One who seemed of more importance now and then took notes in a book as he walked along. This was the president of the jury, Monsieur Derozerays de la Panville. As soon as he recognized Rodolphe he came forward quickly, and smiling amiably, said:

"What! Monsieur Boulanger, you are deserting us?"

Rodolphe protested that he was just coming. But when the president had disappeared:

"*Ma foi!*" said he, "I shall not go. Your company is better than his."

And while poking fun at the show, Rodolphe, to move about more easily, showed the gendarme his blue card, and even stopped now and then in front of some fine beast which Madame Bovary did not at all admire. He noticed this and began jeering at the Yonville ladies and their dresses; then he apologized for the negligence of his own. He had that incongruity of common and elegant in which the habitually vulgar think they see the revelation of an eccentric existence, of the perturbations of sentiment, the tyrannies of art, and always a certain contempt for social conventions, that seduces or exasperates them. Thus his cambric shirt with plaited cuffs was blown out by the wind in the opening of his waistcoat of gray ticking, and his broad-striped trousers disclosed at the ankle nankeen boots with patent leather gaiters. These were so polished that they reflected the grass. He trampled on horses' dung with them, one hand in the pocket of his jacket and his straw hat on one side.

"Besides," added he, "when one lives in the country——"

"It's waste of time," said Emma.

"That is true," replied Rodolphe. "To think that not one of these people is capable of understanding even the cut of a coat!"

Then they talked about provincial mediocrity, of the lives it crushed, the illusions lost there.

"And I too," said Rodolphe, "am drifting into depression."

"You!" she said in astonishment; "I thought you very light-hearted."

"Ah! yes. I seem so, because in the midst of the world I know how to wear the mask of a scoffer upon my face; and yet, how many a time at the sight of a cemetery by moonlight have I not asked myself whether it were not better to join those sleeping there!"

"Oh! and your friends?" she said. "You do not think of them."

"My friends! What friends? Have I any? Who cares for me?" And he accompanied the last words with a kind of whistling of the lips.

But they were obliged to separate from each other because of a great pile of chairs that a man was carrying behind them. He was so overladen with them that one could only see the tips of his wooden shoes and the ends of his two outstretched arms. It was Lestiboudois, the gravedigger, who was carrying the church chairs about among the people. Alive to all that concerned his interests, he had hit upon this means of turning the show to account; and his idea was succeeding, for he no longer knew which way to turn. In fact, the villagers, who were hot, quarreled for these seats, whose straw smelled of incense, and they lent against the thick backs, stained with the wax of candles, with a certain veneration.

Madame Bovary again took Rodolphe's arm; he went on as if speaking to himself:

"Yes, I have missed so many things. Always alone! Ah! if I had some aim in life, if I had met some love, if I had found some one! Oh, how I would have spent all the energy of which I am capable, surmounted everything, overcome everything!"

"Yet it seems to me," said Emma, "that you are not to be pitied."

"Ah! you think so?" said Rodolphe.

"For, after all," she went on, "you are free——" she hesitated, "rich ——"

"Do not mock me," he replied.

And she protested that she was not mocking him, when the report of a cannon resounded. Immediately all began hustling one another pell-mell toward the village.

It was a false alarm. The prefect seemed not to be coming, and the members of the jury felt much embarrassed, not knowing if they ought to begin the meeting or still wait.

At last at the end of the Place a large hired landau appeared, drawn by two thin horses, whom a coachman in a white hat was whipping lustily. Binet had only just time to shout, "Present arms!" and the colonel to imitate him. All ran toward the enclosure; every one pushed forward. A few even forgot their collars; but the equipage of the prefect seemed to anticipate the crowd, and the two yoked jades, trapesing in their harness, came up at a little trot in front of the peristyle of the town hall at the very moment when the National Guard and firemen deployed, beating drums and marking time.

"Present!" shouted Binet.

"Halt!" shouted the colonel. "Left about, march."

And after presenting arms, during which the clang of the band, letting loose, rang out like a brass kettle rolling downstairs, all the guns were lowered. Then were seen stepping down from the carriage a gentleman in a short coat with silver braiding, with bald brow, and wearing a tuft of hair at the back of his head, of a sallow complexion and the most benign appearance. His eyes, very large and covered by heavy lids, were half-closed to look at the crowd, while at the same time he raised his sharp nose, and forced a smile upon his sunken mouth. He recognized the mayor by his scarf, and explained to him that the prefect was not able to come. He himself was a councilor at the prefecture; then he added a few apologies. Monsieur Tuvache answered them with compliments; the other confessed himself nervous; and they remained thus, face to face, their foreheads almost touching, with the members of the jury all round, the municipal council, the notable personages, the National Guard and the crowd. The councilor pressing his little cocked hat to his breast repeated his bows, while Tuvache, bent like a bow, also smiled, stammered, tried to say something, protested his devotion to the monarchy and the honor that was being done to Yonville.

Hippolyte, the groom from the inn, took the head of the horses from the coachman, and, limping along with his club-foot, led them to the door of the "Lion d'Or," where a number of peasants collected to look at the carriage. The drum beat, the howitzer thundered, and the gentlemen one by one mounted the platform, where they sat down in red utrecht velvet armchairs that had been lent by Madame Tuvache.

All these people looked alike. Their fair flabby faces, somewhat tanned by the sun, were the color of sweet cider, and their puffy whiskers emerged from stiff collars, kept up by white cravats with broad bows. All the waistcoats were of velvet, double-breasted; all the watches had, at the end of a long ribbon, an oval cornelian seal; every one rested his two hands on his thighs, carefully stretching the stride of his trousers, whose unsponged glossy cloth shone more brilliantly than the leather of his heavy boots.

The ladies of the company stood at the back under the vestibule between the pillars, while the common herd was opposite, standing up or sitting on chairs. As a matter of fact, Lestiboudois had brought thither all those that he had moved from the field,

and he even kept running back every minute to fetch
others from the church. He caused such confusion
with this piece of business that one had great difficulty in getting to the small steps of the platform.

"I think," said Monsieur Lheureux to the chemist,
who was passing to his place, "that they ought to
have put up two Venetian masts with something
rather severe and rich for ornaments; it would have
been a very pretty effect."

"To be sure," replied Homais; "but what can you
expect? The mayor took everything on his own
shoulders. He hasn't much taste. Poor Tuvache!
and he is even completely destitute of what is called
the genius of art."

Rodolphe, meanwhile, with Madame Bovary, had
gone up to the first floor of the townhall, to the
"council-room," and as it was empty, he declared
that they could enjoy the sight there more comfortably.
He fetched three stools from the round table under the
bust of the monarch, and having carried them to one
of the windows, they sat down by each other.

There was commotion on the platform, long whis-
perings, much parleying. At last the councilor got up.
They knew now that his name was Lieuvain, and in
the crowd the name was passed from one to the
other. After he had collated a few pages, and bent
over them to see better, he began:

"Gentlemen! May I be permitted first of all (before addressing you on the object of our meeting
to-day, and this sentiment, will, I am sure, be shared
by you all), may I be permitted, I say, to pay a
tribute to the higher administration, to the government, to the monarch, gentlemen, our sovereign, to
that beloved king, to whom no branch of public or

private prosperity is a matter of indifference, and who directs with a hand at once so firm and wise the chariot of the state amid the incessant perils of a stormy sea, knowing, moreover, how to make peace respected as well as war, industry, commerce, agriculture, and the fine arts."

"I ought," said Rodolphe, "to get back a little further."

"Why?" said Emma.

But at this moment the voice of the councilor rose to an extraordinary pitch. He declaimed:

"This is no longer the time, gentlemen, when civil discord ensanguined our public places, when the landlord, the business-man, the working-man himself, falling asleep at night, lying down to peaceful sleep, trembled lest he should be awakened suddenly by the noise of incendiary tocsins, when the most subversive doctrines audaciously sapped foundations."

"Well, some one down there might see me," Rodolphe resumed, "then I should have to invent excuses for a fortnight; and with my bad reputation ——"

"Oh, you are slandering yourself," said Emma.

"No! It is dreadful, I assure you."

"But, gentlemen," continued the councilor, "if, banishing from my memory the remembrance of these sad pictures, I carry my eyes back to the actual situation of our dear country, what do I see there? Everywhere commerce and the arts are flourishing; everywhere new means of communication, like so many new arteries in the body of the state, establish within it new relations. Our great industrial centers have recovered all their activity; religion, more consolidated, smiles in all hearts; our ports are full, confidence is born again, and France breathes once more!"

"Besides," added Rodolphe, "perhaps from the world's point of view they are right."

"How so?" she asked.

"What!" said he. "Do you not know that there are souls constantly tormented? They need by turns to dream and to act, the purest passions and the most turbulent joys, and thus they fling themselves into all sorts of fantasies, of follies."

Then she looked at him as one looks at a traveler who has voyaged over strange lands, and went on:

"We have not even this distraction, we poor women!"

"A sad distraction, for happiness isn't found in it."

"But is it ever found?" she asked.

"Yes; one day it comes," he answered.

"And this is what you have understood," said the councilor. "You farmers, agricultural laborers! you pacific pioneers of a work that belongs wholly to civilization! you men of progress and morality, you have understood, I say, that political storms are even more redoubtable than atmospheric disturbances!"

"It comes one day," repeated Rodolphe, "one day suddenly, and when one is despairing of it. Then the horizon expands; it is as if a voice cried, 'It is here!' You feel the need of confiding the whole of your life, of giving everything, sacrificing everything to this being. There is no need for explanations; they understand one another. They have seen each other in dreams!" He looked at her. "In fine, here it is, this treasure so sought after, here before you. It glitters, it flashes; yet one still doubts, one does not believe it; one remains dazzled, as if one went out from darkness into light!"

And as he ended Rodolphe suited the action to the word. He passed his hand over his face, like a man seized with giddiness. Then he let it fall on Emma's. She took hers away.

"And who would be surprised at it, gentlemen? He only who was so blind, so plunged (I do not fear to say it), so plunged in the prejudices of another age as still to misunderstand the spirit of agricultural populations. Where, indeed, is to be found more patriotism than in the country, greater devotion to the public welfare, more intelligence, in a word? And, gentlemen, I do not mean that superficial intelligence, vain ornament of idle minds, but rather that profound and balanced intelligence that applies itself above all else to useful objects, thus contributing to the good of all, to the common amelioration and to the support of the state, born of respect for law and the practice of duty——"

"Ah! again!" said Rodolphe. "Always 'duty.' I am sick of the word. They are a lot of old block-heads in flannel vests and of old women with foot-warmers and rosaries who constantly drone into our ears 'Duty, duty!' Ah! by Jove! one's duty is to feel what is great, cherish the beautiful, and not accept all the conventions of society with the ignominy that it imposes upon us."

"Yet—yet——" objected Madame Bovary.

"No, no! Why cry out against the passions? Are they not the one beautiful thing on the earth, the source of heroism, of enthusiasm, of poetry, music, the arts, of everything, in a word?"

"But one must," said Emma, "to some extent bow to the opinion of the world and accept its moral code."

"Ah! but there are two," he replied. "The small, the conventional, that of men, that which constantly changes, that brays out so loudly, that makes such a commotion here below, of the earth earthy, like the mass of imbeciles you see down there. But the other, the eternal, that is about us and above, like the landscape that surrounds us, and the blue heavens that give us light."

Monsieur Lieuvain had just wiped his mouth with a pocket-handkerchief. He continued:

"And what should I do here, gentlemen, pointing out to you the uses of agriculture? Who supplies our wants? who provides our means of subsistence? Is it not the agriculturist? The agriculturist, gentlemen, who, sowing with laborious hand the fertile furrows of the country, brings forth the corn, which, being ground, is made into a powder by means of ingenious machinery, comes out thence under the name of flour, and from there, transported to our cities, is soon delivered at the baker's, who makes it into food for poor and rich alike. Again, is it not the agriculturist who fattens, for our clothes, his abundant flocks in the pastures? For how should we clothe ourselves, how nourish ourselves, without the agriculturist? And, gentlemen, is it even necessary to go so far for examples? Who has not frequently reflected on all the momentous things that we get out of that modest animal, the ornament of poultry-yards, that provides us at once with a soft pillow for our bed, with succulent flesh for our tables, and eggs? But I should never end if I were to enumerate one after the other all the different products which the earth, well cultivated, like a generous mother, lavishes upon her children. Here it is the vine, elsewhere the appletree for cider, there colza, farther on cheeses and flax. Gentlemen, let us not forget flax, which has made such great strides of late years, and to which I will more particularly call your attention."

He had no need to call it, for all the mouths of the multitude were wide open, as if to drink in his words. Tuvache by his side listened to him with starting eyes. Monsieur Derozerays from time to time softly closed his eyelids, and farther on the chemist, with his son Napoléon between his knees, put his hand behind his ear in order not to lose a syllable. The chins of the other members of the jury went slowly up and down in their waistcoats in sign of approval. The firemen at the foot of the platform rested on their bayonets; and Binet, motionless, stood with out-turned elbows, the point of his sabre in the air. Perhaps he could hear, but certainly he could see nothing, because of the visor of his helmet, that fell down on his nose. His lieutenant, the youngest son of Monsieur Tuvache, had a bigger one, for his was enormous, and shook on his head, and from it an end of his cotton scarf peeped out. He smiled beneath it with a perfectly infantine sweetness, and his pale little face, whence drops were running, wore an expression of enjoyment and sleepiness.

The square as far as the houses was crowded with people. One saw folk leaning on their elbows at all the windows, others standing at doors, and Justin, in front of the chemist's shop, seemed quite transfixed by the sight of what he was looking at. In spite of the silence Monsieur Lieuvain's voice was lost in the air. It reached you in fragments of phrases, and interrupted here and there by the creaking of chairs in the crowd; then you suddenly heard the long bellowing of an ox, or else the bleating of the lambs, who answered one another at street corners. In fact, the cowherds and shepherds had driven their beasts thus far, and these lowed from time to time, while with their tongues they tore down some scrap of foliage that hung above their mouths.

Rodolphe had drawn nearer to Emma, and said to her it a low voice, speaking rapidly:

"Does not this conspiracy of the world revolt you? Is there a single sentiment it does not condemn? The noblest instincts, the purest sympathies are persecuted, slandered; and if at length two poor souls do meet, all is so organized that they cannot blend together. Yet they will make the attempt; they will flutter their wings; they will call upon each other. Oh! no matter. Sooner or later, in six months, ten years, they will come together, will love; for fate has decreed it, and they are born one for the other."

His arms were folded across his knees, and thus lifting his face toward Emma, close by her, he looked fixedly at her. She noticed in his eyes small golden lines radiating from black pupils; she even smelled the perfume of the pomade that made his hair glossy. Then a faintness came over her; she recalled the Viscount who had waltzed with her at Vaubyessard,

and his beard exhaled like this hair an odor of vanilla
and citron, and mechanically she half-closed her eyes
the better to breathe it in.   But in making this movement, as she leaned back in her chair, she saw in the
distance, right on the line of the horizon, the old
diligence the "Hirondelle," that was slowly decending
the hill of Leux, dragging after it a long trail of dust.
It was in this yellow carriage that Léon had so often
come back to her, and by this route down there
that he had gone for ever.   She fancied she saw him
opposite at his window; then all grew confused;
clouds gathered; it seemed to her that she was again
turning in the waltz under the light of the lusters on
the arm of the Viscount, and that Léon was not far
away, that he was coming; and yet all the time she
was conscious of the scent of Rodolphe's head by her
side.   This sweetness of sensation pierced through
her old desires, and these, like grains of sand under
a gust of wind, eddied to and fro in the subtle breath
of the perfume which suffused her soul.   She opened
wide her nostrils several times to drink in the freshness of the ivy round the capitals.   She took off her
gloves, she wiped her hands, then fanned her face
with her handkerchief, while athwart the throbbing
of her temples she heard the murmur of the crowd
and the voice of the councilor intoning his phrases.
He said:

"Continue, persevere; listen neither to the sugges-
tions of routine, nor to the over-hasty councils of a
rash empiricism.   Apply yourselves, above all, to the
amelioration of the soil, to good manures, to the
development of the equine, bovine, ovine, and porcine races.   Let these shows be to you pacific arenas,
where the victor in leaving it will hold forth a hand

to the vanquished, and will fraternize with him in the hope of better success. And you, aged servants, humble domestics, whose hard labor no Government up to this day has taken into consideration, come hither to receive the reward of your silent virtues, and be assured that the state henceforward has its eye upon you; that it encourages you, protects you; that it will accede to your just demands, and alleviate as much as in it lies the burden of your painful sacrifices."

Monsieur Lieuvain then sat down; Monsieur Derozerays got up, beginning another speech. His was not perhaps so florid as that of the councilor, but it recommended itself by a more direct style, that is to say, by more special knowledge and more elevated considerations. Thus the praise of the Government took up less space in it; religion and agriculture more. He showed in it the relations of these two, and how they had always contributed to civilization. Rodolphe with Madame Bovary was talking dreams, presentiments, magnetism. Going back to the cradle of society, the orator painted those fierce times when men lived on acorns in the heart of woods. Then they had left off the skins of beasts, had put on cloth, tilled the soil, planted the vine. Was this a good, and in this discovery was there not more of injury than of gain? Monsieur Derozerays set himself this problem. From magnetism little by little Rodolphe had come to affinities, and while the president was citing Cincinnatus and his plough, Diocletian planting his cabbages, and the emperors of China inaugurating the year by the sowing of seed, the young man was explaining to the young woman that these irresistible attractions find their cause in some previous state of existence.

"Thus we," he said, "why did we come to know one another? What chance willed it? It was because across the infinite, like two streams that flow but to unite, our special bents of mind had driven us toward each other."

And he seized her hand; she did not withdraw it.

"For good farming generally!" cried the president.

"Just now, for example, when I went to your house."

"To Monsieur Bizat of Quincampoix."

"Did I know I should accompany you?"

"Seventy francs."

"A hundred times I wished to go; and I followed you—I remained."

"Manures!"

"And I shall remain to-night, to-morrow, all other days, all my life!"

"To Monsieur Caron of Argueil, a gold medal!"

"For I have never in the society of any other person found so complete a charm."

"To Monsieur Bain of Givry-Saint-Martin."

"And I shall carry away with me the remembrance of you."

"For a merino ram!"

"But you will forget me; I shall pass away like a shadow."

"To Monsieur Belot of Notre-Dame."

"Oh, no! I shall be something in your thought, in your life, shall I not?"

"Porcine race; prizes—equal, to Messrs. Lehérissé and Cullembourg, sixty francs!"

Rodolphe was pressing her hand, and he felt it all warm and quivering like a captive dove that tries to fly away; but, whether she was trying to take it

away or whether she was answering his pressure, she
made a movement with her fingers. He exclaimed—

"Oh, I thank you! You do not repulse me!
You are good! You understand that I am yours!
Let me look at you; let me contemplate you!"

A gust of wind that blew in at the window ruffled
the cloth on the table, and in the square below all
the great caps of the peasant women were uplifted
by it like the wings of white butterflies fluttering.

"Use of oil-cakes," continued the president. He
was hurrying on: "Flemish manure—flax-growing—
drainage—long leases—domestic service."

Rodolphe was no longer speaking. They looked
at one another. A supreme desire made their dry
lips tremble, and softly, without an effort, their fingers
intertwined.

"Catherine Nicaise Elizabeth Leroux, of Sassetot-
la-Guerrière, for fifty-four years of service at the same
farm, a silver medal—value, twenty-five francs!"

"Where is Catherine Leroux?" repeated the councilor.

She did not present herself, and one could hear
voices whispering:

"Go up!"

"Don't be afraid!"

"Oh, how stupid she is!"

"Well, is she there?" cried Tuvache.

"Yes; here she is."

"Then let her come up!"

Then there came forward on the platform a little
old woman with timid bearing, who seemed to
shrink within her poor clothes. On her feet she wore
heavy wooden clogs, and from her hips hung a large
blue apron. Her pale face framed in a borderless cap

was more wrinkled than a withered russet apple, and
from the sleeves of her red jacket hung down two
large hands with knotty joints. The dust of
barns, the potash of washings, and the grease of
wools had so incrusted, roughened, hardened these,
that they seemed dirty, although they had been rinsed
in clear water; and by dint of long service they remained half open, as if to bear humble witness for
themselves of so much suffering endured. Something
of monastic rigidity dignified her face. Nothing of
sadness or of emotion weakened that pale look. In
her constant living with animals she had caught their
dumbness and their calm. It was the first time that
she found herself in the midst of so large a company,
and inwardly scared by the flags, the drums, the gentlemen in frock-coats, and the order of the councilor,
she stood motionless, not knowing whether to advance or run away, nor why the crowd was pushing
her and the jury were smiling at her. Thus stood
before these radiant bourgeois this half-century of
servitude.

"Approach, venerable Catherine Nicaise Elizabeth
Leroux!" said the councilor, who had taken the list
of prize-winners from the president; and, looking at
the piece of paper and the old woman by turns, he
repeated in a fatherly tone:

"Approach! approach!"

"Are you deaf?" said Tuvache, fidgeting in his
armchair; and he began shouting in her ear, "Fifty-
four years of service. A silver medal! Twenty-five
francs! For you!"

Then, when she had her medal, she looked at it,
and a smile of beatitude spread over her face; and as
she walked away they could hear her muttering:

"I'll give it to our curé up home, to say some masses for me!"

"What fanaticism!" exclaimed the chemist, leaning across to the notary.

The meeting was over, the crowd dispersed, and now that the speeches had been read, each one fell back into his place again, and everything into the old grooves; the masters bullied the servants, and these struck the animals, indolent victors, going back to the stalls, a green crown on their horns.

The National Guards, however, had gone up to the first floor of the townhall with buns spitted on their bayonets, and the drummer of the battalion carried a basket with bottles. Madame Bovary took Rodolphe's arm; he saw her home; they separated at her door; then he walked about alone in the meadow while he waited for the time of the banquet.

The feast was long, noisy, ill served; the guests were so crowded that they could hardly move their elbows; and the narrow planks used for forms almost broke down under their weight. They ate hugely. Each one stuffed himself on his own account. Sweat stood on every brow, and a whitish steam, like the vapor of a stream on an autumn morning, floated above the table between the hanging lamps. Rodolphe, leaning against the calico of the tent, was thinking so earnestly of Emma that he heard nothing. Behind him on the grass the servants were piling up the dirty plates; his neighbors were talking; he did not answer them; they filled his glass, and there was silence in his thoughts in spite of the growing noise. He was dreaming of what she had said, of the line of her lips; her face, as in a magic mirror, shone on the plates of the shakos, the folds of her gown fell along the walls, and days of love unrolled to all infinity before him in the vistas of the future.

He saw her again in the evening during the fireworks, but she was with her husband, Madame Homais, and the druggist, who was worrying about the danger of stray rockets, and every moment he left the company to go and give some advice to Binet.

The pyrotechnic pieces sent to Monsieur Tuvache had, through an excess of caution, been shut up in his cellar, and so the damp powder would not light, and the principal set piece, that was to represent a dragon biting his tail, failed completely. Now and then a meager Roman-candle went off ; then the gaping crowd sent up a shout that mingled with the cry of the women, whose waists were being squeezed in the darkness. Emma silently nestled gently against Charles's shoulder ; then, raising her chin, she watched the luminous rays of the rockets against the dark sky. Rodolphe gazed at her in the light of the burning lanterns.

They went out one by one. The stars shone out. A few drops of rain began to fall. She knotted her fichu round her bare head.

At this moment the councilor's carriage came out from the inn. His coachman, who was drunk, suddenly dozed off, and one could see from the distance, above the hood, between the two lanterns, the mass of his body, that swayed from right to left with the giving of the traces.

"Truly," said the chemist, "one ought to proceed most rigorously against drunkenness ! I should like to see written up weekly at the door of the townhall on a board *ad hoc* the names of all those who during the week got intoxicated on alcohol. Besides, with regard to statistics, one would thus have, as it were, public records that one could refer to in case of need. But excuse me!"

And he once more ran off to the captain. The latter was going back to see his lathe again.

"Perhaps you would not do ill," Homais said to him, "to send one of your men, or to go yourself——"

"Leave me alone!" answered the tax-collector. "It's all right!"

"Do not be uneasy," said the chemist, when he returned to his friends. "Monsieur Binet has assured me that all precautions have been taken. No sparks have fallen; the pumps are full. Let us go to rest."

"*Ma foi!* I want it," said Madame Homais, yawning at large. "But never mind; we've had a beautiful day for our fête."

Rodolphe repeated in a low voice, and with a tender look, "Oh, yes! very beautiful."

And having bowed to one another, they separated.

Two days later, in the "Fanal de Rouen," there was a long article on the show. Homais had composed it with *verve* the very next morning.

"Why these festoons, these flowers, these garlands? Whither hurries this crowd like the waves of a furious sea under the torrents of a tropical sun pouring its heat upon our heads?"

Then he spoke of the condition of the peasants. Certainly the Government was doing much, but not enough. "Courage!" he cried to it; "a thousand reforms are indispensable; let us accomplish them!" Then touching on the entry of the councilor, he did not forget "the martial air of our militia," nor "our most merry village maidens," nor the "bald-headed old men like patriarchs who were there, and of whom some, the remnants of our immortal phalanxes, still felt their hearts beat at the manly sound of the drums." He cited himself among the first of the members of the jury, and he even called attention in a note to the fact that Monsieur Homais, chemist, had sent a memoir on cider to the agricultural society. When he came to the distribution of the prizes, he painted the joy of the prize-winners in dithyrambic strophes. "The father embraced the son, the brother the brother, the husband his consort. More than one showed his humble medal with pride ; and no doubt when he got home to his good housewife, he hung it up weeping on the modest walls of his cot.

"About six o'clock a banquet prepared in the meadow of Monsieur Leigeard brought together the principal personages of the fête. The greatest cordiality reigned here. Divers toasts were proposed. Monsieur Lieuvain, the King; Monsieur Tuvache, the Prefect; Monsieur Derozerays, Agriculture; Monsieur Homais, Industry and the Fine Arts, those twin sisters; Monsieur Leplichey, Progress. In the evening some brilliant fireworks on a sudden illumined the air. One would have called it a veritable kaleidoscope, a real operatic scene; and for a moment our little locality might have thought itself transported into the midst of a dream of the 'Thousand and One Nights.'

"Let us state that no untoward event disturbed this family meeting." And he added: "Only the absence of the clergy was remarked. No doubt the priests understand progress in another fashion. Just as you please, messieurs the followers of Loyola !"

IX.

A Woodland Idyll.

SIX weeks passed. Rodolphe did not come again. At last one evening he appeared.

The day after the show he had said to himself:

"We mustn't go back too soon; that would be a mistake."

And at the end of a week he had gone off hunting. After the hunting he had thought he was too late, and then he reasoned thus:

"If from the first day she loved me, she must, from impatience to see me again, love me more. Let's go on with it!"

And he knew that his calculation had been right when, on entering the room, he saw Emma turn pale.

She was alone. The day was drawing in. The small muslin curtain along the windows deepened the twilight, and the gilding of the barometer, on which the rays of the sun fell, shone in the looking-glass between the meshes of the coral.

Rodolphe remained standing, and Emma hardly answered his first conventional phrases.

"I," he said, "have been busy. I have been ill."

"Seriously?" she cried.

"Well," said Rodolphe, sitting down at her side on a footstool, "no; it was because I did not want to come back."

"Why?"

"Can you not guess?"

He looked at her again, but so hard that she lowered her head, blushing. He went on:

"Emma!"

"Sir," she said, drawing back a little.

"Ah! you see," replied he in a melancholy voice, "that I was right not to come back; for this name, this name that fills my whole soul, and that escaped me, you forbid me to use! Madame Bovary! why all the world calls you thus! Besides it is not your name; it is the name of another!" he repeated, "of another!" And he hid his face in his hands. "Yes, I think of you constantly. The memory of you drives me to despair. Ah! forgive me! I will leave you! Farewell! I will go far away, so far that you will never hear of me again; and yet—to-day—I know not what force impelled me toward you. For one does not struggle against Heaven; one cannot resist the smile of angels; one is carried away by that which is beautiful, charming, adorable."

It was the first time that Emma had heard such words spoken to herself, and her pride, like one who reposes bathed in warmth, expanded softly and fully at this glowing language.

"But if I did not come," he continued, "if I could not see you, at least I have gazed long on all that surrounds you. At night—every night—I arose; I came hither; I watched your house, its roof glimmering in the moonlight, the trees in the garden before your window, and the little lamp, a gleam shining through the window-panes in the darkness. Ah! you never knew that there, so near you, so far from you, was a poor wretch!"

She turned toward him with a sob.

"Oh, you are good!" she said.

"No, I love you, that is all! You do not doubt that! Tell me — one word — only one word!"

And Rodolphe imperceptibly glided from the footstool to the floor; but a sound of wooden shoes was heard in the kitchen, and he noticed the door of the room was not closed.

"How kind it would be of you," he went on, rising, "if you would humor a whim of mine." It was to go over her house; he wanted to know it; and Madame Bovary seeing no objection to this, they both rose, when Charles came in.

"Good morning, doctor," Rodolphe said to him.

The doctor, flattered at this unexpected title, launched out into obsequious phrases. Of this the other took advantage to pull himself together a little.

"Madame was speaking to me," he then said, "about her health."

Charles interrupted him; he had indeed a thousand anxieties; his wife's palpitations of the heart were beginning again. Then Rodolphe asked if riding would not be good.

"Certainly! excellent! just the thing! There's an idea! You ought to follow it up."

And as she objected that she had no horse, Monsieur Rodolphe offered one. She refused his offer; he did not insist. Then to explain his visit he said that his ploughman, the man of the blood-letting, still suffered from giddiness.

"I'll call round," said Bovary.

"No, no! I'll send him to you; we'll come; that will be more convenient for you."

"Ah! very good! I thank you."

And as soon as they were alone, "Why don't you accept Monsieur Boulanger's kind offer?"

She assumed a sulky air, invented a thousand excuses, and finally declared that perhaps it would look odd.

"Well, what the deuce do I care for that?" said Charles, making a pirouette. "Health before everything! You are wrong."

"And how do you think I can ride when I haven't got a habit?"

"You must order one," he answered.

The riding-habit decided her.

When the habit was ready, Charles wrote to Monsieur Boulanger that his wife was at his command, and that they counted on his good-nature.

The next day at noon Rodolphe appeared at Charles's door with two saddle-horses. One had pink rosettes at his ears and a deerskin side-saddle.

Rodolphe had put on high soft boots, saying to himself that no doubt she had never seen anything like them. In fact, Emma was charmed with his appearance as he stood on the landing in his great velvet coat and white corduroy breeches. She was ready; she was waiting for him.

Justin escaped from the chemist's to see her start, and the chemist also came out. He was giving Monsieur Boulanger a little good advice.

"An accident happens so easily. Be careful! Your horses perhaps are mettlesome."

She heard a noise above her; it was Félicité drum-

ming on the window-panes to amuse little Berthe.
The child blew her a kiss; her mother answered with
a wave of her whip.

"A pleasant ride!" cried Monsieur Homais. "Prudence! above all, prudence!" And he flourished his
newspaper as he saw them disappear.

As soon as he felt the ground, Emma's horse set off
at a gallop. Rodolphe galloped by her side. Now
and then they exchanged a word. Her figure slightly
bent, her hand well up, and her right arm stretched
out, she gave herself up to the cadence of the movement that rocked her in her saddle. At the bottom
of the hill Rodolphe gave his horse its head; they
started together at a bound, then at the top suddenly the horses stopped, and her large blue veil fell
about her.

It was early in October. There was fog over the
land. Hazy clouds hovered on the horizon between
the outlines of the hills; others, rent asunder, floated
up and disappeared. Sometimes through a rift in the
clouds, beneath a ray of sunshine, gleamed from afar
the roofs of Yonville, with the gardens at the water's
edge, the yards, the walls, and the church steeple.
Emma half closed her eyes to pick out her house, and
never had this poor village where she lived appeared
so small. From the height on which they were, the
whole valley seemed an immense pale lake sending
off its vapor into the air. Clumps of trees here and
there stood out like black rocks, and the tall lines of
the poplars that rose above the mist were like a beach
stirred by the wind.

Beside them, on the turf between the pines, a brown
light shimmered in the warm atmosphere. The earth,
ruddy like the powder of tobacco, deadened the noise

of their steps, and with the edge of their shoes the horses as they walked kicked the fallen fir cones in front of them.

Rodolphe and Emma thus went along the skirt of the wood. She turned away from time to time to avoid his look, and then she saw only the pine trunks in lines, whose monotonous succession made her a little giddy. The horses were panting; the leather of the saddles creaked.

Just as they were entering the forest the sun shone out.

"God protects us!" said Rodolphe.

"Do you think so?" she said.

"Forward! forward!" he continued.

He "tchk'd" with his tongue. The two beasts set off at a trot. Long ferns by the roadside caught in Emma's stirrup. Rodolphe leant forward and removed them as they rode along. At other times to turn aside the branches, he passed close to her, and Emma felt his knee brushing against her leg. The sky was now blue, the leaves no longer stirred. There were spaces full of heather in flower, and plots of violets alternated with the confused patches of the trees that were gray, fawn, or golden colored, according to the nature of their leaves. Often in the thicket was heard the fluttering of wings, or else the hoarse, soft cry of the ravens flying off amid the oaks.

They dismounted. Rodolphe fastened up the horses. She walked on in front on the moss between the paths. But her long habit got in her way, although she held it up by the skirt; and Rodolphe, walking behind her, saw between the black cloth and the black shoe the fineness of her white stocking, that seemed to him as if it were a part of her nakedness.

She stopped. "I am tired," she said.

"Come, try again," he went on. "Courage!"

Then some hundred paces farther on she again stopped, and through her veil, that fell sideways from her man's hat over her hips, her face appeared in a bluish transparency as if she were floating under azure waves.

"But where are we going?"

He did not answer. She was breathing irregularly. Rodolphe looked round him biting his mustache. They came to a larger space where the coppice had been cut. They sat down on the trunk of a fallen tree, and Rodolphe began speaking to her of his love. He did not begin by frightening her with compliments. He was calm, serious, melancholy.

Emma listened to him with bowed head, and stirred the bits of wood on the ground with the tip of her foot.

But at the words, "Are not our destinies now one?——"

"Oh, no!" she replied. "You know that well. It is impossible!"

She rose to go. He seized her by the wrist. She stopped. Then, having gazed at him for a few moments with an amorous and humid look, she said hurriedly:

"Ah! do not speak of it again! Where are the horses? Let us go back."

He made a gesture of anger and annoyance. She repeated:

"Where are the horses? Where are the horses?"

Then smiling a strange smile, his pupils fixed, his teeth set, he advanced with outstretched arms. She recoiled trembling. She stammered:

"Oh, you frighten me! You hurt me! Let us go!"

"If it must be," he went on, his face changing; and he again became respectful, caressing, timid. She gave him her arm. They went back. He said:

"What was the matter with you? Why? I do not understand. You were mistaken, no doubt. In my soul you are as a Madonna on a pedestal, in a place lofty, secure, immaculate. But I want you for my life. I must have your eyes, your voice, your thought! Be my friend, my sister, my angel!"

And he put out his arm around her waist. She feebly tried to disengage herself. He supported her thus as they walked along.

But they heard the two horses browsing on the leaves.

"Oh! one moment!" said Rodolphe. "Do not let us go! Stay!"

He drew her farther on to a small pool where duckweeds made a greenness on the water. Faded waterlilies lay motionless between the reeds. At the noise of their steps in the grass, frogs jumped away to hide themselves.

"I am wrong! I am wrong!" she said. "I am mad to listen to you!"

"Why? Emma! Emma!"

"Oh, Rodolphe!" said the young woman slowly, leaning on his shoulder.

The cloth of her habit caught against the velvet of his coat. She threw back her white neck, swelling with a sigh, and faltering, in tears, with a long shudder and hiding her face, she gave herself up to him.

The shades of night were falling; the horizontal sun passing between the branches dazzled the

eyes. Here and there around her, in the leaves or on
the ground, trembled luminous patches, as if hum-
ming-birds flying about had scattered their feathers.
Silence was everywhere; something sweet seemed to
come forth from the trees; she felt her heart, whose
beating had begun again, and the blood coursing
through her flesh like a stream of milk. Then far
away, beyond the wood, on the other hills, she
heard a vague prolonged cry, a voice which lingered,
and in silence she heard it mingling like music with
the last pulsations of her throbbing nerves. Rodolphe,
a cigar between his lips, was mending with his pen-
knife one of the two broken bridles.

They returned to Yonville by the same road. On
the mud they saw again the traces of their horses
side by side, the same thickets, the same stones in
the grass; nothing around them seemed changed; and
yet for her something had happened more stupendous
than if the mountains had moved in their places.
Rodolphe now and again bent forward and took her
hand to kiss it.

She was charming on horseback—upright, with her
slender waist, her knee bent on the mane of her
horse, her face something flushed by the fresh air
in the red of the evening.

On entering Yonville she made her horse prance
in the road. People looked at her from the windows.

At dinner her husband thought she looked well,
but she pretended not to hear him when he inquired
about her ride, and she remained sitting there with
her elbow at the side of her plate between the two
lighted candles.

"Emma!" he said.

"What?"

"Well, I spent the afternoon at Monsieur Alexandre's. He has an old cob, still very fine, only a little broken-kneed, that could be bought, I am very sure, for a hundred crowns." He added, "And thinking it might please you, I have bespoken it — bought it. Have I done right? Do tell me!"

She nodded her head in assent; then a quarter of an hour later—

"Are you going out to-night?" she asked.

"Yes. Why?"

"Oh, nothing, nothing, my dear!"

And as soon as she had got rid of Charles she went and shut herself up in her room.

At first she felt stunned; she saw the trees, the paths, the ditches, Rodolphe, and she again felt the pressure of his arm, while the leaves rustled and the reeds whistled.

But when she saw herself in the glass she wondered at her face. Never had her eyes been so large, so black, of so profound a depth. Something subtle about her being transfigured her. She repeated, "I have a lover! a lover!" delighting at the idea as if a second puberty had come to her. So at last she was to know those joys of love, that fever of happiness of which she had despaired! She was entering upon marvels where all would be passion, ecstasy, delirium. An azure infinity encompassed her, the heights of sentiment sparkled under her thought, and ordinary existence appeared remote, far below in the shade, through the interspaces of these heights.

Then she recalled the heroines of the books that she had read, and the lyric legion of these adulterous women began to sing in her memory with the voice of sisters that charmed her. She became herself, as it were, an actual part of these imaginings, and realized the love-dream of her youth as she saw herself in this type of amorous women whom she had so envied. Besides, Emma felt a satisfaction of revenge. Had she not suffered enough? But now she triumphed, and the love so long pent up burst forth in full joyous bubblings. She tasted it without remorse, without anxiety, without trouble.

The day following passed with a new sweetness. They made vows to one another. She told him of her sorrows. Rodolphe interrupted her with kisses; and she, looking at him through half-closed eyes, asked him to call her again by her name—to say that he loved her. They were in the forest, as yesterday, in the shed of some wooden-shoe maker. The walls were of straw, and the roof so low they had to stoop. They were seated side by side on a bed of dry leaves.

From that day forth they wrote to one another regularly every evening. Emma placed her letter at the end of the garden, by the river, in a fissure of the wall. Rodolphe came to fetch it, and put another there, that she always found fault with as too short.

One morning, when Charles had gone out before daybreak, she was seized with the fancy to see Rodolphe at once. She would go quickly to La Huchette, stay there an hour, and be back again at Yonville while every one was still asleep. This idea made her pant with desire, and she soon found herself in the middle of the field, walking with rapid steps, without looking behind her.

Day was just breaking. Emma from afar recognized her lover's house. Its two dove-tailed weathercocks stood out black against the pale dawn.

Beyond the farmyard there was a detached building that she thought must be the château. She entered it as if the doors at her approach had opened wide of their own accord. A large straight staircase led up to the corridor. Emma raised the latch of a door, and suddenly at the end of the room she saw a man sleeping. It was Rodolphe. She uttered a cry.

"You here? You here?" he repeated. "How did you manage to come? Ah! your dress is damp."

"I love you," she answered, passing her arms round his neck.

This first piece of daring successful, now every time Charles went out early Emma dressed quickly and slipped on tiptoe down the steps that led to the waterside.

But when the plank for the cows was taken up, she had to go by the walls alongside of the river; the bank was slippery; in order not to fall she caught hold of the tufts of faded wallflowers. Then she went across ploughed fields, in which she sank, stumbling, and clogging her thin shoes. Her scarf, knotted round her head, fluttered to the wind in the meadows. She was afraid of the oxen; she began to run; she arrived out of breath, with rosy cheeks, and breathing out from her whole person a fresh perfume of sap, of verdure, of the open air. At this hour Rodolphe still slept. It was like a spring morning coming into his room.

The yellow curtains along the windows let a heavy, whitish light enter softly. Emma felt about, opening and closing her eyes, while the drops of dew hanging from her hair formed, as it were, a topaz aureole around her face. Rodolphe, laughing, drew her to him and pressed her to his breast.

Then she examined the apartment, opened the drawers of the tables, combed her hair with his comb, and looked at herself in his shaving-glass. Often she even put between her teeth the big pipe that lay on the table by the bed, amongst lemons and pieces of sugar near a bottle of water.

It took them a good quarter of an hour to say good-bye. Then Emma wept. She would have wished never to leave Rodolphe. Something stronger than herself forced her to him; so much so, that one day, seeing her come unexpectedly, he frowned as one put out.

"What is the matter with you?" she said. "Are you ill? Tell me!"

At last he declared with a serious air that her visits were becoming imprudent — that she was compromising herself.

X.

LOVERS' VOWS.

GRADUALLY Rodolphe's fears took possession of her. At first, love had intoxicated her, and she had thought of nothing beyond. But now that he was indispensable to her life, she feared to lose anything of this, or even that it should be disturbed. When she came back from his house, she looked all about her, anxiously watching every form that passed in the horizon, and every village window from which she could be seen. She listened for steps, cries, the noise of the ploughs, and she stopped short, white, and trembling more than the aspen leaves swaying overhead.

One morning as she was thus returning, she suddenly thought she saw the long barrel of a carbine that seemed to be aimed at her. It stuck out sideways from the end of a small tub half-buried in the grass on the edge of a ditch. Emma, half-fainting with terror, nevertheless walked on, and a man stepped out of the tub like a Jack-in-the-box. He had gaiters buckled up to the knees, his cap pulled down over his eyes, trembling lips, and a red nose. It was Captain Binet lying in ambush for wild ducks.

"You ought to have called out long ago!" he exclaimed. "When one sees a gun, one should always give warning."

The tax-collector was thus trying to hide the fright he had had, for a prefectorial order having prohibited duck-hunting except in boats, Monsieur Binet, despite his respect for the laws, was infringing them, and so he every moment expected to see the rural guard turn up. But this anxiety whetted his pleasure, and, all alone in his tub, he congratulated himself on his luck and on his cleverness.

At sight of Emma he seemed relieved from a great weight, and at once entered upon a conversation.

"It isn't warm; it's nipping."

Emma answered nothing. He went on—

"And you're out so early?"

"Yes," she said stammering; "I am just coming from the nurse where my child is."

"Ah! very good! very good! For myself, I am here, just as you see me, since break of day; but the weather is so muggy, that unless one had the bird at the mouth of the gun——"

"Good evening, Monsieur Binet," she interrupted him, turning on her heel.

"Your servant, madame," he replied drily; and he went back into his tub.

Emma regretted having left the tax-collector so abruptly. No doubt he would form unfavorable conjectures. The story about the nurse was the worst possible excuse, every one at Yonville knowing that the little Bovary had been at home with her parents for a year. Besides, no one was living in this direction; this path led only to La Huchette. Binet, then, would guess whence she came, and he would not keep silence; he would talk, that was certain. She remained until evening racking her brain with every conceivable lying project, and had constantly before her eyes that imbecile with the game-bag.

Charles after dinner, seeing her gloomy, proposed, by way of distraction, to take her to the chemist's, and the first person she caught sight of in the shop was the tax-collector again. He was standing in front of the counter, lighted by the gleams of the red bottle, and was saying:

"Please give me half an ounce of vitriol."

"Justin," cried the druggist, "bring us the sulphuric acid." Then to Emma, who was going up to Madame Homais' room, "No, stay here; it isn't worth while going up; she is just coming down. Warm yourself at the stove in the meantime. Excuse me. Good-day, doctor" (for the chemist much enjoyed pronouncing the word "doctor," as if addressing another by it reflected on himself some of the grandeur that he found in it). "Now, take care not to upset the mortars! You'd better fetch some chairs from the little room; you know very well that the arm-chairs are not to be taken out of the drawing-room."

And to put his arm-chair back in its place he was darting away from the counter, when Binet asked him for half an ounce of sugar acid.

"Sugar acid!" said the chemist contemptuously, "don't know it; I'm ignorant of it! But perhaps you want oxalic acid. It is oxalic acid, isn't it?"

Binet explained that he wanted a corrosive to make himself some copper-water with which to remove rust from his hunting things.

Emma shuddered. The chemist began, saying:

"Indeed the weather is not propitious on account of the damp."

"Nevertheless," replied the tax-collector, with a sly look, "there are people who like it."

She was stifling.

"And give me——"

"Will he never go?" thought she.

"Half an ounce of resin and turpentine, four ounces of yellow wax, and three half ounces of animal charcoal, if you please, to clean the varnished leather of my togs."

The chemist was beginning to cut the wax when Madame Homais appeared, Irma in her arms, Napoléon by her side, and Athalie following. She sat down on the velvet seat by the window, and the lad squatted down on a footstool, while his eldest sister hovered round the jujube box near her papa. The latter was filling funnels and corking phials, sticking on labels, making up parcels. Around him all were silent; only from time to time were heard the weights jingling in the balance, and a few low words from the chemist giving directions to his pupil.

"And how's the little woman?" suddenly asked Madame Homais.

"Silence!" exclaimed her husband, who was writing down some figures in his waste-book.

"Why didn't you bring her?" she went on in a low voice.

"Hush! hush!" said Emma, pointing with her finger to the chemist.

But Binet, quite absorbed in looking over his bill, had probably heard nothing. At last he went out. Then Emma, relieved, uttered a deep sigh.

"How hard you are breathing!" said Madame Homais.

"Well, you see, it's rather warm," she replied.

The next day the lovers discussed how to arrange their rendezvous. Emma wanted to bribe her servant with a present, but it would be better to find some safe house at Yonville. Rodolphe promised to look for one.

All through the winter, three or four times a week, in the dead of night he came to the garden. Emma had on purpose taken away the key of the gate, which Charles thought lost.

To call her, Rodolphe threw a sprinkle of sand at the shutters. She jumped up with a start; but sometimes he had to wait, for Charles had a mania for chatting by the fireside, and he would not stop. She was wild with impatience; if her eyes could have done it, she would have hurled him out at the window. At last she would begin to undress, then take up a book, and go on reading very quietly as if the book amused her. But Charles, who was in bed, called to her to come too.

"Come, now, Emma," he said, "it is time."

"Yes, I am coming," she answered.

Then, as the candles dazzled him, he turned to the wall and fell asleep. She escaped, smiling, palpitating, undressed.

Rodolphe had a large cloak; he wrapped her in it, and putting his arm around her waist, he drew her without a word to the end of the garden.

It was in the arbor, on the same seat of old sticks where formerly Léon had looked at her so amorously on the summer evenings. She never thought of him now.

The stars shone through the leafless jasmine branches. Behind them they heard the river flowing, and now and again on the bank the rustling of the dry reeds. Masses of shadow here and there loomed out in the darkness and sometimes, vibrating with one movement, they rose up and swayed like immense black waves pressing forward to engulf them. The cold of the nights made them clasp closer; the sighs of their lips seemed to them deeper; their eyes, that they could hardly see, larger; and in the midst of the silence low words were spoken that fell on their souls sonorous, crystalline, and reverberating in multiplied vibrations.

When the night was rainy, they took refuge in the consulting-room between the car-shed and the stable. She lighted one of the kitchen candles that she had hidden behind the books. Rodolphe settled down there as if at home. The sight of the library, of the bureau, of the whole apartment, in fine, excited his merriment, and he could not refrain from making jokes about Charles, which rather embarrassed Emma. She would have liked to see him more serious, and even on occasions more dramatic; as, for example, when she thought she heard a noise of approaching steps in the alley.

"Some one is coming!" she said.

He blew out the light.

"Have you your pistols?"

"Why?"

"Why, to defend yourself," replied Emma.

"From your husband? Oh, poor devil!" And Rodolphe finished his sentence with a gesture that said, "I could crush him with a flip of my finger."

She was wonder-stricken at his bravery, although

she felt in it a sort of indecency and a naïve coarseness that scandalized her.

Rodolphe reflected a good deal on the affair of the pistols. If she had spoken seriously, it was very ridiculous, he thought, even odious; for he had no reason to hate the good Charles, not being what is called devoured by jealousy; and on this subject Emma had treated him to a lecture, which he did not think in the best taste.

Besides, she was growing very sentimental. She had insisted on exchanging miniatures; they had cut handfuls of hair, and now she was asking for a ring —a real wedding-ring, in sign of an eternal union. She often spoke to him of the evening chimes, of the voices of nature. Then she talked to him of her mother—hers! and of his mother—his! Rodolphe had lost his twenty years ago. Emma none the less consoled him with caressing words as one would soothe a forsaken child, and she sometimes even said to him, gazing at the moon:

"I am sure that above there together they approve of our love."

But she was so pretty! He had possessed so few women of such ingenuousness. This love without debauchery was a new experience for him, and, drawing him out of his lazy habits, caressed at once his pride and his sensuality. Emma's enthusiasm, which his bourgeois good sense disdained, seemed to him in his heart of hearts charming, since it was lavished on him. Then, sure of being loved, he no longer kept up appearances, and insensibly his ways changed.

He had no longer, as formerly, words so gentle that they made her cry, nor passionate caresses that made her mad; so that their great love, which engrossed her life, seemed to lessen beneath her like the water of a stream absorbed into its channel, and she could see the bed of it. She would not believe it; she redoubled in tenderness, and Rodolphe concealed his indifference less and less.

She did not know whether she regretted yielding to him, or whether she did not wish, on the contrary, to enjoy him the more. The humiliation of feeling herself weak was turning to rancour, tempered by their voluptuous pleasures. It was not affection; it was like a continual seduction. He subjugated her; she almost feared him.

Appearances, nevertheless, were calmer than ever, Rodolphe having succeeded in carrying out the adultery after his own fancy; and at the end of six months, when the spring-time came, they were to one another like a married couple, tranquilly keeping up a domestic flame.

It was the time of year when old Rouault sent his turkey in remembrance of the setting of his leg. The present always arrived with a letter. Emma cut the string that tied it to the basket, and read the following lines:—

"MY DEAR CHILDREN,—I hope this will find you in good health, and that it will be as good as the others, for it seems to me a little more tender, if I may venture to say so, and heavier. But next time, for a change, I'll give you a turkey-cock, unless you have a preference for some dabs; and send me back the hamper, if you please, with the two old ones. I have had an accident with my cart-sheds, whose covering flew off one windy night among the trees. The harvest has not been over-good either.

Finally, I don't know when I shall come to see you. It is so difficult now to leave the house since I am alone, my poor Emma."

Here there was a break in the lines, as if the old fellow had dropped his pen to dream a little while.

"For myself, I am very well, except for a cold I caught the other day at the fair at Yvetot, where I had gone to hire a shepherd, having turned away mine because he was too dainty. How we are to be pitied with such a lot of thieves! Besides, he was also rude. I heard from a pedlar, who, traveling through your part of the country this winter, had a tooth drawn, that Bovary was as usual working hard. That doesn't surprise me; and he showed me his tooth; we had some coffee together. I asked him if he had seen you, and he said not, but that he had seen two horses in the stables, from which I conclude that business is looking up. So much the better, my dear children, and may God send you every imaginable happiness! It grieves me not yet to have seen my dear little grand-daughter, Berthe Bovary. I have planted an Orleans plum-tree for her in the garden under your room, and I won't have it touched unless it is to have jam made for her by-and-bye, that I will keep in the cupboard for when she comes.

"Good-bye my dear children. I kiss you, my girl, you too, my son-in-law, and the little one on both cheeks. I am, with best compliments, your loving father,

"THÉODORE ROUAULT."

She held the coarse paper in her fingers for some minutes. The mistakes in spelling interwove with one another, but Emma followed the kindly thought that chattered through it all like a hen half hidden in a hedge of thorns. The writing had been dried with ashes from the hearth, for a little grey powder slipped from the letter on to her dress, and she almost thought she saw her father bending over the hearth to take up the tongs. How long since she had been with him, sitting on the footstool in the chimney-corner, where she used to burn the end of a bit of wood in the great flame of the sea-sedges! She remembered the summer evenings all full of sunshine. The colts neighed when any one passed by, and galloped, galloped. Under her window there was a beehive, and sometimes the bees wheeling round in the light struck against her window like rebounding balls of gold. What happiness she had had at that time, what freedom, what hope! What an abundance of illusions! Nothing was left of them now. She had got rid of them all in her soul's life, in all her successive conditions of life, — maidenhood, her marriage, and her love; — thus constantly losing them all her life through, like a traveller who leaves something of his wealth at every inn along his road.

But what, then, made her so unhappy? What was the extraordinary catastrophe that had transformed her? And she raised her head, looking round as if to seek the cause of that which made her suffer.

An April ray was dancing on the china of the *étagère;* the fire burned; beneath her slippers she felt the softness of the carpet; the day was bright, the air warm, and she heard her child shouting with laughter.

In fact, the little girl was just then rolling on the lawn in the midst of the grass that was being turned.

She was lying flat on her stomach at the top of a rick. The servant was holding her by her skirt. Lestiboudois was raking by her side, and every time he came near she leant forward, beating the air with both her arms.

"Bring her to me," said her mother, rushing to embrace her. "How I love you, my poor child! How I love you!"

Then, noticing that the tips of her ears were rather dirty, she rang at once for warm water, and washed her, changed her linen, her stockings, her shoes, asked a thousand questions about her health, as if on the return from a long journey, and finally, kissing her again and crying a little, she gave her back to the servant, who stood quite thunder-stricken at this excess of tenderness.

That evening Rodolphe found her more serious than usual.

"That will pass over," he concluded; "it's a whim."

And he missed three rendezvous running. When he did come, she showed herself cold and almost contemptuous.

"Ah! you're losing your time, my lady!"

And he pretended not to notice her melancholy sighs, nor the handkerchief she took out.

Then Emma repented. She even asked herself why she detested Charles; if it had not been better to have been able to love him? But he gave her no opportunities for such a revival of sentiment, so that she was much embarrassed by her desire for sacrifice, when the chemist came just in time to provide her with an opportunity.

XI.

An Experiment and a Failure.

H E HAD recently read a eulogy on a new method for curing club-foot, and as he was a partisan of progress, he conceived the patriotic idea that Yonville, in order to keep to the fore, ought to have some operations for strephopody or club-foot.

"For," said he to Emma, "what risk is there? See" (and he enumerated on his fingers the advantages of the attempt), "success, almost certain relief and beautifying the patient, celebrity acquired by the operator. Why, for example, should not your husband relieve poor Hippolyte of the 'Lion d'Or'? Note that he would not fail to tell about his cure to all the travellers, and then" (Homais lowered his voice and looked round him), "who is to prevent me from sending a short paragraph on the subject to the paper? Eh! goodness me! an article gets about; it is talked of; it ends by making a snowball! And who knows? who knows?"

In fact, Bovary might succeed. Nothing proved to Emma that he was not clever; and what a satisfaction for her to have urged him to a step by which his reputation and fortune would be increased ! She only wished to lean on something more solid than love.

Charles, urged by the chemist and by her, allowed himself to be persuaded. He sent to Rouen for Dr. Duval's volume, and every evening, holding his head between both hands, plunged into the reading of it.

While he was studying equinus, varus, and valgus, that is to say, *katastrephopody, endostrephopody,* and *exostrephopody* (or better, the various turnings of the foot downwards, inwards, and outwards, with the *hypostrephopody* and *anastrephopody*), otherwise torsion downwards and upwards, Monsieur Homais, with all sorts of arguments, was exhorting the lad at the inn to submit to the operation.

"You will scarcely feel, probably, a slight pain ; it is a simple prick, like a little blood-letting, less than the extraction of certain corns."

Hippolyte, reflecting, rolled his stupid eyes.

"However," continued the chemist, "it doesn't concern me. It's for your sake, for pure humanity ! I should like to see you, my friend, rid of your hideous deformity, together with that waddling of the lumbar regions which, whatever you say, must considerably interfere with you in the exercise of your calling."

Then Homais represented to him how much jollier and brisker he would feel afterwards, and even gave him to understand that he would be more likely to please the women ; and the stable-boy began to smile heavily. Then he attacked him through his vanity : —

"Aren't you a man? Hang it ! what would you have done if you had had to go into the army, to go and fight beneath the standard? Ah ! Hippolyte !"

And Homais retired, declaring that he could not understand this obstinacy, this blindness in refusing the benefactions of science.

The poor fellow gave way, for it was like a conspiracy. Binet, who never interfered with other people's business, Madame Lefrançois, Artémise, the neighbors, even the mayor, Monsieur Tuvache — every one persuaded him, lectured him, shamed him; but what finally decided him was that it would cost him nothing. Bovary even undertook to provide the machine for the operation. This generosity was an idea of Emma's, and Charles consented to it, thinking in his heart of hearts that his wife was an angel.

So, by the advice of the chemist, and after three fresh starts, he had a kind of box made by the carpenter, with the aid of the locksmith, that weighed about eight pounds, in which iron, wood, sheet-iron, leather, screws, and nuts had not been spared.

But to know which of Hippolyte's tendons to cut, it was necessary first of all to find out what kind of club-foot he had.

He had a foot forming almost a straight line with the leg, which, however, did not prevent it from being turned in, so that it was an equinus together with something of a varus, or else a slight varus with a strong tendency to equinus. But with this equinus, wide in foot like a horse's hoof, with rugose skin, dry tendons, and large toes, on which the black nails looked as if made of iron, the club-foot ran about like a deer from morn till night. He was constantly to be seen on the Place, jumping around the carts, thrusting his limping foot forward. He seemed even stronger on that leg than the other. By dint of hard service it had acquired, as it were, moral qualities of patience and of energy; and when he was doing some heavy work, he stood on it in preference to its fellow.

Now, as it was an equinus, it was necessary to cut the tendo Achillis, and, if need were, the anterior tibial muscle could be seen to afterwards for getting rid of the varus; for the doctor did not dare to risk both operations at once; he was even trembling already for fear of injuring some important region that he did not know.

Neither Ambrose Paré, applying for the first time since Celsus, after an interval of fifteen centuries, a ligature to an artery, nor Dupuytren, about to open an abscess in the brain, nor Gensoul when he first took away the superior maxilla, had hearts that trembled, hands that shook, minds so strained as had the doctor when he approached Hippolyte, his tenotome between his fingers. And, as at hospitals, near by on a table lay a heap of lint, with waxed thread, many bandages — a pyramid of bandages — every bandage to be found at the chemist's. It was Monsieur Homais who since morning had been organising all these preparations, as much to dazzle the multitude as to keep up his illusions. Charles pierced the skin; a dry crackling was heard. The tendon was cut, the operation over. Hippolyte could not get over his surprise, but bent over Bovary's hands to cover them with kisses.

"Come, be calm," said the chemist; "later you will show your gratitude to your benefactor."

And he went down to tell the result to five or six inquirers who were waiting in the yard, and who fancied that Hippolyte would reappear walking properly. Then Charles, having buckled his patient into the machine, went home, where Emma, all anxiety, awaited him at the door. She threw herself on his neck; they sat down to table; he ate much, and at dessert he even wished to take a cup of coffee, a luxury·he permitted himself only on Sundays when there was company.

The evening was charming, full of prattle, of dreams together. They talked about their future fortune, of the improvements to be made in their house; he saw people's estimation of him growing, his comforts increasing, his wife always loving him; and she was happy to refresh herself with a new sentiment, healthier, better, to feel at last some tenderness for this poor fellow who adored her. The thought of Rodolphe for one moment passed through her mind, but her eyes turned again to Charles; she even noticed with surprise that he had not bad teeth.

They were in bed when Monsieur Homais, in spite of the servant, suddenly entered the room, holding·in his hand a sheet of paper just written. It was the paragraph he intended for the "Fanal de Rouen." He brought it them to read.

"Read it yourself," said Bovary.

He read:

"'Despite the prejudices that still cover a part of the face of Europe like a net, the light nevertheless begins to penetrate our country places. Thus on Tuesday our little town of Yonville found itself the scene of a surgical operation which is at the same time an act of loftiest philanthropy. Monsieur Bovary, one of our most distinguished practitioners——'"

"Oh, that is too much! too much!" said Charles, choking with emotion.

"No, no! not at all! What next!"

"'——Performed an operation on a club-footed man.' I have not used the scientific term, because you know in a newspaper every one would not perhaps understand. The masses must——"

"No doubt," said Bovary; "go on!"

"I proceed," said the chemist. "'Monsieur Bovary, one of our most distinguished practitioners, performed an operation on a club-footed man called Hippolyte Tautain, stable-man for the last twenty-five years at the hotel of the "Lion d'Or," kept by Widow Lefrançois, at the Place d'Armes. The novelty of the attempt, and the interest incident to the subject, had attracted such a concourse of persons that there was a veritable obstruction on the threshold of the establishment. The operation, moreover, was performed as if by magic, and barely a few drops of blood appeared on the skin, as if to show that the rebellious tendon had at last given way beneath the efforts of art. The patient, strangely enough—we affirm it as an eye-witness—complained of no pain. His condition up to the present time leaves nothing to be desired. Everything tends to show that his convalescence will be brief; and who knows whether, at our next village festivity, we shall not see our good Hippolyte figuring in the bacchic dance in the midst of a chorus of joyous boon-companions, and thus proving to all eyes by his verve and his capers his complete cure? Honor, then, to the generous savants! Honor to those indefatigable spirits who consecrate their vigils to the amelioration or to the alleviation of their kind! Honor, thrice honor! Is it not time to cry that the blind shall see, the deaf hear, the lame walk? But that which fanaticism formerly promised to its elect, science now accomplishes for all men. We shall keep our readers informed as to the successive phases of this remarkable cure.'"

This did not prevent Mère Lefrançois from coming five days after, scared, and crying out —

"Help! he is dying! I am going crazy!"

Charles rushed to the "Lion d'Or," and the chemist, who caught sight of him passing along the Place hatless, abandoned his shop. He appeared himself breathless, red, anxious, and asking every one who was going up the stairs —

"Why, what's the matter with our interesting strephopode?"

The strephopode was writhing in hideous convulsions, so that the machine in which his leg was enclosed was knocked against the wall enough to break it.

With many precautions, in order not to disturb the position of the limb, the box was removed, and an awful sight presented itself. The outlines of the foot disappeared in such a swelling that the entire skin seemed about to burst, and it was covered with ecchymosis, caused by the famous machine. Hippolyte had already complained of suffering from it. No attention had been paid to him; they had to acknowledge that he had not been altogether wrong, and he was freed for a few hours. But hardly had the œdema gone down to some extent, than the two savants thought fit to put back the limb in the apparatus, strapping it tighter to hasten matters. At last, three days after, Hippolyte being unable to endure it any longer, they once more removed the machine, and were much surprised at the result they saw. The livid tumefaction spread over the leg, with blisters here and there, whence oozed a black liquid. Matters were taking a serious turn. Hippolyte began to worry himself, and Mère Lefrançois had him installed in the little room near the kitchen, so that he might at least have some distraction.

But the tax-collector, who dined there every day, complained bitterly of such companionship. Then Hippolyte was removed to the billiard-room. He lay there moaning under his heavy coverings, pale, with long beard, sunken eyes, and from time to time turning his perspiring head on the dirty pillow, where the flies alighted. Madame Bovary went to see him. She brought him linen for his poultices; she comforted and encouraged him. Besides, he did not want for company, especially on market-days, when the peasants were knocking about the billiard-balls round him, fenced with the cues, smoked, drank, sang, and brawled.

"How are you?" they said, clapping him on the shoulder. "Ah! you're not up to much, it seems, but it's your own fault. You should do this! do that!" And then they told him stories of people who had all been cured by other remedies than his. Then by way of consolation they added:—

"You give way too much! Get up! You coddle yourself like a king! All the same, old chap, you don't smell nice!"

Gangrene, in fact, was spreading more and more. Bovary himself turned sick at it. He came every hour, every moment. Hippolyte looked at him with eyes full of terror, sobbing—

"When shall I get well? Oh, save me! How unfortunate I am! how unfortunate I am!"

And the doctor left, always recommending him to diet himself.

"Don't listen to him, my lad," said Mère Lefrançois. "Haven't they tortured you enough already?
You'll grow still weaker. Here! swallow this."

And she gave him some good beef-tea, a slice of
mutton, a piece of bacon, and sometimes small glasses
of brandy, that he had not the strength to put to his
lips.

Abbé Bournisien, hearing that he was growing
worse, asked to see him. He began by pitying his
sufferings, declaring at the same time that he ought
to rejoice at them since it was the will of the Lord,
and take advantage of the occasion to reconcile himself to Heaven.

"For," said the ecclesiastic in a paternal tone,
"you rather neglected your duties; you were rarely
seen at divine worship. How many years is it since
you approached the holy table? I understand that
your work, that the whirl of the world may have
kept you from care for your salvation. But now is
the time to reflect. Yet don't despair. I have known
great sinners, who, about to appear before God (you
are not yet at this point, I know), had implored His
mercy, and who certainly died in the best frame of
mind. Let us hope that, like them, you will set us a
good example. Thus, as a precaution, what is to
prevent you from saying morning and evening a
'Hail Mary, full of grace,' and 'Our Father which art
in heaven'? Yes, do that, for my sake, to oblige
me. That won't cost you anything. Will you prom-
ise me?"

The poor devil promised. The curé came back
day after day. He chatted with the landlady, and
even told anecdotes interspersed with jokes and puns
that Hippolyte did not understand. Then, as soon as

he could, he fell back upon matters of religion, putting on an appropriate expression of face.

His zeal seemed successful, for the club-foot soon manifested a desire to go on a pilgrimage to Bon-Secours if he were cured; to which Monsieur Bournisien replied that he saw no objection; two precautions were better than one; it was no risk.

The chemist was indignant at what he called the manœuvres of the priest; they were prejudicial, he said, to Hippolyte's convalescence, and he kept repeating to Madame Lefrançois, "Leave him alone! leave him alone! You perturb his morals with your mysticism."

But the good woman would no longer listen to him; he was the cause of it all. From a spirit of contradiction she hung up near the bedside of the patient a basin filled with holy-water and a branch of box.

Religion, however, seemed no more able to succour him than surgery, and the invincible gangrene still spread from the extremities towards the stomach. It was all very well to vary the potions and change the poultices; the muscles each day rotted more and more; and at last Charles replied by an affirmative nod of the head when Mère Lefrançois asked him if she could not, as a forlorn hope, send for Monsieur Canivet of Neufchâtel, who was a celebrity.

A doctor of medicine, fifty years of age, enjoying a good position and self-possessed, Charles's colleague did not refrain from laughing disdainfully when he had uncovered the leg, mortified to the knee. Then having flatly declared that it must be amputated, he went off to the chemist's to rail at the asses who could have reduced a poor man to such a state.

Shaking Monsieur Homais by the button of his coat, he shouted out in the shop:

"These are the inventions of Paris! These are the ideas of those gentry of the capital! It is like strabismus, chloroform, lithotrity, a heap of monstrosities that the Government ought to prohibit. But they want to do the clever, and they cram you with remedies without troubling about the consequences. We are not so clever, not we! We are not savants, coxcombs, fops! We are practitioners; we cure people, and we should not dream of operating on any one who is in perfect health. Straighten club-feet! As if one could straighten club-feet! It is as if one wished, for example, to make a hunchback straight!"

Homais suffered as he listened to this discourse, and he concealed his discomfort beneath a courtier's smile; for he needed to humour Monsieur Canivet, whose prescriptions sometimes came as far as Yonville. So he did not take up the defense of Bovary; he did not even make a single remark, and, renouncing his principles, he sacrificed his dignity to the more serious interests of his business.

This amputation of the thigh by Doctor Canivet was a great event in the village. On that day all the inhabitants got up earlier, and the Grande Rue, although full of people, had something lugubrious about it, as if an execution had been expected. At the grocer's they discussed Hippolyte's illness; the shops did no business, and Madame Tuvache, the mayor's wife, did not stir from her window, such was her impatience to see the operator arrive.

He came in his gig, which he drove himself. But the springs of the right side having at length given way beneath the weight of his corpulence, it happened that the carriage as it rolled along leaned over a little, and on the other cushion near him could be seen a large box covered in red sheep-leather, whose three brass clasps shone grandly.

After he had entered like a whirlwind the porch of the "Lion d'Or," the doctor, shouting very loud, ordered them to unharness his horse. Then he went into the stable to see that he was eating his oats all right; for on arriving at a patient's he first of all looked after his mare and his gig. People even said about this:

"Ah! Monsieur Canivet's a character!"

And he was the more esteemed for this imperturbable coolness. The universe to the last man might have died, and he would not have missed the smallest of his habits.

Homais presented himself.

"I count on you," said the doctor. "Are we ready? Come along!"

But the chemist, turning red, confessed that he was too sensitive to assist at such an operation.

"When one is a simple spectator," he said, "the imagination, you know, is impressed. And then I have such a nervous system!"

"Pshaw!" interrupted Canivet; "on the contrary, you seem to me inclined to apoplexy. Besides, that doesn't astonish me, for you chemist fellows are always poking about your kitchens, which must end by spoiling your constitutions. Now just look at me. I get up every day at four o'clock; I shave with cold water (and am never cold). I don't wear flannels, and I never catch cold; my carcass is good enough! I live now in one way, now in another, like a philosopher, taking pot-luck; that is why I am not squeamish like you, and it is as indifferent to me to carve a Christian as the first fowl that turns up. Then, perhaps, you will say, habit! habit!"

Then, without any consideration for Hippolyte, who was sweating with agony between his sheets, these gentlemen entered into a conversation, in which the chemist compared the coolness of a surgeon to that of a general; and this comparison was pleasing to Canivet, who launched out on the exigencies of his art. He looked upon it as a sacred office, although the ordinary practitioners dishonoured it. At last, coming back to the patient, he examined the bandages brought by Homais, the same that had appeared for the club-foot, and asked for some one to hold the limb for him. Lestiboudois was sent for, and Monsieur Canivet having turned up his sleeves, passed into the billiard-room, while the chemist stayed with Artémise and the landlady, both whiter than their aprons, and with ears strained towards the door.

Bovary during this time did not dare to stir from his house. He kept downstairs in the sitting-room by the side of the fireless chimney, his chin on his breast, his hands clasped, his eyes staring. "What a mishap!" he thought, "what a mishap!" Perhaps, after all, he had made some slip. He thought it over, but could hit upon nothing. But the most famous surgeons also made mistakes; and that is what no one would ever believe! People, on the contrary, would laugh, jeer! It would spread as far as Forges, as Neufchâtel, as Rouen, everywhere! Who could say if his colleagues would not write against him. Polemics would ensue; he would have to answer in the papers. Hippolyte might even prosecute him. He saw himself dishonored, ruined, lost; and his imagination, assailed by a world of hypotheses, tossed amongst them like an empty cask borne by the sea and floating upon the waves.

Emma, opposite, watched him; she did not share his humiliation; she felt another—that of having supposed such a man was worth anything. As if twenty times already she had not sufficiently perceived his mediocrity.

Charles was walking up and down the room; his boots creaked on the floor.

"Sit down," she said; "you fidget me."

He sat down again.

How was it that she—she, who was so intelligent—could have allowed herself to be deceived again? and through what deplorable madness had she thus ruined her life by continual sacrifices? She recalled all her instincts of luxury, all the privations of her soul, the sordidness of marriage, of the household, her dream sinking into the mire like wounded swallows; all that she had longed for, all that she had denied herself, all that she might have had! And for what? for what?

In the midst of the silence that hung over the village a heart-rending cry rose on the air. Bovary turned white to fainting. She knit her brows with a nervous gesture, then went on. And it was for him, for this creature, for this man, who understood nothing, who felt nothing! For he was there quite quiet, not even suspecting that the ridicule of his name would henceforth sully hers as well as his. She had made efforts to love him, and she had repented with tears for having yielded to another!

"But it was perhaps a valgus!" suddenly exclaimed Bovary, who was meditating.

At the unexpected shock of this phrase falling on her thought like a leaden bullet on a silver plate, Emma, shuddering, raised her head in order to find out what he meant to say; and they looked one at the other in silence, almost amazed to see each other, so far sundered were they by their inner thoughts. Charles gazed at her with the dull look of a drunken man, while he listened motionless to the last cries of the sufferer, that followed each other in long-drawn modulations, broken by sharp spasms like the far-off howling of some beast being slaughtered. Emma bit her wan lips, and rolling between her fingers a piece of coral that she had broken, fixed on Charles the burning glance of her eyes like two arrows of fire about to dart forth. Everything in him irritated her now; his face, his dress, what he did not say, his whole person, his existence, in fine. She repented of her past virtue as of a crime, and what still remained of it crumbled away beneath the furious blows of her pride. She revelled in all the evil ironies of triumphant adultery. The memory of her lover came back to her with dazzling attractions; she threw her whole soul into it, borne away towards this image with a fresh enthusiasm; and Charles seemed to her as much removed from her life, as absent for ever, as impossible and annihilated, as if he had been about to die and were passing under her eyes.

There was a sound of steps on the pavement. Charles looked up, and through the lowered blinds he saw at the corner of the market in the broad sunshine Dr. Canivet, who was wiping his brow with his handkerchief. Homais, behind him, was carrying a large red box in his hand, and both were going towards the chemist's.

Then with a feeling of sudden tenderness and discouragement Charles turned to his wife saying to her:

"Oh, kiss me, my own!"

"Leave me!" she said, red with anger.

"What is the matter?" he asked, stupefied. "Be calm; compose yourself. You know well enough that I love you. Come!"

"Enough!" she cried with a terrible look.

And escaping from the room, Emma closed the door so violently that the barometer fell from the wall and smashed on the floor.

Charles sank back into his arm-chair overwhelmed, trying to discover what could be wrong with her, fancying some nervous illness, weeping, and vaguely feeling something fatal and incomprehensible whirling round him.

When Rodolphe came to the garden that evening, he found his mistress waiting for him at the foot of the steps on the lowest stair. They threw their arms round one another, and all their rancour melted like snow beneath the warmth of that kiss.

XII.

Preparations for Flight.

T HEY began to love one another again. Often, even in the middle of the day, Emma suddenly wrote to him, then from the window made a sign to Justin, who, taking his apron off, quickly ran to La Huchette. Rodolphe would come; she had sent for him to tell him that she was bored; that her husband was odious, her life frightful.

"But what can I do?" he cried one day impatiently.

"Ah! if you would—

She was sitting on the floor between his knees, her hair loose, her look lost.

"Why, what?" said Rodolphe.

She sighed.

"We would go and live elsewhere—somewhere!"

"You are really mad!" he said laughing. "How could that be possible?"

She returned to the subject; he pretended not to understand, and turned the conversation.

What he did not understand was all this worry about so simple an affair as love. She had a motive, a reason, and, as it were, a pendant to her affection.

(233)

Her tenderness, in fact, grew each day with her repulsion to her husband. The more she gave up herself to the one, the more she loathed the other. Never had Charles seemed to her so disagreeable, to have such stodgy fingers, such vulgar ways, to be so dull as when they found themselves together after her meeting with Rodolphe. Then, while playing the spouse and virtue, she was burning at the thought of that head whose black hair fell in a curl over the sun-burnt brow, of that form at once so strong and elegant, of that man, in a word, who had such experience in his reasoning, such passion in his desires. It was for him that she filed her nails with the care of a chaser, and that there was never enough cold-cream for her skin, nor of patchouli for her handkerchiefs. She loaded herself with bracelets, rings, and necklaces. When he was coming she filled the two large blue glass vases with roses, and prepared her room and her person like a courtesan expecting a prince. The servant had to be constantly washing linen, and all day Félicité did not stir from the kitchen, where little Justin, who often kept her company, watched her at work.

With his elbows on the long board on which she was ironing, he greedily watched all these women's clothes spread out about him, the dimity petticoats, the fichus, the collars, and the drawers with running strings, wide at the hips and growing narrower below.

"What is that for?" asked the young fellow, passing his hand over the crinoline or the hooks and eyes.

"Why, haven't you ever seen anything?" Félicité answered laughing. "As if your mistress, Madame Homais, didn't wear the same."

"Oh, I daresay! Madame Homais!" And he added with a meditative air, "As if she were a lady like madame!"

But Félicité grew impatient of seeing him hanging round her. She was six years older than he, and Théodore, Monsieur Guillaumin's servant, was beginning to pay court to her.

"Let me alone," she said, moving her pot of starch. "You'd better be off and pound almonds; you are always dangling about women. Before you meddle with such things, bad boy, wait till you've got a beard to your chin."

"Oh, don't be cross! I'll go and clean her boots."

And he at once took down from the shelf Emma's boots, all coated with mud, the mud of the rendez-vous, that crumbled into powder beneath his fingers, and that he watched as it gently rose in a ray of sunlight.

"How afraid you are of spoiling them!" said the servant, who wasn't so particular when she cleaned them herself, because as soon as the stuff of the boots was no longer fresh madame handed them over to her.

Emma had many shoes in her closet that she wore out one after the other, without Charles allowing himself the slightest observation. So also he disbursed three hundred francs for a wooden leg that she thought proper to make a present of to Hippolyte. Its top was covered with cork, and it had spring joints, a complicated mechanism, covered over by black trousers ending in a patent-leather boot. But Hippolyte, not daring to use such a handsome leg every day, begged Madame Bovary to get him another more convenient one. The doctor, of course, had again to defray the expense of this purchase.

So little by little the stable-man took up his work again. One saw him running about the village as before, and when Charles heard from afar the sharp noise of the wooden leg, he at once went in another direction.

It was Monsieur Lheureux, the shopkeeper, who had undertaken the order; this provided him with an excuse for visiting Emma. He chatted with her about the new goods from Paris, about a thousand feminine trifles, made himself very obliging, and never asked for his money. Emma yielded to this lazy mode of satisfying all her caprices. Thus she wanted to have a very handsome riding-whip that was at an umbrella-maker's at Rouen, to give to Rodolphe. The week after Monsieur Lheureux placed it on her table.

But the next day he called on her with a bill for two hundred and seventy francs, not counting the centimes. Emma was much embarrassed; all the drawers of the writing-table were empty; they owed over a fortnight's wages to Lestiboudois, two quarters to the servant, for any quantity of other things, and Bovary was impatiently expecting Monsieur Derozerays' account, which he was in the habit of paying him every year about midsummer.

She succeeded at first in putting off Lheureux. At last he lost patience; he was being sued; his capital was out, and unless he got some in he should be forced to take back all the goods she had received.

"Oh, very well, take them!" said Emma.

"I was only joking," he replied; "the only thing I regret is the whip. My word! I'll ask monsieur to return it to me."

"No, no!" she said.

"Ah! I've got you!" thought Lheureux.

And, certain of his discovery, he went out repeating to himself in an undertone, and with his usual low whistle:

"Good! we shall see! we shall see!"

She was thinking how to get out of this when the servant coming in put on the mantelpiece a small roll of blue paper "from Monsieur Derozerays." Emma pounced upon and opened it. It contained fifteen napoleons; it was the account. She heard Charles on the stairs; threw the gold to the back of her drawer, and took out the key.

Three days after Lheureux reappeared.

"I have an arrangement to suggest to you," he said. "If, instead of the sum agreed on, you would take——"

"Here it is," she said, placing fourteen napoleons in his hand.

The tradesman was astounded. Then, to conceal his disappointment, he was profuse in apologies and proffers of service, all of which Emma declined; then she remained a few moments fingering in the pocket of her apron the two five-franc pieces that he had given her in change. She promised herself she would economise in order to pay back later on. "Pshaw!" she thought, "he won't think about it again."

Besides the riding-whip with its silver-gilt handle, Rodolphe had received a seal with the motto *Amor nel cor;* furthermore, a scarf for a muffler, and, finally, a cigar-case exactly like the Viscount's, that Charles had formerly picked up in the road, and that Emma had kept. These presents, however, humiliated him; he refused several; she insisted, and he ended by obeying, thinking her tyrannical and over-exacting.

Then she had strange ideas.

"When midnight strikes," she said, "you must think of me."

And if he confessed that he had not thought of her, there were floods of reproaches that always ended with the eternal question:

"Do you love me?"

"Why, of course I love you," he answered.

"A great deal?"

"Certainly!"

"You haven't loved any others?"

"Did you think you'd got a virgin?" he exclaimed laughing.

Emma wept, and he tried to console her, adorning his protestations with puns.

"Oh," she went on, "I love you! I love you so that I could not live without you, do you see? There are times when I long to see you again, when I am torn by all the anger of love. I ask myself, where is he? Perhaps he.is talking to other women. They smile upon him; he approaches. Oh no! no one else pleases you. There are some more beautiful, but I love you best. I know how to love best. I am your servant, your concubine! You are my king, my idol! You are good, you are beautiful, you are clever, you are strong!"

He had so often heard these things said that they did not strike him as original. Emma was like all his mistresses; and the charm of novelty, gradually falling away like a garment, laid bare the eternal monotony of passion, that has always the same forms and the same language. He did not distinguish, this man of so much experience, the difference of sentiment beneath the sameness of expression. Because lips libertine and venal had murmured such words to him, he believed but little in the candour of hers; exaggerated speeches hiding mediocre affections must be discounted; as if the fulness of the soul did not sometimes overflow in the emptiest metaphors, since no one can ever give the exact measure of his needs, nor of his conceptions, nor of his sorrows; and since human speech is like a cracked tin kettle, on which we hammer out tunes to make bears dance when we long to move the stars.

But with that superior critical judgment that belongs to him, who, in no matter what circumstance, holds back, Rodolphe saw other delights to be got out of this love. He thought all modesty in the way. He treated her quite *sans façon*. He made of her something supple and corrupt. Hers was an idiotic sort of attachment, full of admiration for him, of voluptuousness for her, a beatitude that benumbed her; her soul sank into this drunkenness, shrivelled up, drowned in it, like Clarence in his butt of Malmsey.

By the mere effect of her love Madame Bovary's manners changed. Her looks grew bolder, her speech more free; she even committed the impropriety of walking out with Monsieur Rodolphe, a cigarette in her mouth, "as if to defy the people." At last those who still doubted doubted no longer when one day they saw her getting out of the "Hirondelle" her waist squeezed into a waistcoat like a man; and Madame Bovary senior, who, after a fearful scene with her husband, had taken refuge at her son's, was not the least scandalised of the women-folk. Many other things displeased her. First, Charles had not attended to her advice about the forbidding of novels; then the "ways of the house" annoyed her; she allowed herself to make some remarks, and there were quarrels, especially one on account of Félicité.

Madame Bovary senior, the evening before, passing along the passage, had surprised her in company of a man — a man with a brown collar, about forty years old, who, at the sound of her step, had quickly escaped through the kitchen. Then Emma began to laugh, but the good lady grew angry, declaring that unless morals were to be laughed at one ought to look after those of one's servants.

"Where were you brought up?" asked the daughter-in-law, with so impertinent a look that Madame Bovary asked her if she were not perhaps defending her own case.

"Leave the room!" said the young woman, springing up with a bound.

"Emma! Mamma!" cried Charles, trying to reconcile them.

But both had fled in their exasperation. Emma was stamping her feet as she repeated —

"Oh! what manners! What a peasant!"

He ran to his mother; she was beside herself. She stammered:

"She is an insolent, giddy-headed thing, or perhaps worse!"

And she was for leaving at once if the other did not apologize.

So Charles went back again to his wife and implored her to give way; he knelt to her; she ended by saying —

"Very well! I'll go to her.

And in fact she held out her hand to her mother-in-law with the dignity of a marchioness as she said:

"Excuse me, madame."

Then having gone up again to her room, she threw herself flat on her bed and cried there like a child, her face buried in the pillow.

She and Rodolphe had agreed that in the event of anything extraordinary occurring, she should fasten a small piece of white paper to the blind, so that if by chance he happened to be in Yonville, he could hurry to the lane behind the house. Emma made the signal; she had been waiting three-quarters of an hour when she suddenly caught sight of Rodolphe at the corner of the market. She felt tempted to open the window and call him, but he had already disappeared. She fell back in despair.

Soon, however, it seemed to her that some one was walking on the pavement. It was he, no doubt. She went downstairs, crossed the yard. He was there outside. She threw herself into his arms.

"Do take care!" he said.

"Ah! if you knew!" she replied.

And she began telling him everything, hurriedly, disjointedly, exaggerating the facts, inventing many, and so prodigal of parentheses that he understood nothing of it.

"Come, my poor angel, courage! Be comforted! be patient!"

"But I have been patient; I have suffered for four years. A love like ours ought to show itself in the face of heaven. They torture me! I can bear it no longer! Save me!"

She clung to Rodolphe. Her eyes, full of tears, flashed like flames beneath a wave; her breast heaved;

he had never loved her so much, so that he lost his head and said:

"What is it? What do you wish?"

"Take me away," she cried, "carry me off! Oh, I entreat you!"

And she threw herself upon his mouth, as if to seize there the unexpected consent it breathed forth in a kiss.

"But——" Rodolphe resumed.

"What?"

"Your little girl!"

She reflected a few moments, then replied—

"We will take her! It can't be helped!"

"What a woman!" he said to himself, watching her as she went. For she had run into the garden. Some one was calling her.

On the following days Madame Bovary senior was much surprised at the change in her daughter-in-law. Emma, in fact, was showing herself more docile, and even carried her deference so far as to ask for a recipe for pickling gherkins.

Was it the better to deceive them both? Or did she wish by a sort of voluptuous stoicism to feel the more profoundly the bitterness of the things she was about to leave?

But she paid no heed to them; on the contrary, she lived as if lost in the anticipated delight of her coming happiness. It was an eternal subject for conversation with Rodolphe. She leant on his shoulder murmuring—

"Ah! when we are in the mail-coach! Do you think about it? Can it be? It seems to me that the moment I feel the carriage start, it will be as if we were rising in a balloon, as if we were setting out for the clouds. Do you know that I count the hours? And you?"

Never had Madame Bovary been so beautiful as at this period; she had that indefinable beauty that results from joy, from enthusiasm, from success, and that is only the harmony of temperament with circumstances. Her desires, her sorrows, the experience of pleasure, and her ever-young illusions, that had, as soil and rain and winds and the sun make flowers grow, gradually developed her, and she at length blossomed forth in all the plenitude of her nature. Her eyelids seemed chiselled expressly for her long amorous looks in which the pupil disappeared, while a strong inspiration expanded her delicate nostrils and raised the fleshy corner of her lips, shaded in the light by a little black down. One would have thought that an artist apt in conception had arranged the curls of hair upon her neck; they fell in a thick mass, negligently, and with the changing chances of their adultery, that unbound them every day. Her voice now took more mellow inflections, her figure also; something subtle and penetrating escaped even from the folds of her gown and from the line of her foot. Charles, as when they were first married, thought her delicious and quite irresistible.

When he came home in the middle of the night, he did not dare to wake her. The porcelain nightlight threw a round trembling gleam upon the ceiling, and the drawn curtains of the little cot formed, as it were, a white hut standing out in the shade, and by the bedside Charles looked at them. He seemed to hear the light breathing of his child. She would grow big now; every season would bring rapid progress. He already saw her coming from school as the day drew in, laughing, with ink-stains on her jacket, and carrying her basket on her arm. Then she would have to be sent to a boarding-school; that would cost much; how was it to be done? Then he reflected. He thought of hiring a small farm in the neighborhood, that he would superintend every morning on his way to his patients. He would save up what he brought in; he would put it in the savings-bank. Then he would buy shares somewhere, no matter where; besides, his practice would increase; he counted upon that, for he wanted Berthe to be well-educated, to be accomplished, to learn to play the piano. Ah! how pretty she would be later on when she was fifteen, when, resembling her mother, she would, like her, wear large straw hats in the summer-time; from a distance they would be taken for two sisters. He pictured her to himself working in the evening by their side beneath the light of the lamp; she would embroider him slippers; she would look after the house; she would fill all the home with her charm and her gaiety. At last, they would think of her marriage; they would find her some good young fellow with a steady business; he would make her happy; this would last for ever.

Emma was not asleep; she pretended to be; and while he dozed off by her side she awakened to other dreams.

To the gallop of four horses she was carried away for a week towards a new land, whence they would return no more. They went on and on, their arms entwined, without a word. Often from the top of a mountain there suddenly glimpsed some splendid city with domes, and bridges, and ships, forests of citron trees, and cathedrals of white marble, on whose pointed steeples were storks' nests. They went at a walking-pace because of the great flag-stones, and on the ground there were bouquets of flowers, offered you by women dressed in red bodices. They heard the chiming of bells, the neighing of mules, together with the murmur of guitars and the noise of fountains, whose rising spray refreshed heaps of fruit arranged like a pyramid at the foot of pale statues that smiled beneath playing waters. And then, one night they came to a fishing village, where brown nets were drying in the wind along the cliffs and in front of the huts. It was there that they would stay; they would live in a low, flat-roofed house, shaded by a palm-tree, in the heart of a gulf, by the sea. They would row in gondolas, swing in hammocks, and their existence would be easy and large as their silk gowns, warm and star-spangled as the nights they would contemplate. However, in the immensity of this future that she conjured up, nothing special stood forth; the days, all magnificent, resembled each other like waves; and it swayed in the horizon, infinite, harmonized, azure, and bathed in sunshine. But the child began to cough in her cot or Bovary snored more loudly, and Emma did not fall asleep till morning, when the dawn whitened the window, and when little Justin was already in the square taking down the shutters of the chemist's shop.

She had sent for Monsieur Lheureux, and had said to him—

"I want a cloak—a large lined cloak with a deep collar."

"You are going on a journey?" he asked.

"No; but—never mind. I may count on you, may I not, and quickly?"

He bowed.

"Besides, I shall want," she went on, "a trunk—not too heavy—handy."

"Yes, yes, I understand. About three feet by a foot and a half, as they are being made just now."

"And a travelling bag."

"Decidedly," thought Lheureux, "there's a row on here."

"And," said Madame Bovary, taking her watch from her belt, "take this; you can pay yourself out of it."

But the tradesman cried out that she was wrong; they knew one another; did he doubt her? What childishness!

She insisted, however, on his taking at least the chain, and Lheureux had already put it in his pocket and was going, when she called him back.

"You will leave everything at your place. As to the cloak"—she seemed to be reflecting—"do not bring it either; you can give me the maker's address, and tell him to have it ready for me."

It was the next month that they were to run away. She was to leave Yonville as if she was going on some business to Rouen. Rodolphe would have booked the seats, procured the passports, and even have written to Paris in order to have the whole mail-coach reserved for them as far as Marseilles, where they would buy a carriage, and go on thence without stopping to Genoa. She would take care to send her luggage to Lheureux', whence it would be taken direct to the "Hirondelle," so that no one would have any suspicion. And in all this there never was any allusion to the child. Rodolphe avoided speaking of her; perhaps he no longer thought about it.

He wished to have two more weeks before him to arrange some affairs; then at the end of a week he wanted two more; then he said he was ill; next he went on a journey. The month of August passed, and, after all these delays, they decided that it was to be irrevocably fixed for the 4th September — a Monday.

At length the Saturday before arrived.

Rodolphe came in the evening earlier than usual.

"Everything is ready?" she asked him.

"Yes."

Then they walked round a garden-bed, and went to sit down near the terrace on the curb-stone of the wall.

"You are sad," said Emma.

"No; why?"

And yet he looked at her strangely in a tender fashion.

"Is it because you are going away?" she went on; "because you are leaving what is dear to you — your life? Ah! I understand. I have nothing in the world! You are all to me; so shall I be to you. I will be your people, your country; I will tend, I will love you!"

"How sweet you are!" he said, seizing her in his arms.

"Really!" she said with a voluptuous laugh. "Do you love me? Swear it then!"

"Do I love you — love you? I adore you, my love!"

The moon, full and purple-colored, was rising right out of the earth at the end of the meadow. She rose quickly between the branches of the poplars, that hid her here and there like a black curtain pierced with holes. Then she appeared dazzling with whiteness in the empty heavens that she lit up, and now sailing more slowly along, let fall upon the river a great stain that broke up into an infinity of stars; and the silver sheen seemed to writhe through the very depths like a headless serpent covered with luminous scales; it also resembled some monster candelabra all along which sparkled drops of diamonds running together. The soft night was about them; masses of shadow filled the branches. Emma, her eyes half-closed, breathed in with deep sighs the fresh wind that was blowing. They did not speak, lost as they were in the rush of their reverie. The tenderness of the old days came back to their hearts, full and silent as the flowing river, with the softness of the perfume of the syringas, and threw across their memories shadows more immense and more sombre than those of the still willows that lengthened out over the grass. Often some night-animal, hedgehog or weasel, setting out on the hunt, disturbed the lovers, or sometimes they heard a ripe peach falling all alone from the espalier.

"Ah! what a lovely night!" said Rodolphe.

"We shall have others," replied Emma; and, as if speaking to herself, "Yes, it will be good to travel. And yet, why should my heart be so heavy? Is it dread of the unknown? The effect of habits left? Or rather——? No; it is the excess of happiness. How weak I am, am I not? Forgive me!"

"There is still time!" he cried. "Reflect! perhaps you may repent!"

"Never!" she cried impetuously. And coming closer to him: "What ill could come to me? There is no desert, no precipice, no ocean I would not traverse with you. The longer we live together the more it will be like an embrace, every day closer, more heart to heart. There will be nothing to trouble us, no care, no obstacle. We shall be alone, all to ourselves eternally. Oh, speak! Answer me!"

At regular intervals he answered, "Yes — Yes —" She had passed her hands through his hair, and she repeated in a childlike voice, despite the big tears which were falling, "Rodolphe! Rodolphe! Ah! Rodolphe! dear little Rodolphe!"

Midnight struck.

"Midnight!" said she. "Come! it is to-morrow! One day more!"

He rose to go; and as if the movement he made had been the signal for their flight, Emma said, suddenly, assuming a gay air —

"You have the passports?"

"Yes."

"You are forgetting nothing?"

"No."

"Are you sure?"

"Certainly."

"It is at the Hôtel de Provence, is it not, that you will wait for me at mid-day?"

He nodded.

"Till to-morrow then!" said Emma, in a last caress; and she watched him go.

He did not turn round. She ran after him, and, leaning over the water's edge between the bulrushes —

"To-morrow!" she cried.

He was already on the other side of the river and walking fast across the meadow.

After a few moments Rodolphe stopped; and when he saw her with her white gown gradually fade away in the shade like a ghost, he was seized with such a beating of the heart that he leant against a tree lest he should fall.

"What an imbecile I am!" he said with a fearful oath. "No matter! she was a pretty mistress!"

And immediately Emma's beauty, with all the pleasures of their love, came back to him. For a moment he softened; then he rebelled against her.

"For, after all," he exclaimed gesticulating, "I can't exile myself—have a child on my hands."

He was saying these things to give himself firmness.

"And besides, the worry, the expense! Ah! no, no, no, no! a thousand times no! It would have been too stupid."

XIII.

Deserted.

O SOONER was Rodolphe at home than he sat down quickly at his bureau under the stag's head that hung as a trophy on the wall. But when he had the pen between his fingers, he could think of nothing, so that, resting on his elbows, he began to reflect. Emma seemed to him to have receded into a far-off past, as if the resolution he had taken had suddenly placed a distance between them.

To get back something of her, he fetched from the cupboard at the bedside an old Rheims biscuit-box, in which he usually kept his letters from women, and from it came an odor of dry dust and withered roses. First he saw a handkerchief with pale little spots. It was a handkerchief of hers. Once when they were walking her nose had bled ; he had forgotten it. Near it, chipped at all the corners, was a miniature given him by Emma : her toilette seemed to him pretentious, and her languishing look in the worst possible taste. Then, from looking at this image and recalling the memory of its original, Emma's features little by little grew confused in his remembrance, as if the living and the painted face, rubbing one against the other, had effaced each other. Finally, he read some of her letters; they were full of explanations relating to their journey, short, technical, and urgent, like business notes. He wanted to see the long ones again, those of old times. In order to find them at the bottom of the box, Rodolphe disturbed all the others, and mechanically began rumaging amidst this mass of papers and things, finding pell-mell bouquets, garters, a black mask, pins, and hair—hair! dark and fair, some even, catching in the hinges of the box, broke when it was opened.

Thus dallying with his souvenirs, he examined the writing and the style of the letters, as varied as their orthography. They were tender or jovial, facetious, melancholy; there were some that asked for love, others that asked for money. A word recalled faces to him, certain gestures, the sound of a voice; sometimes, however, he remembered nothing at all.

In fact, these women, rushing at once into his thoughts, cramped each other and lessened, as reduced to a uniform level of love that equalized them all. So taking handfuls of the mixed-up letters, he amused himself for some moments with letting them fall in cascades from his right into his left hand. At last, bored and weary, Rodolphe took back the box to the cupboard, saying to himself, "What a lot of rubbish!" Which summed up his opinion; for pleasures, like schoolboys in a school courtyard, had so trampled upon his heart that no green thing grew there, and that which passed through it, more heedless than children, did not even, like them, leave a name carved upon the wall.

"Come," said he, "let's begin."

He wrote —

"Courage, Emma! courage! I would not bring misery into your life."

"After all, that's true," thought Rodolphe. "I am acting in her interest; I am honest."

"Have you carefully weighed your resolution? Do you know to what an abyss I was dragging you, poor angel? No, you do not, do you? You were coming confident and fearless, believing in happiness in the future. Ah! unhappy that we are — insensate!"

Rodolphe stopped here to think of some good excuse.

"If I told her all my fortune is lost? No! Besides that would stop nothing. It would all have to be begun over again later on. As if one could make women like that listen to reason!" He reflected, then went on —

"I shall not forget you, oh! believe it; and I shall ever have a profound devotion for you; but some day, sooner or later, this ardour (such is the fate of human things) would have grown less, no doubt. Lassitude would have come to us, and who knows if I should not even have had the atrocious pain of witnessing your remorse, of sharing it myself, since I should have been its cause? The mere idea of the grief that would come to you tortures me, Emma. Forget me! Why did I ever know you? Why were you so beautiful? Is it my fault? O my God! No, no! accuse only fate."

"That's a word that always tells," he said to himself.

"Ah! if you had been one of those frivolous women that one sees, certainly I might, through egotism, have made an experiment, in that case without danger for you. But that delicious exaltation, at once your charm and your torment, has prevented you from understanding, adorable woman that you are, the falseness of our future position. Nor had I reflected upon this at first, and I rested in the shade of that ideal happiness as beneath that of the manchineel tree, without foreseeing the consequences."

"Perhaps she'll think I'm giving it up from avarice. Ah, well! so much the worse; it must be stopped!"

"The world is cruel, Emma. Wherever we might have gone, it would have persecuted us. You would have had to put up with indiscreet questions, calumny, contempt, insult, perhaps. Insult to you! Oh! And I, who would place you on a throne! I who bear with me your memory as a talisman! For I am going to punish myself by exile for all the ill I have done you. I am going away. Whither I know not. I am mad. Adieu! Be good always. Preserve the memory of the unfortunate who has lost you. Teach my name to your child; let her repeat it in her prayers."

The wicks of the candles flickered. Rodolphe got up to shut the window, and when he had sat down again —

"I think it's all right. Ah! and this for fear she should come and hunt me up."

"I shall be far away when you read these sad lines, for I have wished to flee as quickly as possible to shun the temptation of seeing you again. No weakness! I shall return, and perhaps later we shall talk together very coldly of our old love. Adieu!"

And there was a last 'adieu' divided into two words: "A Dieu!" which he thought in very excellent taste.

"Now how am I to sign?" he said to himself. "'Yours devotedly?' No! 'Your friend?' Yes, that's it."

"YOUR FRIEND."

He re-read his letter. He considered it very good. "Poor little woman!" he thought with emotion. "She'll think me harder than a rock. There ought to have been some tears on this; but I can't cry; it isn't my fault." Then, having emptied some water into a glass, Rodolphe dipped his finger into it, and let a big drop fall on the paper, that made a pale stain on the ink. Then looking for a seal, he came upon the one "*Amor nel cor.*"

"That doesn't at all fit in with the circumstances. Pshaw! never mind!"

After which he smoked three pipes and went to bed.

The next day when he was up (at about two o'clock—he had slept late), Rodolphe had a basket of apricots picked. He put his letter at the bottom under some vine leaves, and at once ordered Girard, his ploughman, to take it with care to Madame Bovary. He made use of this means for corresponding with her, sending according to the season fruits or game.

"If she asks after me," he said, "you will tell her that I have gone on a journey. You must give the basket to her herself, into her own hands. Get along and take care!"

Girard put on his new blouse, knotted his handkerchief round the apricots, and, walking with great heavy steps in his thick iron-bound galoshes, made his way to Yonville.

Madame Bovary, when he got to her house was arranging a bundle of linen on the kitchen-table with Félicité.

"Here," said the ploughboy, "is something for you from master."

She was seized with apprehension, and as she sought in her pocket for some coppers, she looked at the peasant with haggard eyes, while he himself looked at her with amazement, not understanding how such a present could so move any one. At last he went out. Félicité remained. Emma could bear it no longer; she ran into the sitting-room as if to take the apricots there, overturned the basket, tore away the leaves, found the letter, opened it, and, as if some fearful fire were behind her, she flew to her room terrified.

Charles was there; she saw him; he spoke to her; she heard nothing, and she went on quickly up the stairs, breathless, distraught, dumb, and ever holding this horrible piece of paper, that crackled between her fingers like a plate of sheet-iron. On the second floor she stopped before the attic-door, that was closed.

Then she tried to calm herself; she recalled the letter; she must finish it; she did not dare to. And

where? How? She would be seen! "Ah, no! here,"
she thought, "I shall be all right."

Emma pushed open the door and went in.

The slates threw straight down a heavy heat that
gripped her temples, stifled her; she dragged herself
to the closed garret-window. She drew back the
bolt, and the dazzling light burst in with a leap.

Opposite, beyond the roofs, stretched the open
country until it was lost to the sight. Underneath
her, the village square was empty; the stones of the
pavement glittered, the weathercocks on the houses
were motionless. At the corner of the street, from a
lower story, rose a kind of humming with strident
modulations. It was Binet turning.

She leant against the embrasure of the window, and
re-read the letter with angry sneers. But the more
she fixed her attention upon it, the more confused
were her ideas. She saw him again, heard him, en-
circled him with her arms, and the throbs of her
heart, that beat against her breast like blows of a
sledge-hammer, grew faster and faster, with uneven
intervals. She looked about her with the wish that
the earth might crumble into pieces. Why not end
it all? What restrained her? She was free. She advanced, looked at the paving-stones, saying to herself,
"Come! come!"

The luminous ray that came straight up from below
drew the weight of her body towards the abyss. It
seemed to her that the ground of the oscillating
square went up the walls, and that the floor dipped
on end like a tossing boat. She was right at the
edge, almost hanging, surrounded by vast space. The
blue of the heavens suffused her, the air was whirling
in her hollow head; she had but to yield, to let her-

self be taken; and the humming of the lathe never ceased, like an angry voice calling her.

"Emma! Emma!" cried Charles.

She stopped.

"Wherever are you? Come!"

The thought that she had just escaped from death almost made her faint with terror. She closed her eyes; then she shivered at the touch of a hand on her sleeve; it was Félicité.

"Master is waiting for you, madame; the soup is on the table."

And she had to go down to sit at table.

She tried to eat. The food choked her. Then she unfolded her napkin as if to examine the darns, and she really thought of applying herself to this work, counting the threads in the linen. Suddenly the remembrance of the letter returned to her. How had she lost it? Where could she find it? But she felt such weariness of spirit that she could not even invent a pretext for leaving the table. Then she became a coward; she was afraid of Charles; he knew all, that was certain! Indeed he pronounced these words in a strange manner:

"We are not likely to see Monsieur Rodolphe soon again, it seems."

"Who told you?" she said, shuddering.

"Who told me!" he replied, rather astonished at her abrupt tone. "Why, Girard, whom I met just now at the door of the Café-Français. He has gone on a journey, or is to go."

She gave a sob.

"What surprises you in that? He absents himself like that from time to time for a change, and, ma foi, I think he's right, when one has a fortune and is a bachelor. Besides, he has jolly times, has our friend. He's a bit of a rake. Monsieur Langlois told me——"

He stopped for propriety's sake because the servant came in. She put back into the basket the apricots scattered on the sideboard. Charles, without noticing his wife's color, had them brought to him, took one, and bit into it.

"Ah! perfect!" said he; "just taste!"

And he handed her the basket, which she put away from her gently.

"Do just smell! What an odor!" he remarked, passing it under her nose several times.

"I am choking," she cried, leaping up. But by an effort of will the spasm passed; then—

"It is nothing," she said, "it is nothing! It is nervousness. Sit down and go on eating." For she dreaded lest he should begin questioning her, attending to her, that she should not be left alone.

Charles, to obey her, sat down again, and he spat the stones of the apricots into his hands, afterwards putting them on his plate.

Suddenly a blue tilbury passed across the square at a rapid trot. Emma uttered a cry and fell back rigid to the ground.

In fact, Rodolphe, after many reflections, had decided to set out for Rouen. Now, as from La Huchette to Buchy there is no other way than by Yonville, he had to go through the village, and Emma had recognized him by the rays of the lanterns, which like lightning flashed through the twilight.

The chemist, at the tumult which broke out in the house, ran thither. The table with all the plates was upset; sauce, meat, knives, the salt, and cruet-

stand were strewn over the room; Charles was calling for help; Berthe, scared, was crying; and Félicité,
whose hands trembled, was unlacing her mistress,
whose whole body shivered convulsively.

"I'll run to my laboratory for some aromatic vinegar," said the chemist.

Then as she opened her eyes on smelling the bottle:

"I was sure of it," he remarked; "that would
wake any dead person for you!"

"Speak to us," said Charles; "collect yourself; it
is I — your Charles, who loves you. Do you know
me? See! here is your little girl! Oh, kiss her!"

The child stretched out her arms to her mother to
cling to her neck. But turning away her head, Emma
said in a broken voice —

"No, no! no one!"

She fainted again. They carried her to her bed.
She lay there stretched at full length, her lips apart,
her eyelids closed, her hands open, motionless, and
white as a waxen image. Two streams of tears flowed
from her eyes and fell slowly upon the pillow.

Charles, standing up, was at the back of the alcove, and the chemist, near him, maintained that
meditative silence that is becoming on the serious occasions of life.

"Do not be uneasy," he said, touching his elbow;
"I think the paroxysm is past."

"Yes, she is resting a little now," answered
Charles, watching her sleep. "Poor girl! poor girl!
She has gone off now!"

Then Homais asked how the accident had come
about. Charles answered that she had been taken ill
suddenly while she was eating some apricots

"Extraordinary!" continued the chemist. "But it might be that the apricots had brought on the syncope. Some natures are so sensitive to certain smells; and it would even be a very fine question to study both in its pathological and physiological relation. The priests know the importance of it, they who have introduced aromatics into all their ceremonies. It is to stupefy the senses and to bring on ecstasies — a thing, moreover, very easy in persons of the weaker sex, who are more delicate than the other. Some are cited who faint at the smell of burnt hartshorn, of new bread——"

"Take care ; you'll wake her!" said Bovary in a low voice.

"And not only," the chemist went on, "are human beings subject to such anomalies, but animals also. Thus you are not ignorant of the singularly aphrodisiac effect produced by the *Nepeta cataria,* vulgarly called cat-mint, on the feline race ; and, on the other hand, to quote an example whose authenticity I can answer for, Bridaux (one of my old comrades, at present established in the Rue Malpalu) possesses a dog that falls into convulsions as soon as you hold out a snuff-box to him. He often even makes the experiment before his friends at his summer-house at Guillaume Wood. Would any one believe that a simple sternutation could produce such ravages on a quadrupedal organism? It is extremely curious, is it not?"

"Yes," said Charles, who was not listening to him.

"This shows us," went on the other, smiling with benign self-sufficiency, "the innumerable irregularities of the nervous system. With regard to madame, she has always seemed to me, I confess, very susceptible. And so I should by no means recommend to you, my dear friend, any of those so-called remedies that, under the pretence of attacking the symptoms, attack the constitution. No; no useless physicking! Diet, that is all; sedatives, emollients, dulcification. Then, don't you think that perhaps her imagination should be worked upon?"

"In what way? How?" said Bovary.

"Ah! that is it. Such is indeed the question. 'That is the question,' as I lately read in a newspaper."

But Emma, awaking, cried out—

"The letter! the letter!"

They thought she was delirious; and she was by midnight. Brain-fever had set in.

For forty-three days Charles did not leave her. He gave up all his patients; he no longer went to bed; he was constantly feeling her pulse, putting on sinapisms and cold-water compresses. He sent Justin as far as Neufchâtel for ice; the ice melted on the way; he sent him back again. He called Monsieur Canivet into consultation; he sent for Dr. Larivière, his old master, from Rouen; he was in despair. What alarmed him most was Emma's prostration, for she did not speak, did not listen, did not even seem to suffer, as if her body and soul were both resting together after all their troubles.

About the middle of October she could sit up in bed supported by pillows. Charles wept when he saw her eat her first bread-and-jelly. Her strength returned to her; she got up for a few hours of an afternoon, and one day, when she felt better, he tried to take her, leaning on his arm, for a walk round the garden. The sand of the paths was disappearing beneath the dead leaves; she walked slowly, dragging along her slippers, and leaning against Charles's shoulder. She smiled all the time.

They went thus to the bottom of the garden near the terrace. She drew herself up slowly, shading her eyes with her hand to look. She looked far off, as far as she could, but on the horizon were only great bonfires of grass smoking on the hills.

"You will tire yourself, my darling!" said Bovary. And pushing her gently to make her go into the arbour, "Sit down on this seat; you'll be comfortable."

"Oh! no; not there!" she said in a faltering voice.

She was seized with giddiness, and from that evening her illness recommenced, with a more uncertain character, it is true, and more complex symptoms. Now she suffered in her heart, then in the chest, the head, the limbs; she had vomitings, in which Charles thought he saw the first signs of cancer.

And besides this, the poor fellow was worried about money matters.

XIV.

O BEGIN with, he did not know how he could pay Monsieur Homais for all the physic supplied by him, and though, as a medical man, he was not obliged to pay for it, he nevertheless blushed a little at such an obligation. Then the expenses of the household, now that the servant was mistress, became terrible. Bills rained in upon the house; the tradesmen grumbled; Monsieur Lheureux especially harassed him. In fact, at the height of Emma's illness, the latter, taking advantage of the circumstances to make his bill larger, had hurriedly brought the cloak, the travelling-bag, two trunks instead of one, and a number of other things. It was very well for Charles to say he did not want them. The tradesman answered arrogantly that these articles had been ordered, and that he would not take them back; besides, it would vex madame in her convalescence; the doctor had better think it over; in short, he was resolved to sue him rather than give up his rights and take back his goods. Charles subsequently ordered them to be sent back to the shop. Félicité forgot; he had other things to attend to; then thought no more about them. Monsieur Lheureux returned to the charge, and, by turns threatening and whining, so managed that Bovary ended by signing a bill at six months. But hardly had he signed this bill than a bold idea occurred to him: it was to borrow a thousand francs from Lheureux. So, with an embarrassed air, he asked if it were possible to get them, adding that it would be for a year, at any interest he wished. Lheureux ran off to his shop, brought back the money and dictated another bill, by which Bovary undertook to pay to his order on the 1st of September next the sum of one thousand and seventy francs, which, with the hundred and eighty already agreed to, made just twelve hundred and fifty, thus lending at six per cent. in addition to one-fourth for commission; and the things bringing him in a good third at the least, this ought in twelve months to give him a profit of a hundred and thirty francs. He hoped that the business would not stop there; that the bills would not be paid; that they would be renewed; and that his poor little money, having thriven at the doctor's as at a hospital, would come back to him one day considerably more plump, and fat enough to burst his bag.

Everything, moreover, succeeded with him. He was adjudicator for a supply of cider to the hospital at Neufchâtel; Monsieur Guillaumin promised him some shares in the turf-pits of Gaumesnil, and he dreamt of establishing a new diligence service between Arcueil and Rouen, which no doubt would not be long in ruining the ramshackle van of the "Lion d'Or," and that, travelling faster, at a cheaper rate, and carrying more luggage, would thus put into his hands the whole commerce of Yonville.

Charles several times asked himself by what means he should next year be able to pay back so much money. He reflected, imagined expedients, such as applying to his father or selling something. But his father would be deaf, and he—he had nothing to sell. Then he foresaw such worries that he quickly dismissed so disagreeable a subject of meditation from his mind. He reproached himself with forgetting Emma, as if, all his thoughts belonging to this woman, it was robbing her of something not to be constantly thinking of her.

The winter was severe, Madame Bovary's convalescence slow. When it was fine they wheeled her arm-chair to the window that overlooked the square, for she now had an antipathy to the garden, and the blinds on that side were always down. She wished the horse to be sold; what she formerly liked now displeased her. All her ideas seemed to be limited to the care of herself. She stayed in bed taking little meals, rang for the servant to inquire about her gruel or to chat with her. The snow on the market-roof threw a white, still light into the room; then the rain began to fall; and Emma waited daily with a mind full of eagerness for the inevitable return of some trifling events which nevertheless had no relation to her. The most important was the arrival of the "Hirondelle" in the evening. Then the landlady shouted out, and other voices answered, while Hippolyte's lantern, as he fetched the boxes from the boot, was like a star in the darkness. At mid-day Charles came in; then he went out again; next she took some beef-tea, and towards five o'clock, as the day drew in, the children coming back from school, dragging their wooden shoes along the pavement, knocked the clapper of the shutters with their rulers one after the other.

It was at this hour that Monsieur Bournisien came to see her. He inquired after her health, gave her news, exhorted her to religion in a coaxing little gossip that was not without its charm. The mere thought of his cassock comforted her.

One day, when at the height of her illness, she had thought herself dying, and had asked for the communion; and, while they were making the preparations in her room for the sacrament, while they were turning the night-table covered with sirups into an altar, and while Félicité was strewing dahlia flowers on the floor, Emma felt some power passing over her that freed her from her pains, from all perception, from all feeling. Her body, relieved, no longer thought; another life was beginning; it seemed to her that her being, mounting toward God, would be annihilated in that love like a burning incense that melts into vapour. The bed-clothes were sprinkled with holy water, the priest drew from the holy pyx the white wafer; and it was fainting with a celestial joy that she put out her lips to accept the body of the Saviour presented to her. The curtains of the alcove floated gently round her like clouds, and the rays of the two tapers burning on the night-table seemed to shine like dazzling halos. Then she let her head fall back, fancying she heard in space the music of seraphic harps, and perceived in an azure sky, on a golden throne in the midst of saints holding green palms, God the Father, resplendent with majesty, who with a sign sent to earth angels with wings of fire to carry her away in their arms.

This splendid vision dwelt in her memory as the

most beautiful thing that it was possible to dream, so that now she strove to recall her sensation, that still lasted, however, but in a less exclusive fashion and with a deeper sweetness. Her soul, tortured by pride, at length found rest in Christian humility, and, tasting the joy of weakness, she saw within herself the destruction of her will, that must have left a wide entrance for the inroads of heavenly grace. There existed, then, in the place of happiness, still greater joys,—another love beyond all loves, without pause and without end, one that would grow eternally! She saw amid the illusions of her hope a state of purity floating above the earth mingling with heaven, to which she aspired. She wanted to become a saint. She bought chaplets and wore amulets; she wished to have in her room, by the side of her bed, a reliquary set in emeralds that she might kiss it every evening.

The curé marvelled at this humour, although Emma's religion, he thought, might, from its fervour, end by touching on heresy, extravagance. But not being much versed in these matters, as soon as they went beyond a certain limit he wrote to Monsieur Boulard, bookseller to Monsignor, to send him "something good for a lady who was very clever." The bookseller, with as much indifference as if he had been sending off hardware to niggers, packed up, pell-mell, everything that was then the fashion in the pious book trade. There were little manuals in questions and answers, pamphlets of aggressive tone after the manner of Monsieur de Maistre, and certain novels in rose-coloured bindings and with a honied style, manufactured by troubadour seminarists or penitent blue-stockings. There were the "Think of it; the

Man of the World at Mary's Feet, by Monsieur de
* * *, *décoré* with many Orders;" "The Errors of
Voltaire, for the Use of the Young," &c.

Madame Bovary's mind was not yet sufficiently
clear to apply herself seriously to anything; moreover, she began this reading in too much hurry. She
grew provoked at the doctrines of religion; the arro-
gance of the polemic writings displeased her by their
inveteracy in attacking people she did not know;
and the secular stories, relieved with religion, seemed
to her written in such ignorance of the world, that
they insensibly estranged her from the truths for
whose proof she was looking. Nevertheless, she
persevered; and when the volume slipped from her
hands, she fancied herself seized with the finest Cath-
olic melancholy that an ethereal soul could conceive.

As for the memory of Rodolphe, she had thrust it
back to the bottom of her heart, and it remained there
more solemn and more motionless than a king's
mummy in a catacomb. An exhalation escaped from
this embalmed love, that, penetrating through everything, perfumed with tenderness the immaculate
atmosphere in which she longed to live. When she
knelt on her Gothic prie-Dieu, she addressed to the
Lord the same suave words that she had murmured
formerly to her lover in the outpourings of adultery.
It was to make faith come; but no delights descended
from the heavens, and she arose with tired limbs and
with a vague feeling of a gigantic dupery.

This searching after faith, she thought, was only
one merit the more, and in the pride of her devout-
ness Emma compared herself to those grand ladies of
long ago whose glory she had dreamed of over a
portrait of La Vallière, and who, trailing with so

much majesty the lace-trimmed trains of their long gowns, retired into solitudes to shed at the feet of Christ all the tears of hearts that life had wounded.

Then she gave herself up to excessive charity. She sewed clothes for the poor, she sent wood to women in childbed; and Charles one day, on coming home, found three good-for-nothings in the kitchen seated at the table eating soup. She had her little girl, whom during her illness her husband had sent back to the nurse, brought home. She wanted to teach her to read; even when Berthe cried, she was not vexed. She had made up her mind to resignation, to universal indulgence. Her language about everything was full of ideal expressions. She said to her child, "Is your stomach-ache better, my angel?"

Madame Bovary senior found nothing to censure except perhaps this mania of knitting jackets for orphans instead of mending her own house-linen; but, harassed with domestic quarrels, the good woman took pleasure in this quiet house, and she even staid there till after Easter, to escape the sarcasms of old Bovary, who never failed on Good Friday to order chitterlings.

Besides the companionship of her mother-in-law, who strengthened her a little by the rectitude of her judgment and her grave ways, Emma almost every day had other visitors. These were Madame Langlois, Madame Caron, Madame Dubreuil, Madame Tuvache, and regularly from two to five o'clock the excellent Madame Homais, who, for her part, had never believed any of the tittle-tattle about her neighbor. The little Homais also came to see her; Justin accompanied them. He went up with them to her bed-room, and remained standing near the door, motionless and mute. Often even Madame Bovary, taking no heed of him, began her toilette. She began by taking out her comb, shaking her head with a quick movement, and when he for the first time saw all this mass of hair that fell to her knees unrolling in black ringlets, it was to him, poor child! like a sudden entrance into something new and strange, whose splendour terrified him.

Emma, no doubt, did not notice his silent attentions or his timidity. She had no suspicion that the love vanished from her life was there, palpitating by her side, beneath that coarse holland shirt, in that youthful heart open to the emanations of her beauty. Besides, she now enveloped all things with such indifference, she had words so affectionate with looks so haughty, such contradictory ways, that one could no longer distinguish egotism from charity, or corruption from virtue. One evening, for example, she was angry with the servant, who had asked to go out, and stammered as she tried to find some pretext. Then suddenly—

"So you love him?" she said.

And without waiting for any answer from Félicité, who was blushing, she added, "There! run along; enjoy yourself!"

In the beginning of spring she had the garden turned up from end to end, despite Bovary's remonstrances. However, he was glad to see her at last manifest a wish of any kind. As she grew stronger she displayed more wilfulness. First, she found occasion to expel Mère Rollet, the nurse, who during her convalescence had contracted the habit of coming too often to the kitchen with her two nurslings and her boarder, better off for teeth than a cannibal. Then she got rid of the Homais family, successively dismissed all the other visitors, and even frequented church less assiduously, to the great approval of the chemist, who said to her in a friendly way —

"You were going in a bit for the cassock!"

As formerly, Monsieur Bournisien dropped in every day when he came out after catechism class. He preferred staying out of doors to taking the air "in the grove," as he called the arbour. This was the time when Charles came home. They were hot; some sweet cider was brought out, and they drank together to madame's complete restoration.

Binet was there; that is to say, a little lower down against the terrace wall, fishing for cray-fish. Bovary invited him to have a drink, and he thoroughly understood the uncorking of the stone bottles.

"You must," he said, throwing a satisfied glance all round him, even to the very extremity of the landscape, "hold the bottle perpendicularly on the table, and after the strings are cut, press up the cork with little thrusts, gently, gently, as indeed they do seltzer-water at restaurants."

But during his demonstration the cider often spurted right into their faces, and then the ecclesiastic, with a thick laugh, never missed this joke —

"It's goodness strikes the eye!"

He was, in fact, a good fellow, and one day he was not even scandalised at the chemist, who advised Charles to give madame some distraction by taking her to the theatre at Rouen to hear the illustrious tenor, Lagardy. Homais, surprised at this silence, wanted to know his opinion, and the priest declared that he considered music less dangerous for morals than literature.

But the chemist took up the defence of letters. The theatre, he contended, served for railing at prejudices, and, beneath a mask of pleasure, taught virtue. "*Castigat ridendo mores,* Monsieur Bournisien! Thus, consider the greater part of Voltaire's tragedies; they are cleverly strewn with philosophical reflections, that make them a very school of morals and diplomacy for the people."

"I," said Binet, "once saw a piece called the 'Gamin de Paris,' in which there was the character of an old general that is really hit off to a T. He sets down a young swell who had seduced a working girl, who at the end——"

"Certainly," continued Homais, "there is bad literature as there is bad pharmacy, but to condemn in a lump the most important of the fine arts seems to me a stupidity, a Gothic idea, worthy of the abominable times that imprisoned Galileo."

"I know very well," objected the curé, "that there are good works, good authors. However, if it were only those persons of different sexes together in a bewitching apartment, decorated with worldly pomp, and then, those pagan disguises, that rouge, those lights, those effeminate voices, all this must, in the long run, engender a certain mental libertinage, give rise to immodest thoughts, and impure temptations. Such, at any rate, is the opinion of all the Fathers. Finally," he added, suddenly assuming a mystic tone of voice, while he rolled a pinch of snuff between his fingers, "if the Church has condemned the theatre, she must be right; we must submit to her decrees."

"Why," asked the chemist, "should she excommunicate actors? For formerly they openly took part in religious ceremonies.　Yes, in the middle of the chancel they acted; they performed a kind of farce called 'Mysteries,' which often offended against the laws of decency."

The ecclesiastic contented himself with uttering a groan, and the chemist went on —

"It's just as it is in the Bible; for there, you know, are more than one piquant detail, matters really libidinous!"

And on a gesture of irritation from Monsieur Bournisien —

"Ah! you'll admit that it is not a book to place in the hands of a young girl, and I should be sorry if Athalie —— "

"But it is the Protestants, and not we," cried the other impatiently, "who recommend the Bible."

"No matter," said Homais. "I am surprised that in our days, in this century of enlightenment, any one should still persist in proscribing an intellectual relaxation that is inoffensive, moralising, and sometimes even hygienic; is it not, doctor?"

"No doubt," replied the doctor carelessly, either because, sharing the same ideas, he wished to offend no one, or else because he had not any ideas.

The conversation seemed at an end when the chemist thought fit to shoot a Parthian arrow.

"I've known priests who put on ordinary clothes to go and see dancers kicking about."

"Come, come!" said the curé.

"Ah! I've known some!" And separating the words of his sentence, Homais repeated, "I — have — known — some!"

"Well, they did wrong," said Bournisien, resigned to anything.

"By Jove! they go in for more than that," exclaimed the chemist.

"Sir!" replied the ecclesiastic, with such angry eyes that Homais was intimidated by them.

"I only mean to say," he replied in less brutal a tone, "that toleration is the surest way to draw people to religion."

"That is true! that is true!" agreed the good fellow, sitting down again on his chair. But he stayed only a few moments.

Then, as soon as he had gone, Monsieur Homais said to the doctor—

"That's what I call a cock-fight. I beat him, did you see, in a way!—Now take my advice. Take madame to the theatre, if it were only for once in your life, to enrage one of these ravens, hang it! If any one could take my place, I would accompany you myself. Be quick about it. Lagardy is only going to give one performance; he's engaged to go to England at a high salary. From what I hear, he's a regular dog; he's rolling in money; he's taking three mistresses and a cook along with him. All these great artists burn the candle at both ends; they require a dissolute life, that stirs the imagination to some extent. But they die at the hospital, because they haven't the sense when young to lay by. Well, a pleasant dinner! Good-bye till to-morrow."

The idea of the theatre quickly germinated in Bovary's head, for he at once communicated it to his wife, who at first refused, alleging the fatigue, the worry, the expense; but, for a wonder, Charles did not give in, so sure was he that this recreation would be good for her. He saw nothing to prevent it: his mother had sent them three hundred francs which he had no longer expected; the current debts were not very large, and the falling in of Lheureux's bills was still so far off that there was no need to think about them. Besides, imagining that she was refusing from delicacy, he insisted the more; so that by dint of worrying her she at last made up her mind, and the next day at eight o'clock they set out in the "Hirondelle."

The chemist, whom nothing whatever kept at Yonville, but who thought himself bound not to budge from it, sighed as he saw them go.

"Well, a pleasant journey!" he said to them; "happy mortals that you are!"

Then addressing himself to Emma, who was wearing a blue silk gown with four flounces—

"You are as lovely as a Venus. You'll cut a figure at Rouen."

The diligence stopped at the "Croix-Rouge" in the Place Beauvoisine. It was the inn that is in every provincial faubourg, with large stables and small bedrooms, where one sees in the middle of the court chickens pilfering the oats under the muddy gigs of the commercial travellers;—a good old house with worm-eaten balconies that creak in the wind on winter nights, always full of people, noise, and feeding, whose black tables are sticky with coffee and brandy, the thick windows made yellow by the flies, the damp napkins stained with cheap wine, and that always smells of the village, like ploughboys dressed in Sunday-clothes, has a café on the street, and towards the country-side a kitchen-garden. Charles at once set out. He muddled up the stage-boxes with the gallery, the pit with the boxes: asked for explanations, did not understand them; was sent from the box-office to the acting-manager; came back to the inn, returned to the theatre, and thus several times traversed the whole length of the town from the theatre to the boulevard.

Madame Bovary bought a bonnet, gloves, and a bouquet. The doctor was much afraid of missing the beginning, and, without having had time to swallow a plate of soup, they presented themselves at the doors of the theatre, which were still closed.

XV.

A New Delight.

HE crowd was waiting against the wall, symmetrically enclosed between the balustrades. At the corner of the neighbouring streets huge bills repeated in quaint letters "Lucia de Lammermoor — Lagardy — Opera — &c." The weather was fine, the people were hot, perspiration trickled amid the curls, and handkerchiefs taken from pockets were mopping red foreheads ; and now and again a warm wind that blew from the river gently stirred the border of the tick awnings hanging from the doors of the public-houses. A little lower down, however, one was refreshed by a current of icy air that smelt of tallow, leather, and oil. This was an exhalation from the Rue des Charrettes, full of large black ware-houses where they make casks.

For fear of seeming ridiculous, Emma before going in wished to have a little stroll in the harbour, and Bovary prudently kept his tickets in his hand, in the pocket of his trousers, which he pressed against his stomach.

Her heart began to beat as soon as she reached the vestibule. She involuntarily smiled with vanity on seeing the crowd rushing to the right by the

other corridor while she went up the staircase to the
reserved seats. She was as pleased as a child to push
with her finger the large tapestried door. She
breathed in with all her might the dusty smell of the
lobbies, and when she was seated in her box she
bent forward with the air of a duchess.

The theatre was beginning to fill; opera-glasses
were taken from their cases, and the subscribers,
catching sight of one another, were bowing. They
came to seek relaxation in the fine arts after the
anxieties of business; but "business" was not forgotten; they still talked cotton, spirits of wine, or indigo.
The heads of old men were to be seen, inexpressive
and peaceful, with their hair and complexions looking
like silver medals tarnished by steam of lead. The
young beaux were strutting about in the pit, showing
in the opening of their waistcoats their pink or apple-
green cravats, and Madame Bovary from above admired them leaning on their canes with golden knobs
in the open palm of their yellow gloves.

Now the lights of the orchestra were lit, the lustre,
let down from the ceiling, throwing by the glimmering of its facets a sudden gaiety over the theatre;
then the musicians came in one after the other; and
first there was the protracted hubbub of the basses
grumbling, violins squeaking, cornets trumpeting, flutes
and flageolets fifing. But three knocks were heard on
the stage, a rolling of drums began, the brass instruments played some chords, and the curtain rising,
discovered a country-scene.

It was the cross-roads of a wood, with a fountain
shaded by an oak to the left. Peasants and lords
with plaids on their shoulders were singing a hunting-
song together; then a captain suddenly came on, who

evoked the spirit of evil by lifting both his arms to heaven. Another appeared; they went away, and the hunters started afresh.

She felt herself transported to the reading of her youth, into the midst of Walter Scott. She seemed to hear through the mist the sound of the Scotch bagpipes re-echoing over the heather. Then her remembrance of the novel helping her to understand the libretto, she followed the story phrase by phrase, while vague thoughts that came back to her dispersed at once again with the bursts of music. She gave herself up to the lullaby of the melodies, and felt all her being vibrate as if the violin bows were drawn over her nerves. She had not eyes enough to look at the costumes, the scenery, the actors, the painted trees that shook when any one walked, and the velvet caps, cloaks, swords — all those imaginary things that floated amid the harmony as in the atmosphere of another world. But a young woman stepped forward, throwing a purse to a squire in green. She was left alone, and the flute was heard like the murmur of a fountain or the warbling of birds. Lucia attacked her cavatina in G major bravely. She plained of love; she longed for wings. Emma too, fleeing from life, would have liked to fly away in an embrace. Suddenly Edgar-Lagardy appeared.

He had that splendid pallor that gives something of the majesty of marble to the ardent races of the South. His vigorous form was tightly clad in a brown-coloured doublet; a small chiselled poniard hung against his left thigh, and he cast around laughing looks showing his white teeth. They said that a Polish princess having heard him sing one night on the beach at Biarritz. where he mended boats, had fallen in love with him. She had ruined herself for him. He had deserted her for other women, and this sentimental celebrity did not fail to enhance his artistic reputation. The diplomatic mummer took care always to slip into his advertisements some poetic phrase on the fascination of his person and the susceptibility of his soul. A fine organ, imperturbable coolness, more temperament than intelligence, more power of emphasis than of real singing, made up the charm of this admirable charlatan nature, in which there was something of the hairdresser and the toréador.

From the first scene he evoked enthusiasm. He pressed Lucia in his arms, he left her, he came back, he seemed desperate; he had outbursts of rage, then elegiac gurglings of infinite sweetness, and the notes escaped from his bare neck full of sobs and kisses. Emma leant forward to see him, clutching the velvet of the box with her nails. She was filling her heart with these melodious lamentations that were drawn out to the accompaniment of the double-basses, like the cries of the drowning in the tumult of a tempest. She recognized all the intoxication and the anguish that had almost killed her. The voice of the prima donna seemed to her to be but echoes of her conscience, and this illusion that charmed her as some very thing of her own life. But no one on earth had loved her with such love. He had not wept like Edgar that last moonlit night when they said, "To-morrow! to-morrow!" The theatre rang with cheers; they recommenced the entire movement; the lovers spoke of the flowers on their tomb, of vows, exile, fate, hopes; and when they uttered the final adieu, Emma gave a sharp cry that mingled with the vibrations of the last chords.

"But why," asked Bovary, "does that gentleman persecute her?"

"No, no!" she answered; "he is her lover!"

"Yet he vows vengeance on her family, while the other one who came on before said, 'I love Lucia and she loves me!' Besides, he went off with her father arm in arm. For he certainly is her father, isn't he —the ugly little man with a cock's feather in his hat?"

Despite Emma's explanations, as soon as the recitative duet began in which Gilbert lays bare his abominable machinations to his master Ashton, Charles, seeing the false troth-ring that is to deceive Lucia, thought it was a love-gift sent by Edgar. He confessed, moreover, that he did not understand the story because of the music, which interfered very much with the words.

"What does it matter?" said Emma. "Do be quiet!"

"Yes, but you know," he went on, leaning against her shoulder, "I like to understand things."

"Be quiet! be quiet!" she cried impatiently.

Lucia advanced, half supported by her women, a wreath of orange blossoms in her hair, and paler than the white satin of her gown. Emma dreamed of her marriage-day; she saw herself at home again amid the corn in the little path as they walked to the church. Oh, why had not she, like this woman, resisted, implored? She, on the contrary, had been joyous, without seeing the abyss into which she was throwing herself. Ah! if in the freshness of her beauty, before the soiling of marriage and the disillusions of adultery, she could have anchored her life upon some great, strong heart, then virtue, tenderness, voluptuousness,

and duty blending, she would never have fallen from
so high a happiness. But that happiness, no doubt,
was a lie invented for the despair of all desire. She
now knew the smallness of the passions that art exaggerated. So, striving to divert her thoughts, Emma
determined now to see in this reproduction of her
sorrows only a plastic fantasy, well enough to please
the eye, and she even smiled internally with disdain-
ful pity when at the back of the stage under the velvet hangings a man appeared in a black cloak.

His large Spanish hat fell at a gesture he made,
and immediately the instruments and the singers began the sextet. Edgar, flashing with fury, dominated
all the others with his clearer voice ; Ashton hurled
homicidal provocations at him in deep notes ; Lucia,
uttered her shrill plaint, Arthur, at one side, his
modulated tones in the middle register, and the bass
of the minister pealed forth like an organ, while the
voices of the women repeating his words took them
up in chorus delightfully. They were all in a row
gesticulating, and anger, vengeance, jealousy, terror,
and stupefaction breathed forth at once from their
half-opened mouths. The outraged lover brandished
his naked sword ; his guipure ruffle rose with jerks
to the movements of his chest, and he walked from
right to left with long strides, clanking against the
boards the silver-gilt spurs of his soft boots, widening
out at the ankles. He, she thought, must have an
inexhaustible love to lavish it upon the crowd with
such effusion. All her small fault-findings faded before the poetry of the part that absorbed her ; and,
drawn towards this man by the illusion of the character,
she tried to imagine to herself his life — that life
resonant, extraordinary, splendid, and that might have

been hers if fate had willed it. They would have known one another, loved one another. With him, through all the kingdoms of Europe she would have travelled from capital to capital, sharing his fatigues and his pride, picking up the flowers thrown to him, herself embroidering his costumes. Then each evening, at the back of a box, behind the golden trellis-work, she would have drunk in eagerly the expansions of this soul that would have sung for her alone ; from the stage, even as he acted he would have looked at her. But the mad idea seized her that he was looking at her ; it was certain. She longed to run to his arms, to take refuge in his strength, as in the incarnation of love itself, and to say to him, to cry out, "Take me away! carry me with you! let us go! Thine, thine! all my ardour and all my dreams!"

The curtain fell.

The smell of the gas mingled with that of the breaths, the waving of the fans, made the air more suffocating. Emma wanted to go out ; the crowd filled the corridors, and she fell back in her arm-chair with palpitations that choked her. Charles, fearing that she would faint, ran to the refreshment-room to get a glass of barley-water.

He had great difficulty in getting back to his seat, for his elbows were jerked at every step because of the glass he held in his hands, and he even spilt three-fourths on the shoulders of a Rouen lady in short sleeves, who feeling the cold liquid running down to her loins, uttered cries like a peacock, as if she were being assassinated. Her husband, who was a mill-owner, railed at the clumsy fellow, and while she was with her handkerchief wiping up the stains from her handsome cherry-coloured taffeta gown, he angrily muttered about indemnity, costs, reimbursement. At last Charles reached his wife, saying to her, quite out of breath :

"*Ma foi!* I thought I should have had to stay there. There is such a crowd—*such* a crowd!"

He added—

"Just guess whom I met up there! Monsieur Léon!"

"Léon?"

"Himself! He's coming along to pay his respects." And as he finished these words the ex-clerk of Yonville entered the box.

He held out his hand with the ease of a gentleman; and Madame Bovary extended hers, without doubt obeying the attraction of a stronger will. She had not felt it since that spring evening when the rain fell upon the green leaves, and they had said good-bye standing at the window. But soon recalling herself to the necessities of the situation, with an effort she shook off the torpor of her memories, and began stammering a few hurried words.

"Ah, good-day! What! you here?"

"Silence!" cried a voice from the pit, for the third act was beginning.

"So you are at Rouen?"

"Yes."

"And since when?"

"Turn them out! turn them out!" People were looking at them. They were silent.

But from that moment she listened no more; and the chorus of the guests, the scene between Ashton and his servant, the grand duet in D major, all were for her as far off as if the instruments had grown less sonorous and the characters more remote. She remembered the games at cards at the chemist's, and the walk to the nurse's, the reading in the arbour, *tête-à-tête* by the fireside—all that poor love, so calm and so protracted, so discreet, so tender and that she had nevertheless forgotten. And why had he come back? What combination of circumstances had brought him back into her life. He was standing behind her, leaning with his shoulder against the wall of the box; now and again she felt herself shuddering beneath the hot breath from his nostrils falling upon her hair.

"Does this amuse you?" he said, bending over her so closely that the end of his moustache brushed her cheek. She replied carelessly:

"Oh, dear me, no, not much."

Then he proposed that they should leave the theatre and go and take an ice somewhere.

"Oh, not yet; let us stay," said Bovary. "Her hair's undone; this is going to be tragic."

But the mad scene did not at all interest Emma, and the acting of the singer seemed to her exaggerated.

"She screams too loud," said she, turning to Charles, who was listening.

"Yes—perhaps—a little," he replied, undecided between the frankness of his pleasure and his respect for his wife's opinion.

Then with a sigh Léon said:

"The heat is——"

"Unbearable! Yes!"

"Do you feel unwell?" asked Bovary.

"Yes, I am stifling; let us go."

Monsieur Léon put her long lace shawl carefully about her shoulders, and all three went off to sit down in the harbour, in the open air, outside the windows of a café.

First they spoke of her illness, although Emma interrupted Charles from time to time, for fear, she said, of boring Monsieur Léon; and the latter told them that he had come to spend two years at Rouen in a large office, in order to get practice in his profession, which was different in Normandy and Paris. Then he inquired after Berthe, the Homais, Mère Lefrançois, and as they had, in the husband's presence, nothing more to say to one another, the conversation soon came to an end.

People coming out of the theatre passed along the pavement, humming or shouting at the top of their voices, *" O bel ange, ma Lucie!"* Then Léon playing the dilettante, began to talk music. He had seen Tamburini, Rubini, Persiani, Grisi, and compared with them, Lagardy, despite his grand outbursts, was nowhere.

"Yet," interrupted Charles, who was slowly sipping his rum-sherbet, "they say that he is quite admirable in the last act. I regret leaving before the end, because it was beginning to amuse me."

"Why," said the clerk, "he will soon give another performance."

But Charles replied that they were going back next day.

"Unless," he added, turning to his wife, "you would like to stay alone, pussy?"

And changing his tactics at this unexpected opportunity that presented itself to his hopes, the young man sang the praises of Lagardy in the last number. It was really superb, sublime. Then Charles insisted—

"You would get back on Sunday. Come, make up your mind. You are wrong not to stay if you feel that this is doing you the least good."

The tables round them, however, were emptying; a waiter came and stood discreetly near them. Charles, who understood, took out his purse; the clerk held back his arm, and did not forget to leave two more pieces of silver that he made chink on the marble.

"I am really sorry," said Bovary, "about the money which you are——"

The other made a careless gesture full of cordiality, and taking his hat said—

"It is settled, isn't it? To-morrow at six o'clock?"

Charles explained once more that he could not absent himself longer, but that nothing prevented Emma——

"But," she stammered, with a strange smile, "I am not sure——"

"Well, you must think it over. We'll see. Night brings counsel." Then to Léon, who was walking along with them, "Now that you are in our part of the world, I hope you'll come and ask us for some dinner now and then."

The clerk declared he would not fail to do so, being obliged, moreover, to go to Yonville on some business for his office. And they parted before the Saint-Herbland Passage just as the cathedral struck half-past eleven.